DESTINY FULFILLED

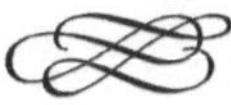

UNOMA NWANKWOR

KEVSTEL PUBLICATIONS

ISBN : 9781733086325

First printing March 2022

Printed in the United States of America

www.kevstel.com

ACKNOWLEDGMENTS

To my Lord and Savior Jesus Christ. I thank you for paying the ultimate price that I may have life and for your grace which I do not deserve. Thank You for the gift of writing and I humbly pray I continue to be a vessel in this journey.

To my family, my husband Kevin who's my number one fan, cheering me along every step of the way. I love you and thank you. To my kids Fumnanya and Ugo, my gang, my pookies, my munchkins who keep me sane when insanity sometimes abound. I love you both more than words can express. I pray for God's continued protection over you.

To my parents and mother in-law, *Daalu.* Thank you for your constant prayers and speaking words of life, courage and hope upon me.

To my readers, author friends and sistah writers thank you, thank you. Sometimes support doesn't always come from the people or places you expect but trust in God and He will send the right people to you.

NOTE FROM THE AUTHOR

Hey there!

We're headed back to my first FICTIONAL town, Tweede Kans Cove. This town, although fictional, borders the real city it was mirrored after: Ifrane. The cultures and traditions are based on facts although a little loose. There's enough given in the book that will ground you. However, I highly suggest you go here to read about the town.

When we were here last, we learned about Yasmine and Kojo in A Promise Fulfilled. Now we get to read about the leader of the DuBois-Arazi pack; Mustafa DuBois-Arazi

As usual, most of the language, Arabic (which is never capitalized), French and Swahili can be contextually deduced. However, all translations are in the glossary. Also, there might be a few British slang (Zaina lived in London).

Without further delay...enjoy!

Unoma

Ultimatum is a great read for anytime of the year" ~ **Norma Jarrett Essence Best Selling author of Sunday Bruch**

"**When You Let Go** is a true testament of the power of God within ourselves and our marriage. Although, we are tested every day, it is up to us to lean on our faith to get through those difficult times and offer forgiveness to those who may have hurt us in the process. Amara and Ejike's faith was tested throughout this novel but once they learned to put God at the forefront of their household, they were able to weather the storm." ~ **Diva's Literary World**

CHAPTER 1

"That your demons don't appear as scarlet letters across your chest doesn't mean they don't exist. Everyone has some darkness. To prevent it from overtaking you, acknowledge it, then use it in your favor, to help others. Don't let your pain go to waste."

Mustafa DuBois-Arazi lifted his eyes from the tablet in his hand. He studied the look on Salma's face. His baby sister was better with these things. The annual event he held for the kids at Beautiful Eyes, Tweede Kans Cove orphanage, and missions house was taking place the next day. He wanted, or rather needed, her opinion on his speech, but she didn't seem to be paying attention.

"*aikhti alsaghira*, are you listening to me?"

Her eyes met his and her brows furrowed. Mustafa smirked. Grown-up Salma disliked being referred to as little sister. But being the lastborn, that's exactly what she was and would always be to him. His eyes narrowed at what she had in her hand. A bowling trophy he could never bring himself to get rid of.

"Yes. It's good, but don't make it too long." She strolled over to him with the trophy she'd picked up from his bookshelf. "These are thirteen to seventeen-year-olds you're talking to. The last thing you want to do is bore them."

Mustafa grunted, set his tablet on the sofa, and rose to his feet. He met Salma halfway across the room. Taking the trophy out of her hand, he passed her and replaced it on the book-shelf. His fingers caressed the names at the bottom of the gold-plated cup. The memory of how it was acquired was bittersweet.

Heavy on the bitter.

"I don't know why you keep that thing," Salma said.

"Because it's mine, and I want to."

"But I don't understand. She—"

"It's not meant for you to understand. Don't touch it again." Mustafa walked out of the room. He shook his head at the real-ization that his sister was hot on his trail. He didn't turn to acknowledge her. Instead, he headed for the kitchen.

Salma pulled out one of the barstools at the island and sat. "Well, all I'm saying—"

"Have you heard from Yasmine?" Mustafa opened the cupboard and removed two bowls from it.

He'd barely had ten hours of sleep in the last two days. Having returned to Morocco from his trip to America in the wee hours of the morning, he wasn't in the mood to hear his sister whine about things she didn't understand. Things he didn't care to explain. His memories, good or bad, were for him alone. To cherish or neglect. Currently, he didn't care to do either. The only thing on his mind was to eat lunch and take a well-deserved rest before the next day.

"I see what you did there."

Mustafa removed the chicken tagine from the warmer and dished two bowls of the traditional Moroccan stew. He handed one to Salma.

"If you don't want to talk about it, I'll leave it alone."

He hiked his brow. "I never want to talk about it. Yet you still find a way to insert yourself."

"Shoot me. I'm looking out for my big brother." She took the spoon he handed her. "The one who thinks it's his job to look out for everyone but himself."

"Adorable, but unnecessary." He placed two bottles of water and some tea in front of them, then took his seat beside her. They said grace and began to eat.

"So?" Mustafa asked.

"I talked to Yas right before I got here. She's fine. Misses home. At least Omar is now in Accra with her." Salma shrugged. "Since Kojo's been on tour, she keeps complaining about being lonely."

Mustafa made a mental note to call his other sister before he retired for the night. He missed having her around, but she was happily married with a budding family. Something he'd always wanted for her after the loss they had experienced. He turned his head to Salma.

"Tell me about tomorrow."

Salma was the Director of Guest Services and Events at their family owned Luxury Spa & Resort, Grand Amour. Originally located in Tweede Kans Cove where the DuBois-Arazis called home, the decades old resort also had locations in West, East, and Southern Africa. It had fifty villas with a beachfront view, two restaurants, three pools, media rooms, gyms, spas, and outside activities for the kids.

When his grandfather, Sir Marcelle DuBois, passed seven years ago, Mustafa, along with his three siblings, took over the reins of the resort. He was the Managing Director and Chairman; Yasmine was the Director of Operations; Omar and Salma, who were fraternal twins, ran the food/beverages and guest services, respectively.

"All guest speakers for the weekend have been checked into their villas." She took a sip of water. "The kids will arrive with the chartered bus. They'll eat breakfast in the usual hall, you'll speak, then they'll be broken out into groups for the various activities. Omar is so sad he won't be the one cooking for the kids this year."

Mustafa nodded. "Well done."

He knew without a doubt that Grand Amour wouldn't be as great as it was, and maintain its place as the number one, five-star resort in Africa, without his staff. Especially his siblings.

"Remember, don't make the speech long. When we were in the orphanage, we had zero desire to listen to long stories by adults."

"We were there for only a few months, and I heard you when you said it the first time." Mustafa tweaked her nose and carried his bowl to the sink.

Salma walked up behind him and placed her hand over the faucet. "You fed me, the least I can do is wash up."

He allowed her to take his place and picked up his phone from the island. The email he was waiting for from Gray Holdings had arrived. His trip to America was to Las Vegas for a conference hosted by Darius Gray of Gray Holdings. He was an American billionaire hotelier who had amassed hotels all around the world. The three-day conference brought together great minds in the marketing and hospitality industry to discuss the latest trends in security, technology, and customer service.

Grand Amour was his family's legacy—a resort his grandfather had built from scratch. Mustafa's goal was to take the resorts to heights he knew would make his grandfather proud. That he did, however, he always had his eye on new and personal investment opportunities outside of Morocco and Africa as a whole. One of his most recent investments was in Africa's biggest motorway located in Lagos, Nigeria. Now, he had his eyes overseas and Darius told him he had someone who could make his desires happen. The email contained contact information for Hakeem Richardson, an investment manager.

Mustafa typed out a quick response of receipt as Salma shut off the faucet and dried her hands with a dishtowel.

They walked into the living room of his villa together as she updated him on other things that had gone on while he was away. Minutes later, she picked up her purse and headed for the door.

"I must really love you to ditch my date and hang out with you on a Friday night."

Mustafa chuckled, walking behind her. "You do love me. And I don't want to hear about dates until you have someone serious."

Salma rolled her eyes. "Typical. How will I have someone serious if I don't date?"

"I never said you can't date, Little One. I said I don't want to hear about them." Mustafa placed a kiss on her forehead and opened the door. "The sun is almost setting."

She shook her head. "I guess I'll take it. You're way better than Omar."

"He's your twin and big brother. It's his job to get on your nerves. As the oldest, I won't allow it to get too far."

Salma laughed.

"Call me when you get to your villa."

As he watched his sister stroll into the evening, he fought the need to trail her. He and his siblings each had their own villa that sat collectively on a five-acre plot. Their homes were located a few miles away from the resort. It was a secluded and safe area, but she was still his little sister. No matter how grown she claimed to be, he couldn't separate her from that scared little girl he'd fiercely protected throughout the years. His aim had always been to ensure the incident that shifted the trajectory of their lives didn't have a lasting effect on her.

To the outside observer, he'd done well, with the help of his grandparents. Underneath, he still struggled with the anxiety of the unknown. Control wasn't something he could afford to give away. Walking to his bedroom, his eyes darted towards the bookshelf and the trophy. It was a constant reminder of why giving up control would not only be to his detriment, but that of his whole family.

~

The following evening, Mustafa stood at the steps of the resort as the last kid boarded the chartered bus taking them back to Beautiful Eyes. Day one of the event had concluded and Salma, who stood by him, had made it spectacular. Grand Amour was one of the pillars of Tweede Kans Cove, employing almost fifty percent of the small town's population. Located in the middle of the Atlas Mountains in Morocco, the town was about three hours from Marrakech. Giving back to the community was one of the resort's and his family's cornerstones. But H.O.M.E., Helping Ourselves to Money & Education, was his baby. It was an event he'd started three years ago.

"You did good, *al'akh al'akbar*," Salma spoke in Arabic.

Due to their upbringing, he and his siblings spoke Arabic, English, and French fluently. Their early childhood was spent with their nomadic parents. With a Moroccan father and French mother, they learned to speak both languages. Their father, who was more than a decade older than their mother, often got his way and forbade them from speaking French. After their mother's death when Mustafa was twelve, they settled in Tweede Kans Cove with their maternal grandparents. That was when they perfected their French.

Mustafa shook his head, sending the memories of those bitter years to the recesses of his mind. His eyes went to the scar on his forearm. He'd mastered blocking out the emotional pain, but the physical scars were a constant reminder.

Salma nudged his shoulder. "Hello?"

He turned his gaze to her. "This was all you. I only showed up and smiled."

"And what a nice smile it is. But to keep it on, we better hurry to Grandma Olly's. You know how you get when she's upset. And that's what she'll be if we are late for dinner."

Mustafa chuckled and led his sister down the steps. Their grandmother, Lady Olivia DuBois never joked around about Saturday dinners, a tradition she continued once they were all back to living in Tweedes after college. Mustafa and Yasmine schooled in France while Omar and Salma went to college in America.

"I'll never tell Omar this, but I miss not having him around."

Mustafa opened the car door for his sister then walked around to the driver's side. Settled in, he pulled out his phone and Facetimed his brother.

"What are you doing? You know you don't always have to fix things?"

"Nonsense. You have a problem that I can fix, it's done." With no answer after three rings, he called Yasmine next.

"Uncle 'Stafa. I miss you." His eight-year-old niece, Anisa's face appeared on the phone.

"I miss you too. Where's your mother?"

"She's in the kitchen with Kwame. Hold on. Where's Aunty Salma?"

"I'm here, Sweet Pea. How are you enjoying Ghana?" Salma leaned over so she could be in the camera's frame.

"It's okay. But it's only mommy here with me and Kwame. My new daddy has gone to sing."

Salma laughed and Mustafa joined in, amused by the simplification of what her stepdad did for a living. Yasmine had been widowed, then reconnected with and married her childhood love a few years back. Kojo "Keyz' Sarbah was the owner of an indie label, New Sound records, and an award-winning producer/songwriter for the 891 Crew, a neo-gospel group known around the world. The group recently announced their retirement with a world tour. They were currently on the African leg of the tour which was to be their last. Kojo, a divorced, Ghanaian father of one son, Kwame, Yasmine, and Anisa made Accra their home. A move that worked well as Yasmine worked out of the newly built Grand Amour location.

"How many times have I told you not to answer my phone?" Yasmine appeared on camera.

"I'm sorry, Mummy. I wanted to talk to Uncle 'Stafa."

"The snacks are on the table. Go join your brother." Yasmine watched her leave before turning her attention to them. "Hey, guys. I miss you."

Salma took the phone as Mustafa began to drive. "We miss you too sis. Where is O?"

"Don't tell me you miss him?" Yasmine joked.

"I wondered the same thing," Mustafa chimed in.

"Don't tell him, but yes I do."

"He's somewhere about town, chasing skirts, I'm sure. He'll be over later because I leave for Abidjan later tonight."

"Is that where your husband is?" Mustafa inquired.

"Yes. Their concert is tomorrow night."

"Don't turn up pregnant," Salma chuckled.

"Too late."

Salma's ear piercing scream gave Mustafa an instant headache, causing him to narrow his eyes at her. Ignoring her silliness, he addressed Yasmine.

"Congratulations, Yas. Do you need to take time off? Your deputy here should be able to temporarily relocate to Accra." He paused when another thought occurred. "Should you be traveling? Does Kojo know this?"

"Musa, breathe. Please, I can't handle you and KJ breathing down my neck. I'm fine. Trust me. And yes, of course he knows, and I'm only six weeks."

Mustafa acquiesced, not willing to belabor the issue further.

He'd give his brother-in-law a call instead. Yasmine was stubborn and determined to do things her way. But he knew what she went through with his niece. They talked a little bit more, then said their goodbyes as he approached the gates of the DuBois Manoir. The twelve-room mansion that sat on a large piece of land was the first home they'd lived in for more than a year.

~

A few hours later, dinner was done. Mustafa made his way to the living room where his grandmother sat knitting. Salma had succumbed to the aftereffects of the feast their grandmother provided and was sleeping in her upstairs bedroom. He stopped at the picture wall; one he had seen a million times before. He stared at the picture he had committed to memory. His late mother, Bella DuBois, as a fresh college graduate. As he studied the picture, he narrowed in on her light green eyes. So innocent and full of life. A sharp contrast from who he remembered.

For the umpteenth time in his adulthood, he wondered what made her leave the comfort of her home to roam the country with his father, Ahmed Arazi, an older man for whom his admiration had long turned to hate. His mother was the only child of his grandparents who were descendants of French expatriates. The DuBois were wealthy by all measures, still, their only child had fallen into the hands of a lazy man. One whose need for her was based on the money she provided. That decision ultimately led to her death.

As a child, Mustafa never understood why his family always had to move often. It wasn't until later that he discovered their moves were forced by his grandparents locating their runaway daughter. That was when his father would urge them to move. Until his young wife ran out of funds. Then the violence started.

Before those memories could take over, Mustafa heard soft footsteps behind him.

"You do know that your mother loved you very much." His grandmother placed her hand on his back.

Mustafa turned and smiled at her. She, like them, had suffered because of his parents' decisions. Now she no longer had their grandfather.

"You always say that, but how could you know that?"

She moved her hand and palmed his cheek. "Because she came from my womb and there was no way she couldn't."

He'd just turned twelve when his father mistakenly killed his mother. An argument over money turned deadly. She was in a coma for a few days before she died. Their father was taken away and the four of them were shipped off to an orphanage in Rabat. Three months later, his grandparents found them. It was a season of firsts. The first time they'd seen or known they had living grandparents. The first time they knew of their French heritage, or the town known as Tweede Kans Cove. The first time Mustafa knew of the opulence they came from. He traced his fingers over his mother's picture before leading his grandmother back to her seat.

He sat next to her. It had only been a few days since he had seen her, but he wanted to make sure she was recovering well from hip surgery and not worrying about him. They talked a little about her upcoming follow-up appointments before she went back to the topic he was trying to forget.

"There was nothing you could've done," she said softly. It was a sentence he'd heard so many times before but had a hard time accepting.

"You were a child," she continued. "It wasn't your place to be the adult or the protector of your siblings. Leave the blame where it's supposed to be…with your parents."

"I've done that."

"*Avez-vous?* Have you? Even with the help of your grandfather and me, you still watch over your siblings like a hawk. They are all grown now. You need to live your own life."

Mustafa groaned; this was his cue to get going. Despite a job that kept him busy, he managed to have a healthy social life and his faith walk was becoming stronger. He had a life. But his grandmother didn't want him to have a life, she wanted him to have a wife. With one disastrous proposal under his belt, he wasn't ready to try again.

Mustafa kissed her cheek and stood.

"One day, I'll tie you down so we can have this conversation."

"*Je ne peux pas attendre*." Telling her he couldn't wait; Mustafa kissed her hair and left the room in search of Salma. As he approached the spiral staircase, his phone rang. His brows came together at the caller's identity—Ben Moseki, his college friend turned Minister of Environment for Natural Resources Conservation and Tourism in Botswana.

"Ben? How are you, my friend?" he asked once he answered the call.

"I'm well. But you're not going to like what I have to say," he said.

Mustafa rolled his shoulders, a feeling of unease coming over him. "That you deem it fit to call so late on a weekend, I know I won't."

"There's no easier way to say this. Your resort is in trouble. You need to get to Botswana immediately."

Mustafa leaned against the railing as he digested what Ben had relayed and the reason why. In this house, seven years ago, his grandfather handed the responsibility of Grand Amour to him. Failure wasn't an option then and it wasn't one now. Someone on his staff was going to have to explain to him how the disaster he'd been appraised of could've happened.

CHAPTER 2

"As we begin a new week my brothers and sisters, I encourage you to stay in a place where you're living by God's power. As I said at the beginning of service, we all have voids we would like filled. Big or small. Relationships, finances, health—anything you can imagine—many of us have voids. Filling them without leaning on God's power is a set up for failure." The pastor paused and nodded to the shouts of "Hallelujah" and "Amen" from the congregation.

"Trust in God, that whatever season you're in and feel lack, He will fill. Through your life, let the God you represent shine. Let us pray."

Zaina Bakari muttered, "Amen" as she stood with the rest of the congregation. It was good to be back in her home church. She'd forgotten how long-winded Pastor Stephen could be. If she'd remembered, she would've had breakfast before leaving her apartment.

For the past fifteen months, she'd been in Botswana for work. She'd let out a huge sigh of relief when she touched down in Abuja, Nigeria two days ago.

The inside of her stomach twisted in knots causing her to

open one eye and peek at the phone in her hand. The pastor was still praying, but her stomach needed food now. She had a brunch date with her girls. One she would be too weak to drive to if the man of God didn't conclude his prayer soon.

Pastor Stephen finally got to the end right as her phone buzzed. She glanced over the text, picked up her Bible and purse, and headed for the exit.

Boma: Leaving the hotel now.

Despite her best efforts to leave, Zaina was stopped along the way by familiar faces wanting to know when she got back. Desperately trying not to be rude, she answered their questions. All the while her stomach squeezed, reminding her that it wasn't thrilled about being kept empty for this long. Finally making her escape, she crossed the parking lot with dark shades shielding her from the mid May sun.

She entered her car and started the engine. As she backed out of the parking space, the melodic chords of "Breathe" by Dusin Onyekan were interrupted by her phone ringing through the car speakers. She weighed the pros and cons of sending the caller to voicemail. Just before the ringing stopped, the cons won the day.

"Good afternoon, Mother."

"You seem to forget you have a mother," came the curt response from her mother, Mrs. Ima Bakari.

Like you forgot you had a child.

Zaina rolled her eyes at the annoyance in her mother's tone. She always wished she could say those words out loud. However, the satisfaction she'd get wouldn't be worth the guilt trip and tears from her mother.

Instead, she replied, "Mother, I'm still getting used to being in my home. I was going to call you when I settled."

Zaina honked at the pedestrian crossing the road with his attention on his phone. This was the reason she hated driving on the backroads. People popped out from nowhere and dashed across the road.

"Your father told me you've been back in Abuja for two days. How much time do you need to call your mother?"

Her father, Chief Phillip Bakari, only knew because her older brother did. Growing up, Zaina was used to not expecting her parents to be genuinely concerned about what she did. However, something about them getting older had them both now smothering her.

"How are you doing, Mother?"

Her mind drifted as her mother continued to fuss. As the last child of seven children, Zaina was the forgotten one. The one her parents were too tired, busy, or old to raise. Her closest sibling was eight years older than her. Her mother was her dad's trophy wife. He married her at a time when he and his first wife, who birthed four girls, were estranged. By the time her mother got pregnant with Zaina's first brother, they'd reconciled. To make life easier for him, her father bought her mother a house in Kensington, London where she still lived. While he and his first wife lived in Tanzania. In quick succession, her mother had another son, and they were done. Six children all together and the Bakari clan was complete. Zaina shook her head at the story her mother always told of the surprise they got when eight years later; she was conceived.

"Are you going to talk, or do you plan to keep scolding me?" Zaina asked.

"I'm really knackered."

"Hmm. You won't be so tired if you stop galivanting all over the world. You have a very—"

"Not this again, I don't want to work for my father. I'm very good at what I do, and I love it. I'm happy." Zaina almost wept at having to keep reiterating her desires. The fact that she was starving also took the fight out of her.

"Okay! But must they keep sending you all over the place?"

"It's part of the job." As an environmental consultant, she traveled a lot, but it wasn't as bad as her mother was making it out to be.

Her mother sighed, signaling her defeat. "I'm fine. When will I see you?"

Zaina circled the parking lot of Bisso Bites looking for a vacant space. She was always in awe of how big the place was. They'd added an additional parking lot because everyone wanted to dine in the exclusive restaurant.

"I'm not sure. When I go into the office tomorrow, I'll know what my schedule will look like. If I have time before the next assignment, I'll be on the next flight out."

"Please make the time. I haven't seen my only daughter in almost two years."

"You know, you could've come to visit me." Finding a spot, Zaina pulled in.

She checked her appearance in the visor's mirror. She reapplied her strawberry-mango lip gloss and fluffed her auburn coils as she listened to her mother read down the litany of reasons why she hadn't made it to Botswana for a visit. Starting with the distance and ending with her feet swelling.

Her Nigerian mother was so bourgeoisie that no one would guess she came from humble beginnings, growing up in the Southeast region of the country. Zaina blamed her father. Their story was almost Cinderella-like. A wealthy, titled Tanzanian man met a farmer's daughter, during a trip to Nigeria—a fresh college graduate working at a coffee shop of all places. He wooed her, married her, and continued to give her anything her heart desired. The only time Ima Bakari left her throne in London was if Zaina was in Abuja or when she had to make her quarterly visit to Tanzania to see her father.

"Okay, mother. I'll let you know tomorrow."

"Don't forget your sister is getting married in a couple of months."

Zaina's eyes bugged at the car speakers as though her mother could see her. "Again?"

"Don't be rude." Her mother sucked her teeth. "I'm still waiting for you to get married for the first time."

"If I do, it will be the *only* time. What number are we on now?"

"Three and—"

Changing her mind on wanting the details, Zaina cut her mother off. "I love you mother, but I really have to go. Call you tomorrow."

Zaina blew her mother kisses and disconnected the call. The circus that was her family needed its own Netflix series. She would think about them later. Now all she wanted was to enjoy a delicious meal, a mimosa, and girl talk. Entering the restaurant, she walked up to the vacant hostess stand. Her eyes darted across the room. Soft music floated through the air. Chatter from patrons and the aroma of different dishes heightened her senses. The easy and natural colors calmed her rattled state. A young woman hurried up to her. Zaina smiled, recognizing one of her favorites.

"Aunty Sam, welcome," Risi greeted.

She addressed Zaina by the short form of her middle name, Samantha. She'd started introducing herself as Sam in high school in defiance of her father. He hated it, so mission accomplished.

A broad smile plastered Risi's face. "I'm happy that you're back."

"Aww, it's good to be back, my dear. How are you?"

"I'm fine. We thank God. Madam is waiting for you. She said to escort you to the upstairs section. Aunty Boma is already here," she said.

Zaina nodded and followed Risi to the secluded area on the second floor. Moments later, Zaina stepped behind the partition and her girls screamed.

"She's back!"

Zaina laughed and spread her arms for a group hug from her friends, Boma Kadiri and Ibiso Danjuma. After the last several months, she really needed this.

~

*H*ours later, Zaina scooped the remaining crème brûlée from her bowl and set the spoon down. She could hear the giggles of her friend as she closed her eyes and leaned back in her chair. She moaned as the last of the decadent dessert exploded in her mouth, providing the oral warmth and comfort she'd been missing.

"SoSo, you've outdone yourself again," she said.

"Thanks. I should hope so after that performance you just put on."

They all laughed.

"Anyway *sha*, for real. My girls were coming to town. I had to step up my game," Ibiso replied.

"I'll be coming to Abuja more often then, if this is what we get," Boma chimed in.

The world was indeed small. Five years ago, in need of a change, Zaina moved from London to Abuja. She'd made a pit stop in Geneva, but it wasn't meant to be a long-term plan. It wasn't even supposed to be part of the plan. She'd gambled and it backfired—a mistake she'd always regret.

When Safi Kijani Consulting, an environmental consulting firm offered her a job, she was ecstatic about the new beginning. Her first assignment on arriving in Abuja was to co-lead a waste mitigation enhancement project for a manufacturing company called the Danjuma Group.

At the end of the project, the CEO held a gala for the share-holders and investors. Zaina was shocked speechless when her college friend, Ibiso, walked in as his wife. The ladies reconnected and Boma, whom she didn't know as well, completed their trio.

"B, I'm just going to ignore you. It's like pulling teeth to get you to leave Port Harcourt," Ibiso replied.

Boma waved her off and turned to Zaina. "Sam, see you survived Botswana. The months passed by just like that." She snapped her fingers. "Have you shipped your things back?"

Zaina shook her head and placed her napkin on the table. "No, not yet. I was so ready to come home that I got on the first flight out. It was only by His grace. Hopefully, now that the project is done, my boss will fulfill his promise. Honestly, Lawrence was the last straw. I'm tired of underqualified men being promoted ahead of me simply because of their gender or connections."

Ibiso shook her head. "I don't even see how you got over the sting of that Lawrence guy."

"I know. One month into the job and you get moved to a position someone has been working three years to qualify for," Boma said.

The reminder from her friends solidified her resolve. Zaina took a sip of her drink. "I went there and managed the highway project for the Ministry of Transportation successfully. My promotion or I'm out."

"Girl don't worry about it. I'm sure they'll do right by you," Boma said.

"Not to be a downer, but if I remember correctly, this job wasn't the original plan. Interior design was," Ibiso said.

Zaina shrugged. "I'm still weighing my options."

"Code word for she's scared," Ibiso added.

Zaina cut her eyes at her. Ibiso knew her better, but even she didn't know the real reason for her hesitancy. Her love for the earth and art led her to pursue degrees in environmental engineering and interior design. Which birthed her dream to own an interior design firm with an emphasis on environmental stewardship. That dream died exactly seven years ago.

"Scared of what? Branching out? With your family's wealth, money shouldn't be an issue," Boma said, searching for her ringing phone. "I have to take this, it's the hubby."

Boma walked away from the table as a waiter was walking toward Ibiso. The young man greeted them before bending to whisper something to his boss.

"Sam, I'll be back. Hubby is in my office."

Zaina idly stirred her zobo with a straw. Even if money was her problem, she'd get a loan rather than ask her father. With the reprieve from her inquisitive friends, her mind wandered to the real reason her dream wasn't yet a reality. She remembered the countless days and nights she'd spent sharing her dreams with the love of her life. Unwarranted fear drove her to self-sabotage and fumble the best thing that had happened to her. Subconsciously, her feeling of unworthiness of anything good caused her to stifle those dreams.

For the last several years, her life had become predictable. Work, home, gym, church. Not necessarily in that order, but those four places were always a constant. On occasion, she'd indulge in a carefree time with the few friends she had or attended a mandatory family gathering. Still, work had practically taken up any room for a personal relationship. Her job was the perfect lifesaver when she needed it to be. However, it was never supposed to be the end game.

The scraping of Boma's chair being pulled out brought Zaina back from her unpleasant trip down memory lane.

"Sorry about that," she said. "Where's SoSo?"

Zaina smiled. "She was summoned by the hubby."

"Rasheed is here?"

"Yeah, in her office."

"Anyway, as we were saying, I can't claim to know the fears behind starting a business. That entrepreneurial spirit isn't in me. I'm content working a nine to five. I'll say this *sha*, my pastor says that your victory is on the opposite side of your fear. So, if you keep running from your fears, you delay the fulfillment of your destiny."

Zaina contemplated her statement. She was approaching thirty-five. It might be time to let go of the thing she couldn't change, forgive herself and get back to being whole.

~

"You look good. Are you sure you went down there to work?" Kate, her coworker asked.

Zaina lowered her tea filled travel cup and looked across the conference table to make eye contact with the older woman. She would never get used to the shade disguised as a compliment most Nigerians tended to give.

What does my work and appearance have to do with each other? Before she could think of the appropriate response, two additional people entered the conference room.

"Ah Sam, welcome back," one of the men said.

Acknowledging them with a nod and a faint smile, Zaina took a seat as Mr. Ladi, their boss entered the room. She gave Kate a dry smile and turned to the head of the table, waiting for the weekly Monday meeting to commence.

"Good morning, everyone. Miss Bakari, welcome back," Mr. Ladi said. "From the preliminary report, the client is very satisfied, and you came in under budget. Well, done."

Zaina smiled and bowed her head in respect. "Thank you, Sir."

He clapped and others joined in.

After this, they had a formal, one-on-one debrief, but she was thankful he affirmed her hard work in public. When her work success chipped away at the narrative that she got the job through her father's connections and not her abilities, she felt a level of satisfaction that couldn't be put into words.

The meeting continued with the normal agenda. Updates on existing projects, new assignments, and brainstorming on difficult projects. About forty-five minutes into the meeting, Zaina looked up from her notes and locked eyes with her boss. His phone was in his hand, and she could almost detect the look of pity in his eyes. Her heart thudded against her chest. Was he going to renege on the promise of the Regional Manager position? She'd gone to Botswana and done a stellar job. There were many sleepless nights to ensure that happened. They couldn't do this to her.

For the remainder of the meeting, Zaina couldn't concentrate with unanswered questions floating in her mind. She let out a sigh of relief when the meeting concluded. As the others filed out of the room, Zaina packed up and waited for Mr. Ladi to get off the phone. He walked toward her and the look she saw earlier returned.

"Miss. Bakari, have you shipped your things back?"

"No, sir. They ship next week," she said. Her voice shook as a shiver crept up her spine.

"Please cancel it. You have to go back."

Zaina shook her head. "Why, Sir? I don't understand."

"Let's go to my office. This wasn't my call."

Go back? For how long? This wasn't what she was told when she gave up her life in Abuja to go there in the first place. So much for the company doing right by her.

CHAPTER 3

Tuesday morning, with both hands nestled in the pockets of his navy blue pants, Mustafa stared out the window of his second-floor office. From this spot which offered him the perfect view of the Atlas Mountains, he mulled over most big decisions. The serene image served as a backdrop to the resort and currently contrasted with the chaos wreaking havoc in his mind.

Over the last two days, he'd scoured the unofficial environmental audit report Ben sent over. Even after a few hours on the phone with his friend, he was still perplexed over how this could have happened. He prided Grand Amour with hiring best-in-class managers who were supposed to ensure disasters like this never happened. Somewhere along the line, someone got careless, and he needed to know the weak link.

A light rap on the door paused his next thought. Mustafa's eyes darted to the wall clock. It was time.

"Enter."

"Sir, everyone's waiting in the conference room. Your sister and brother are on Zoom from Accra. The Motswana general manager is also on video."

Mustafa nodded. "Thank you, Juliet."

His assistant left and Mustafa took a few cleansing breaths. He needed to rein in his annoyance. He hated surprises. The unpleasantness of this one doubled his irritation. Picking up his phone and the folder containing the report, Mustafa made the short walk to the conference room.

Pulling open the double doors, he was hit with the tension that filled the atmosphere. After a quick browse of the room and a few head nods of acknowledgement, he took his seat at the head of the large, rectangular, mahogany table. The assistant manager of operations, the security and technology heads and the head of the green initiative department were all present. Not wishing to waste any more time, he addressed the room.

"Morning everyone."

Murmured responses traveled through the air. The anxiety in their voices mirrored the look of anticipation their eyes held. Mustafa glanced at Salma and the general manager of the Tweedes location who sat at his right and left, respectively.

"You might be wondering why I gathered you all here this early and on such short notice. Over the weekend, I received a disturbing call from Botswana. By the end of the week, the environmental audit results of the Grand Amour Resort & Safari in the Okavango Delta will be released. We will fail the audit with a code yellow warning."

A few beats passed as Mustafa scanned the faces in the room. Low gasps, murmurs and the rustle of paper could be heard as the group digested the gravity of the news. He'd barely had a full twelve hours of sleep over the last couple of days. After failing to convince Ben to stall on releasing the report, Mustafa had been on the phone with his team trying to figure out next steps. The Botswanan government, saddled with corruption, had hired an independent body to conduct the audits of the lodges and resorts of the area. The most Ben could do was call and give him a heads up so that the findings wouldn't catch him by surprise.

"I don't have to tell you the impact such a report will have on the resort. Our integrity, favorable ecofriendly rating, and the exclusivity we've enjoyed from the government are all in jeopardy. This will boil over into revenue loss…it's a domino effect."

After sitting with the news, speaking with Ben again and doing basic research to understand what he was up against, Mustafa had called his siblings. So, this wasn't the first time they were hearing of the issue at hand. Mustafa inclined his head toward Juliet who began handing out the one pager she'd put together.

"From the summaries in front of you, the water levels for the wildlife aren't up to the acceptable standard requirements. Our advantage over other lodges in the area is the appeal we have because of the exclusive part of the delta we occupy. With that exclusivity comes a large variety of wildlife in our safaris. But with that also comes the responsibility to ensure they aren't in danger. Lack of water is a risk.

"Water deprivation has always been an issue. I won't bore you with the environmental details, but we had a company that was supposed to make up for the low rainfall level we anticipated this season. Despite the assurances they gave, they failed. So, here we are."

Salma sighed. "This is sad. As if human exploitation isn't enough of a threat, now Mother Nature is acting up with the water?"

"Agreed, but we had a way to mitigate the risk and we failed," Mustafa said.

He looked at the hanging monitors where the remote participants were. Mr. Phiri, the Botswana general manager and Mr. Nkosi, his Green Initiative director had been instructed to prepare a full report on how the error was made.

"Sir, I've concluded logistic arrangements with the replacement. The consultant should be here within a couple of days of your arrival," Mr. Phiri said.

"Great. Perfect segue. Safi Kijani Green Consultancy, head-quartered in London, but with a main office in Nigeria will take over the project. Because of the importance and urgency of this, you might have to step into roles that aren't necessarily yours as people are pulled to provide support. It's all hands-on deck until further notice," Mustafa concluded.

After a few more minutes of questions, the meeting ended with Mustafa asking his siblings to stay back. Once everyone else had exited the room, Mustafa leaned back in his chair. He took in a deep measured breath and released. His greatest fear was disappointing his grandfather, a man who molded him when the one from whose loins he came failed.

"Musa, I know exactly where you're headed," Yasmine said.

Over the years, the effect of his childhood and the weight of the responsibility he shouldered manifested in the form of anxiety. Control was necessary to avert the panic uncertainty created. He wasn't so arrogant as to think he could control the elements, but this should've been something he had a handle on. The buck stopped with him.

"Besides, you hire people and expect them to do their jobs," Omar chimed in.

Salma placed her hand over his and squeezed. "We have a solution, so that's a start."

Mustafa, who had his eyes fixed on the ceiling, sat upright, and faced his siblings. "I talked to Ben. He advised that there's a way for us to maintain our rating if we can be up to code in six months."

"I thought you said the lake needs to be recharged. I did a little research and that takes a year plus. How's that gonna happen in six months?" Omar asked.

"Ben is the one that recommended this company. They did some work for another ministry. He said they worked a miracle, and we need one." Mustafa took a sip of the mint tea in front of him. "We've been promised that their guy will be able to lead the project as well as provide training to our team. Because this…it cannot happen again."

"Do you need me to return to Tweedes since you'll be in Botswana for a while?" Yasmine asked.

"No, Yas. Stay in Accra. This isn't the best time for your husband and I to get into a war of wills."

Mustafa smirked when Yasmine rolled her eyes. Omar and Salma made matters worse with their laughter. His sister was so used to traveling on Grand Amour business, but now she had a family. He knew she could do both, but he would rather she not. Especially in her current condition.

"Omar will be done with training the kitchen staff soon. He'll head home after that. In the meantime, Salma can handle everything here with the rest of the department heads."

For the next several minutes, the siblings discussed a few more business items before chatting about the surprise eightieth birthday celebration they were planning for their grandmother. By the time they dispersed, Mustafa felt his spirits lift. He was aware of siblings who couldn't stand each other and was thankful that they weren't those siblings. For him, family was everything.

With the boost of energy, Mustafa went about the rest of his day. With immediate Grand Amour business handled, he was headed to downtown Tweede Kans Cove. Later, he'd make the three-hour drive to Marrakech. Mustafa sat on the board of some other businesses and two advisory committees for the Moroccan government. Considering all he had going on, he wanted to send his regrets, but this would be the second time he'd cancelled in the past three months.

Advising on a committee aimed at increasing the attraction for Moroccans schooling in the Diaspora to return home with their knowledge was an honor he didn't take lightly. After obtaining his degree in business administration from Sorbonne University, and later obtaining his master's in hospitality management, Mustafa always knew he would return home. However, he, unlike most, had employment waiting for him. The contribution to the family legacy was his attraction. Many others didn't have the privilege he did and opted to remain abroad. If he could do his part to help make a return more appealing to the great, young Moroccan minds that resided abroad, he would do that. Whether it was his time or money, giving back was something he was always honored to do.

Later that night, Mustafa folded the last of his clothing into the suitcase. He was leaving Tweedes in the morning. He had a few stops to make before he arrived in Botswana. The buzz of his phone sliced through the smooth jazz playing in the background. After training his ear to assess the location of his device, Mustafa strolled to the living room. A text notification caused his brows to crease.

Hi Musa, are we still on for this weekend?

Sitting on the sofa, he gazed at the text. Monica Bennani was the granddaughter of one of his grandmother's friends. She'd returned from Brazil a couple of months ago to help her grandmother run their travel agency business. Despite his reservations, he succumbed to his grandmother's request to show her around the town. Mustafa knew his grandmother's real intentions, so he was up front with Monica about his stance on anything other than a simple friendship. She was a beautiful woman, but he wasn't interested or available for anything more. Of course, he wanted a family—at thirty-nine, he knew it was time. Coming home to an empty villa wasn't something he was fond of anymore. However, it wouldn't be with someone his grandmother picked out for him.

On for?

He responded. As he watched the three little dots signaling her incoming response, he mentally made a note to check his email. He was expecting a response from Hakeem Richardson on an updated investment portfolio.

You were going to take me to the Tourtite festival. You don't remember?

He shook his head at the laughing, surprised and two other, unfamiliar emojis that followed her response. He didn't remember because he made no such commitment. With the bits of the conversation that lingered in his mind, he knew he didn't. She raved about the festival that her grandmother talked about, and he told her that he and his siblings attended every year. In that moment, it dawned on him that this would be the first year that all of them didn't attend. Not being one to deliberately hurt anyone's feelings, he simply replied.

I leave out on business tomorrow, not sure when I will be back.

Uh oh.

She followed her response with a sad face and a crying emoji. Mustafa had never in his life communicated with someone who used so many emojis. It was juvenile. He exited the text thread and headed back to his bedroom to finish packing. His goal was to make up for the lack of sleep he had endured for the past couple of days. He wasn't sure of what awaited him when he got to Botswana, but he needed to be well rested for it. Losing their ecofriendly rating wasn't an option he was willing to accept.

CHAPTER 4

Zaina flung her head back, closed her eyes and released a loud sigh. It was all she could do to stop herself from screaming.

"This was not the plan."

Turning her head slightly to the side, she opened one eye and glanced at Ibiso. Tuesday wasn't their regular spa day, but after her meltdown the previous night, Ibiso decided they needed one.

"You know this hydrotherapy pool isn't doing whatever it is you thought it would," Zaina whined. She didn't even recognize her own voice. She sounded like a five-year-old, but right now, she couldn't be bothered. *This isn't fair.*

"If you stop whining and relax, maybe it will." Ibiso sighed. "Plans change Sam. The bottom line is, do you want the promotion or not?"

Zaina groaned and rolled her eyes. Left with the job of entertaining herself growing up, she didn't have a lot of friends. She'd learned to be a loner. One who was very comfortable with her own company. Moving back to Abuja, running into Ibiso, renewing their friendship, and deepening their bond was a new experience for her. The sisterhood was a welcomed addition to her life, so when her boss told her that she had to return to Botswana, Ibiso was the first person she called.

"I was supposed to be promoted anyway. That was the promise they made after almost a year and a half over there."

"Agreed. But you, my friend, have always wanted to go back to London. They know this and so they used the managerial position in the London office to get you. That's a double promotion." Ibiso lifted the glass flute to her lips and sipped.

When she first got to Nigeria, Zaina couldn't deal with the patriarchy. It was everywhere, but for someone who relocated from London, Zaina had that to deal with, as well as the ugliness from some women who decided she didn't deserve her position. It was one thing to be harassed in a foreign country, but when you're harassed in your own, it's worse. Granted, she was only half Nigerian, but still. So, she wanted to go back. The move would also allow her to rebuild her relationship with her mother. But another stay in Botswana, that wasn't the move. It was a lovely country, but she was done.

"But still—"

Ibiso sat up straight and narrowed her eyes. "Okay, level with me. What's the real problem?"

It's not what. It's who.

Nothing prepared her for the shock she received when she was debriefed on her new assignment. Grand Amour Resort & Safari in Botswana. A lake recharge. She had done that only once in her career. That time, she was part of the team, not in charge of it. Her boss countered her objections by informing her that she wouldn't have to start from scratch. More like a redesign of what a former company had done. Those were sometimes more difficult, but she knew that wasn't the real reason for her objection. Dealing with new vendors, the locals, signing mini contracts and all the other work it would take to get the job done would be a walk in the park compared to coming face to face with Mustafa DuBois-Arazi.

When she saw his name on the paperwork, her knees almost gave way. Seven years ago, she had made the greatest mistake of her life. He refused to forgive her then. Would he still hold a grudge against her now? The memories she'd suppressed for her sanity rose to the surface, driving her to Google. She'd spent the last twenty-four hours trying to dig up anything on him. What plagued her most was wondering if he was now with someone. After using all relevant search words, she came up empty.

"Earth to Sam?" Ibiso's voice cut through her reflection.

"I'm sorry."

"Spill. What's really bothering you?"

Zaina had never told anyone what happened between her and Mustafa. The pages of her journal had a play-by-play, but that didn't count. Deciding she could really use another voice apart from the ones in her head, she waited a few beats then spoke.

"It's not what. It's who."

Ibiso's brows creased. Any time she brought up a man, Zaina sidestepped the issue, so she understood the reaction.

"The job is for Grand Amour Spa—"

"The luxury resort in Morocco? I've heard of them. There was a high-profile wedding there a couple of years ago."

"Do you know the family?"

"No. My brother-in-law has a friend who knows…never mind. Continue, tell me what's bothering you."

"I was in a relationship with the oldest son of the family." The mere thought of him caused her chest to tighten.

"What?" Ibiso changed her position. "I saw a picture of him. Does he smile?" Ibiso looked around the secluded area. "He's fine but looks mean."

Zaina chuckled. "You checking to make sure Rasheed won't pop out of the corner? You scared SoSo?"

Ibiso rolled her eyes. "Whatever…there's not a scary bone in my body. But still, I don't want that kind of *wahala*. Continue, what happened with Mr. Grumpy?"

Zaina's lips curled up in a faint smile. "He's different with me. Or should I say, was. We met in London and had a glorious, three-year relationship until my immaturity happened." She slumped her shoulders. I didn't think he loved me the way I ought to be loved. And he was so absorbed with his family. I mean, we could be out and one of his siblings calls. If they needed something, whatever we had going on stopped. They were grown. Why was he treating them like children? I hated it. I also assumed he wasn't moving fast enough in the marriage department. Anyway, I tricked him. My deception came to light, and he broke off our relationship. That was the last I saw of him. He never looked back."

Her throat was raw from the ball of emotion she struggled to suppress. She rubbed her chest, trying to alleviate the pain the clamp on her heart inflicted. Her thoughts went back to the night everything came crashing down. Mustafa didn't argue, but his anger was visible He never raised his voice. He simply ended their evening, made sure she got to her apartment and that was it. His aloof demeanor always annoyed her, but in that moment, it pierced her deep. When she stepped out of the car, her eye caught the tiny, black velvet box.

He was going to propose.

The shame of that she would never reveal. If only she had used her words to communicate her concerns instead of being manipulative, everything would've been different.

"Wow? That's a lot to unpack. Do you still love him?"

Zaina didn't know what she felt. It'd been a while and she had succeeded in not dealing with the situation. After the breakup, she tried to fill the void he left with another, and that ended up being a greater disaster, leaving her confused on what she really wanted.

"Truthfully, I don't know. What I do know is, I regret the way I handled things. But what does it say about what we had, if he didn't even give me a second thought? Just like that, he left."

"I suggest you do some self-reflection before you get there. I'm still stunned."

"Why?"

"You never share, at least not in detail. So, for you to tell me all that has me speechless."

Zaina shrugged. "You know how I am. It's not personal."

"I do and I know. I don't take your confidence lightly. Okay, my two cents. I understand how you grew up; your family isn't close. But family is a deal breaker for most people. Especially African first-born sons. In the family I grew up in and the one I'm married into, family is everything."

"You're right." She shrugged. "That's just not my experience. I learned that lesson the hard way."

"Something from his past might've made him that way with his siblings. I say that based on my husband and his brothers. They had residual childhood trauma. When I met my hubby, he was like the sacrificial lamb for the family. He had the load of the world on his shoulders. He swore he couldn't cloud his focus with love. I was dealing with stuff of my own, so I put my foot down. I would help him carry his baggage, but only if he knew what he wanted and wasn't afraid to get it.

Zaina contemplated Ibiso's words. Thinking back, Mustafa was always so guarded. They did have times when he was fun and light. But if she wasn't so wrapped up in what she wanted, she would've inquired more when he suddenly fell off the grid for days. He always offered his apologies via text, promising to make up, which he did. She knew he didn't have another woman, so maybe he didn't trust her enough to feel safe showing her all sides of him.

She lowered her eyes. "I broke my own heart."

"And we thank God for second chances. That's if you want

one. You deserve to be loved the way you think you should be, but you can't ask him to turn off his loyalty to his family. At the very least, this is your chance to talk. It's been seven years. I'm sure a lot has changed."

"I hope so."

Ibiso drew her in for a hug. Then she placed both hands on Zaina's shoulders. "Well, you need to put on your big girl panties and find out. If you want this promotion you must return to Botswana. If Mustafa is open to it, talk, and get the awkwardness out of the way. Then do the stellar job I know you're capable of." She shrugged. "Who knows Mr. Fine Meanie may forgive you? If not, it's his loss. You know I've been dying to hook you up. Now I know why you've always refused."

Zaina lips curved up in a smile. "The only guys I would've considered are your brothers-in-law and they're all taken."

Ibiso grimaced. "I'm going to pretend I didn't hear that. My sisters are nothing to play with, and I love you too much to have you at their mercy."

Both ladies laughed and shifted their remaining time to other topics. The heaviness Zaina carried around the last two days lifted. Although she had told her boss she would think about it, it was never her intention to tell him that she wouldn't take on the project. She wouldn't give the people in her office the satisfaction of later implying she didn't get her promotion based on merit. She had a point to prove, not only to her employer, but to herself and hopefully to Mustafa.

After several unsuccessful attempts to reach him over the years, she'd be face to face with him in a few short days. How would he receive her? Did he know she was the one coming? He hated the nickname Sam and never called her by it, so maybe he'd forgotten she went by that name sometimes.

She'd been deeply in love with him once and despite what she told herself, she knew those feelings lingered.

God help me.

~

*T*hree days later, Zaina grabbed the chair handle to keep from falling over. She blinked a couple of times to clear the lightheadedness that washed over her. Her lungs begged for a break from the combined smell of musk, cigarette smoke and somebody's overused vanilla and mango fragrance. Her heart palpitated as the walls of the medium-sized room seemed to be closing in on her. She never considered herself claustrophobic, but if this was what it felt like, she wanted no parts of it. Her eyes scanned the crowd of vacationers whose electrifying excitement would've been contagious if she didn't have so much pent-up anxiety.

"Ladies and gentlemen, welcome to the Okavango Delta."

The sparse crowd erupted in applause as the Grand Amour Resort & Safari guide stepped onto a raised platform. Two other members of the staff passed out water bottles and biscuits.

"As you know, this is Maun. Soon you'll board a shuttle flight that will take you to the Grand Amour Resort & Safari strip where a bus will be waiting to take you to the entrance of the resort. Before you're allowed to board the plane, you must give the attendant the signed copy of the form you received upon entry into this room. You should've also received one electronically when you booked your stay. If you have a signed printed copy of that one, it's fine. Your flight time is forty-five minutes. Your adventure starts now. So, during the flight, look down and gaze at reeds beds, wildlife, palm tree islands, and thousands of square miles of waterways."

Zaina lowered her eyes to her signed form. She adjusted her crossbody bag. This was like the doctor prescribing medicine but telling you about all the side effects that could also kill you.

"Please remember, you are now entering into territory that's a natural habitat for wild animals. This is not, I repeat, not like television. The instructions, rules, and regulations you have on the paper in your hand must be followed to the letter. Grand Amour has taken all the necessary steps to protect you, but your cooperation is required to make sure you're safe and don't end up as dinner for the hippos."

Many of the other guests laughed, but nothing was funny to Zaina. If she was being honest with herself, it wasn't the poor man's fault. He was doing his job. She was in a foul mood. It was about noon, and she hadn't had anything to eat since the one slice of toast and juice she took before leaving her rented apartment in Gaborone. She'd arrived late the previous evening from Abuja. Instead of waiting until Monday morning to make this trip, she'd thrown common sense out the window and took the ninety-minute flight to Maun.

At the time, using the element of surprise seemed like a good idea. No one was expecting her at Grand Amour until next week, so she could get an unbiased lay of the land. Unfortunately, she'd grossly miscalculated the hassle it took to get here, especially in her sleep deprived delirium. For the umpteenth time today, she chided herself for not accepting the on-site accommodation Grand Amour had reserved for the Safi Kijani consultant. Her boss warned her the rejection was not a good idea and now she knew why. How fool hardy of her to think she could make this commute every day? She had to correct that blunder as soon as possible.

Who am I kidding? He's the reason I turned it down.

Mustafa was already affecting her rational decision making and she couldn't have that. Not after all the work she had put in through therapy. There was too much at stake to allow that to happen. She needed to get herself together before she saw him on Monday. Zaina blew out a cleansing breath to expel the anxiety running through her veins.

Hours later, Zaina leaned back in the lounge chair in the lobby of the resort. Through the large glass windows, she had a picturesque view of the reddish orange skies announcing the setting of the sun. She was awaiting the shuttle that would take her to the airstrip beginning her return journey to the city. The fresh smell of the lagoon in the distance wafted up her nostrils as the sliding door opened to people walking in and out of the resort. For all the time she lived in Botswana, she'd never visited the Delta. On the flight over, she now understood why the Okavango was known as the "Jewel of Kalahari." She'd done some research before she arrived, but nothing prepared her for what she saw. It was a mass wetland surrounded by the Kalahari dessert.

Earlier on arrival, they were greeted by a group of traditional dancers, singing in the native language. After check-in for the vacationers and a quick bathroom break for her, the group was given a brief guided tour. According to the guide, unlike other lodges in the area that offered a total commune with a nature theme, Grand Amour balanced modern luxury and a connection to nature the lodgers desired. One could visit the resort without going on a safari and still have tons to do to enjoy themselves. That however was something he jokingly told them never happened.

There were fifteen villas, a restaurant, gift shop, spa, lap pool, and a fishing deck. Some distance from the resort was where the safari began. They could see the gates from the raised deck. While there, Zaina used her binoculars to eyeball the waterbody. The level did look low. The lagoon, they were told, attracted a variety of wildlife like elephants, lions, wildebeests, impalas, hippos, and countless birds. The correct water level was key for sustenance. After the tour, Zaina found herself in the restaurant where she indulged in an early dinner of pan-fried kingklip with lemon parsley and vegetables.

Nursing her bottle of water, Zaina took out her notebook. Armed with the knowledge of the audit report she'd read and the little she saw earlier she wrote down some ideas. She wasn't surprised the resort lost its favorable ecofriendly rating. The issue now was how to rectify the problem before the next audit.

Zaina remembered what this resort meant to Mustafa. If he was still the man she remembered, he wouldn't hold back until the resort was in good standing. Regardless of her promotion, or if he allowed her to finally apologize and explain her past mistakes, she was going to do everything in her power to get the rating restored. It was the least she could do, and although it pained her to admit it, she had something to prove.

The announcement of the last shuttle's arrival was made over the speakers, causing Zaina to lift her eyes from the notebook in her lap. She closed and returned it to her bag before standing. The spa visit of two days ago seemed like a distant memory as she stretched her achy body. The passengers in the bus alighted as she and a family of five moved forward. The bus driver rushed in telling them he would be right back and headed to the direction of the restrooms. Zaina glanced at her Apple watch. Barring no other delays, she'd be in her bed before eleven p.m.

Zaina noticed her shoelaces had come undone and knelt to retie them. Seconds later, head still bowed, her hands stilled as a pair of brown, Berluti oxfords stopped in front of her. There was only one person she knew who wore those.

Jesus it can't be.

Even though her visit to the resort was a rash decision, she'd called ahead to verify that he wasn't here. Her heart thudded against her chest.

"Zaina?"

Yep, it's him. That voice still had its potent power.

The hesitancy to lift her eyes or stand lingered as Zaina willed the floor to swallow her whole. After all these years, the first time they meet, she had to be dressed like an extra in a Gap summer commercial.

CHAPTER 5

From the back office, Mustafa walked down the hallway with Mr. Phiri by his side. His schedule had to be adjusted for several impromptu, yet important meetings, but he finally made it to the resort about an hour ago. Turning into the lobby, he listened as the general manager gave him updates on outstanding items from their meeting. Knowing that he probably wouldn't get anything done this late, Mustafa was headed to his car to take him to his villa in the resort.

He'd nearly reached the double doors when he heard the announcement of the shuttle. He slowed his pace, indulging in his habit of observing the staff when they weren't aware of his presence. The hospitality industry ran on customer service. The advantage he had as a family owned resort was the intimacy and service which he was uncompromising in maintaining.

Mustafa frowned. In his peripheral, he caught a glimpse of a woman who looked eerily familiar. His frown deepened as his eyes narrowed in on her caramel skin made visible by the off the shoulder casual tee shirt she wore over denim Bermuda shorts. She hurriedly tucked loose strands of her dark auburn curly hair behind her ear. As soon as she bent to tie her laces,

Mustafa redirected his steps. Whatever Mr. Phiri was saying had now turned to gibberish as his laser focus was on the woman ahead of him.

Her. It can't be. What are the odds? Did I talk her up with Salma?

Mustafa came to a halt in front of her and his suspicions were confirmed by the mole on her shoulder. One his fingers once loved to caress.

Adjusting his stance, he whispered. "Zaina?"

He watched as her body tensed and her hands froze—a nonverbal confirmation that it was her. She rose in slow motion. Her familiar, delicate floral fragrance attacked his senses. Their eyes locked for a second until he broke the connection for a brief sweep of her body. Zaina hadn't changed much over the years. Her round nose, full lips, high cheekbones, and bright brown eyes had matured some. Gracefully.

Time stood still as their vivid memories played in his head like a movie reel. Their first meeting in Central London at a jazz concert, after which they seemed to run into each other everywhere. He'd been working as a general manager for one of the top hotels in London—experience his grandfather insisted he needed. He remembered her sultry eyes when he spoke to her in Arabic, and her boisterous laughter when they played rummy. The passion in her voice when she talked about the earth. Zaina fascinated him and he pursued her, never one to be shy about getting what he wanted. And he wanted her. After three years, she proved not to be worth the effort.

"Hello, Ms. Bakari. I wasn't expecting you 'til Sunday."

Mr. Phiri broke the trance they were stuck in. Mustafa momentarily tore his gaze from Zaina. His brows creased as he waited for an explanation of how the man knew her or what he was talking about. Was she the consultant? He didn't linger on the details of who the consultant was. That had been his general manager's job. But he would have remembered hearing her name.

"Hi. I know. I wanted to look around myself without all the fuss." She took his outstretched hand in a brief handshake.

"Oh, I see. Allow me to make the introductions. This is Mr. Mustafa DuBois-Arazi, owner of the resort. Sir, this is Miss Sam Bakari, the environmental consultant and project lead from Safi Kijani."

Sam. The name she used to spite her father and the one Mustafa hated.

Mustafa raised a brow. Her lips turned up in a weary smile. He extended a hand to her, reading the trepidation in her eyes.

"Hello, Ms. Bakari. Welcome to Grand Amour."

She cleared her throat and placed her hand in his. Her eyes danced at the spark from their contact. She quickly withdrew her hand and he smirked.

"Err... thank you."

His next statement was halted as the final announcement was made for those leaving on the last shuttle to the airstrip.

Zaina's eyes darted around the lobby as she clenched the leather bag across her shoulders. "That's me. I have to get going."

Her eagerness to escape his presence amused him. It was late and he was certain there had been the offer of accommodations. Returning his hands to his pockets, he turned to the manager.

"What about her accommodations?"

The sternness of his tone wasn't intentional, but he was sure it was what got Zaina in defense mode.

"It's not his fault. I refused it."

Mustafa studied her but didn't respond. His pulse thumped. Turning to the general manager, he said, "Ms. Bakari stays. Instruct the bus driver to leave if the last person has boarded."

"Yes, sir." Mr. Phiri made his way to the exit.

"Why would you do that? I have to be on that bus."

Mustafa returned his eyes to her. "Where do you live?"

She folded her arms across her chest. "Gaborone."

"That's more than two hours away. Why would you turn down the room?"

Zaina bit down on her bottom lip, something she used to do when she was nervous. Her unease wasn't his intention; her safety was. With no response from her, he pulled out his cell phone and dialed his pilot.

"Have you left the airstrip yet?" Mustafa asked once the call connected.

"We're about to take off, sir."

"Hold on. How long will it take to get a permit to fly to Gaborone airport?"

"I can make a call, sir. It shouldn't be long."

"Do it. I have someone that needs to get to Gaborone." After a few more instructions, Mustafa thanked him and disconnected.

"You didn't have to do that. Thank you."

"I never do what I don't want to. No matter how much I'm pushed."

Mustafa noticed her recoil as the meaning of his last statement settled on her. He regretted his reference to their failed relationship. She was the solution to his resort problem, so he had to find a way to put the past behind and work with her. The six-month clock on the next audit had already started ticking. Besides, from what he remembered, she was exceptionally smart and dedicated.

"What I should've said is, you're welcome. That didn't come out right."

"That's fine. It's good to see you, Mustafa," she whispered.

He lowered his head lightly. "Come, let's sit while we wait."

He ushered her to the corner of the lobby, offering them some privacy. He unbuttoned his suit jacket, and they took a seat. He leaned back in his chair.

"Environmental consultant? What happened to interior design?"

Zaina pulled in a deep breath, then her eyes met his. "I still have it as a goal. It's delayed for now."

He nodded. "Do you want something to drink?"

"No, I'm fine." She looked around the lobby. "Mustafa, this place is gorgeous. You did it. I'm sure the other locations are too. I'm so proud of you."

Massaging his beard, he acknowledged her praise with a nod. "Thank you. Tweedes remains our original location, but we are expanding. No major problems, until now."

Her eyes softened. "I looked around, and from what I could see of the—"

"I'll wait to read your official analysis. In the meantime, tell me, what you've been up to since we saw each other last?'

"You mean since you dropped me off at my apartment and never looked back?"

Mustafa had never been a fan of small talk. The indulgence in meaningless utterances irritated him. However, to tone down the awkwardness between them, he was willing to tolerate it. Her accusatory tone told him that he shouldn't have indulged her.

He was apathetic. "Not my finest moment, but a necessary one."

"How? You wouldn't even let me explain," she said.

His eyes turned serious and dark as he pinned her in a stare. "There shouldn't have been anything *to* explain."

He hadn't allowed it then, neither was he in the mood to allow it now. He'd memorized the voicemail she'd left him years ago. He didn't buy her explanation then and was sure it wouldn't be much different now. Zaina opened her mouth, most likely to counter his words, but the buzz from his phone halted the conversation.

Zaina had always hated his phone and from the roll of her eyes, he could tell she still did. Unperturbed, he answered the call.

"Great," Mustafa said after listening for a few moments. He disconnected the call and signaled over a staff member. "Please have my car pull up to the front."

Zaina still sported a pout. Ignoring what he knew was her issue, he stood and extended his hand to her. "Let's go. My driver will take you to the airstrip. There you'll meet my pilot who will fly you to Gaborone. Once you arrive, a car service will be waiting to take you home."

She stayed seated; her eyes trained on him. A beat passed before she placed her hand in his, allowing him to help her up.

"Musa...," she started.

"We'll talk." His voice was even, but the finality couldn't be missed.

Her eyes longed to finish their conversation, but he couldn't indulge her. He had an international call to be on in a few minutes. Accepting, albeit reluctantly, his stance, she followed him towards the exit. After settling her in the back seat, he gave the driver some instructions.

His eyes found hers. "Give me your phone."

"Why?" Frowning, she handed him the device.

"So, you can call me when you get in." Mustafa tapped on the screen a few times and handed the phone back. "Zaina, be prepared to move in on Sunday. Someone will be at your apartment by noon to get you."

Mustafa closed the door and tapped on the roof signaling the driver to move. He had no desire to hear the argument he knew she'd have.

Later that night in his home office, Mustafa absentmindedly participated in another call as he browsed the Safi Kijani website. After Ben's recommendation, he'd gone on their website only to find out who they were and what they did. Impressed with their stellar reviews and awards of excellence, his research ended. Now his cursor hovered over the "staff" icon with a need to know more. He clicked and found her name on the second page.

Zaina Samantha Bakari.

There was no headshot, but she did have a few reviews. All of them sang her praises. He had firsthand knowledge of her passion, so the praise didn't come as a surprise. Other than that, there wasn't any other information. Opening another tab on his browser, he went to Google and typed in her name. His pulse quickened as he waited for the results to come in.

The night he left Zaina, Mustafa received a call that his grandfather was on his death bed. He no longer wanted to undergo treatment for his ailment. The following morning, he left London for Tweede Kans Cove. His grandfather died two weeks later. There was no time to dwell on the fact that a woman he'd allowed in his heart intentionally decided to be reckless with it. There was work to be done. His family needed him. His grandfather had entrusted them to him. Mustafa forced himself to forget anything that had to do with that time in his life. Including the need to check on Zaina's whereabouts.

The top result from the search was her LinkedIn profile. The next was her family's furniture empire, Bakari Furniture & Design. Mustafa had always admired her desire to stand her ground against what she'd called the pressure to join the family business. She always wanted to provide sustainable, ecofriendly designs. From what she shared earlier, that dream had been deferred.

Mustafa clicked on her profile and was transfixed on her headshot. A warm sensation rose within him. The same one he ignored when he saw her earlier. He picked up his reading glasses and scanned her work history. From the timeline, after their breakup, Zaina went to Geneva where she worked for six months before heading back to London. It was there she started working for Safi Kijani before transferring to their office in Abuja.

She told him she lived in Gaborone, so she must have been here on assignment. The search engine hadn't returned any information about her social life. He saw she had an Instagram account but didn't post regularly. Her last post was a few weeks ago. She didn't seem to be attached to anyone.

His heart rate slowed, and he frowned. The contradicting reactions to his findings upset him. Granted, it appeared she wasn't attached to anyone, but the relief he got from his findings was unwanted. He shouldn't care.

On paper, Zaina looked flawless. Educated, hardworking and smart. From the organizations she volunteered in, one would say she was also compassionate, giving and kind. She was all those things, but he knew another side of her. The spoiled, manipulative, and deceitful side. He would do well to remember that when they eventually talked, and Zaina wanted to rewrite history.

CHAPTER 6

"*I'm telling you. These Arab men can't be faithful for anything.*"

"*Ava, stop saying that. Mustafa seems different,*" *Emma said.*

Zaina, sandwiched between her coworkers, crossed the busy London intersection to the wing shop they often frequented for lunch. For almost two weeks, she hadn't spent quality time with her man. She understood Mustafa worked for a busy, five-star hotel. She also knew how much excellence meant to him. It was mid-June and the high season for tourists. But still. Was he cheating on her? This weekend, he was supposed to be off. Instead of spending it with her, he was off to the United States to see his brother and sister. They had to talk about her potential Geneva job offer, but he never had the time.

As a response to her unanswered call, she would get a text hours later, with a one liner: I apologize, will make it up. *Not even an I love you. She knew he loved her, although rare, he had said the words. He also showered her with gifts. It was his time she had a hard time getting lately. Flashbacks of her childhood and the relationship she had with her father conjured up a feeling of unease.*

"*Sam, are you listening?*"

Zaina blinked her eyes. She had been so caught up in her thoughts that she was oblivious to them entering the bistro and securing a table. Zaina glanced around, taking in the lunch time crowd before returning her attention to the women seated with her. Their expressions mirrored each other. Why did she say anything to them in the first place? They weren't her friends. She had no friends, but when they walked in on her sobbing in the restroom and started badgering her, she had a weak moment.

"What did you say? Where is the menu?" Zaina asked.

"Stop trying to change the topic. We're trying to help you," Ava said. "You guys have shagged right?"

"That's none of your business," Zaina responded. She rubbed her neck that had prickled at the thought of the last time she and Mustafa were in bed together. Passionate wasn't the word she'd use. Sensual... that was a better term. That man knew how to...

"I'll take that as a yes. Anyway, I read somewhere that if an Arab man sleeps with you, then you're nothing but a plaything to him," Ava said.

Zaina caught Emma's frown. It mirrored hers.

"That's not a fair generalization. I've heard that too, but it's still a stereotype. From what I see, that man loves you. Your African love is the envy of the office. We all secretly want to have his baby."

Zaina gave a faint chuckle. She didn't know if Emma thought that was a compliment. Zaina was caught somewhere between irritation and pride that she had the man. But did she?

"That's true, but that's not the point. Have you met his family?" Ava asked.

"Yes." Memories of one Christmas in Tweede Kans Cove came flooding back.

"You see, I told you Mustafa was different. Those kind of men never take women to see their family unless it's serious," Emma added.

"Well, to be sure. Use the Geneva job to force his hand," Ava suggested.

Zaina contemplated for a few moments. Getting words out of

Mustafa was like pulling teeth. Maybe that would do it. A plan formed in her head.

The melodic chords of the church piano pulled Zaina out of the dreaded memory. In retrospect, she wished she'd made a different choice. However, that choice and the subsequent ones she made were things she had to go through to become a better version of herself. The message from the day's sermon floated through her mind. No matter how many emotions we've had, life doesn't stop. If we don't process that hurt, we are bound to get stuck in whatever time period it occurred. The pain was initially too difficult to process, but eventually she did, and now it was time to move on.

She turned to the flat screen television mounted on the wall. Sunday service was over. It was now time for the closing song before the benediction. She'd connected her iPad to it so she would be able to stream the service on a wider screen. From the furnished deck where she started off admiring the pool before she got sidetracked, Zaina strolled back into the deluxe, tented room.

True to his word, Mustafa's driver was waiting for her outside her apartment by ten a.m. After the three-hour journey, factoring in the two-hour time difference between Botswana and Ghana, she was just in time to stream the eleven a.m. service. Her own church didn't have online service, so she'd been an e-member of Calvary Is the Way pastored by Pastor Mensah since she moved to Botswana.

Saturday had been a complete blur. Exhaustion prevented her from spiraling after seeing Mustafa again. She woke up in the early hours of the morning to pack. Now, with nothing else to do but think, she concluded that she wasn't ready. The man was beautiful. Her lips curled up in a smile at Ibiso's name for Mustafa.

She thought of his burly arms, broad shoulders, his low-cut black hair she noticed was now peppered with some gray. So were his moustache and beard that connected in the perfect trim. She used to love running her fingers through his beard. His onyx eyes maintained the aura of danger and darkness she knew he was capable of.

When Mustafa called her name, the deep, husky timbre of his voice sent her insides racing. His outfit was always impeccable, but she was surprised when she saw he had on an ash-colored blazer over a white dress shirt and khaki pants. He was almost always in a suit. Zaina remembered her skin tingling at the awareness of his presence. The delicious mix of his signature cologne and soap had given her a warm, familiar sensation.

Plopping down on the king-sized bed that had white satin sheets, Zaina hummed the melody playing in the background as she took in the massive room. There was no way that this kind of room was reserved for contractors. She'd checked the resort's website, confirming that this room went for fifteen hundred dollars per night. She shook her head. At that rate, she marveled at how the resort was booked out a year in advance.

The room was worth the price. It was an open floor plan. The sleeping area connected to an ensuite bathroom containing a large tub, toilet, and sink with a separate outside shower. The view it provided was priceless. The deck had a deep daybed with a small side table, perfect for a lazy day. The interior was airconditioned, had a television and Wi-Fi. The sitting area was a good size with a small corner desk for working. The kitchenette, which looked too beautiful to even think about cooking in, tied the place together. The warm colors that ran through the space gave that home away from home feel, almost making one forget that wild animals resided mere miles away.

True to what she remembered; Mustafa had gone out of his way to ensure her comfort. Even in his vexed state, which was evident by the way he'd dismissed her the other night.

Her eyes darted back to the television as Kojo Sarbah

wrapped up the cover to "Refiner" by Maverick City Music. Zaina knew about the 891 crew when they toured London some years ago. Finding out he was a member of the church was interesting, but now knowing he was married to Mustafa's sister was mind-blowing. The cliché of the world being small had never been truer. The last she knew, Yasmine had been married to a French man. The celebrity blogs called the couple childhood sweethearts...but how? Yasmine got her second chance so maybe she could too. Was Ibiso right? Maybe her being here was destiny or was it another steppingstone in her journey.

Instead of continuing to daydream, Zaina walked over to her desk, set up her laptop and decided to get to work. The formal start of the project was by nine a.m. the following morning. Her primary reason for being here was to do a job and knowing how shrewd of a businessman Mustafa was, she intended to be prepared. For the next several minutes, she busied herself with her presentation template. She adjusted the order, reworded sentences, and resized pictures. Lifting her eyes, she reached for her buzzing phone

Mustafa: Hello Zaina, I trust you've settled in okay.

Her heart fluttered as she stared at the text. He was so formal, yet familiar. He was often a walking contradiction which made it hard to read him.

Hey there!

She typed, then shaking her head, she immediately hit backspace to delete. What was she thinking?

Hi Mustafa, yes, I have. Thank you.

Satisfied, she sent her response. That was much better. Zaina bit her lower lip as she second guessed her response. Should she have said more? Like gush over the luxurious accommodations? Before she could obsess over it further, her phone rang. Zaina smiled and answered the call.

"Good afternoon, Mother."

"I wasn't the best, but God knows I tried," her mother's voice quaked over the phone.

Zaina bit down on her fist to stifle the laughter that threatened to erupt. Her thoughts went back to a time Mustafa told her she was over the top. If she was, she got it from her mama. Ima Bakari was the most dramatic woman she knew.

"What did I do now?"

"Didn't we discuss your trip to London for a visit?" She sighed. "I cancelled my trip to the U.S to see your brother and his wife because of it."

Zaina gasped. "You gave up seeing your precious son... for me?"

"Stop being snarky, young lady."

Her mother was wrong on both accounts. At thirty-four, she was far from young and snarky she sure wasn't either. It was the truth. Her older brothers, Hashim and Zane, were never skipped over because of little ol' her. Opting for peace this afternoon, Zaina didn't correct her mother on either charge.

"I promised to *think* about making the trip, but things changed. Important things like my job." Zaina placed the phone on speaker and set it down to free up her hands.

"So how long are you there for this time?"

"I'm not sure yet. But the contract is for six months." Her eyes went over her document detecting a typo. She silently reread the statement and corrected it.

"Samantha..."

Zaina's attention snapped back to the person at the other end of the line. For her mother to use her middle name, Zaina knew she was about to say something she already knew was a hard sell.

"The first time you were there, you never went to see your father. Not even one time. When will you let the past go?"

"I have let it go. That's why his approval is no longer my desire."

"Darling, remember when you told me some years ago that you've accepted Christ's salvation? As I recall, you said part of your healing involved you telling your dad and I how our actions impacted your life and your resentment. I'm trying hard to rebuild my connection with you. Your father is too. But it won't succeed if you keep penalizing us for sins you claim to have forgiven."

The resignation in her mother's voice tugged at her heart. She had been angry with and resentful of them for so many years. She acted out and blamed them for her insecurities. The fact remained that even though she had forgiven them, it was still hard to forget. Besides, forgiveness didn't mean reconciliation. But these were her parents. She wanted them in her life, but it was going to take time.

"Mother, I need time."

"I understand but life is too short, darling."

Huh? That's true but what's this sudden fascination with mortality.

"Mother, are you okay? Is there something I should know? Have you gone for your annual checkup?"

Her mother chuckled. "I'm fine."

Her tone wasn't convincing, but Zaina decided not to push. "I have this really important presentation to give in the morning, so I can't deal with daddy's talk right now. But I promise I'll call him."

"Better yet, answer the phone when he calls you," her mother said.

Zaina opted to offer no response. A few beats went by before the discussion moved to other things. Her mother gave her an update on the lives of her siblings, — things she'd never had known otherwise. From there, the conversation moved to her mother's latest project. Surprisingly, Zaina's relationship status was left alone. Her mother refrained from meddling, and she was impressed.

"Okay darling, I'll let you get back to preparing for tomorrow."

"Okay, mother."

"Please be safe out there. Don't go close to those animals. No one is ready for the war that'll ensue if Chief Bakari's child is harmed in any way."

That much was true. After a few more air kisses, promises to call soon and a blessing, the call was disconnected.

Zaina tried to refocus on the task at hand, but the growling of her stomach interrupted her. The hunger pang reminded her that she hadn't had a warm meal since the previous night. In the busyness of earlier, she'd skipped a warm breakfast, opting for a breakfast bar and a smoothie. Her new mission was to search for some food. First, she needed to freshen up.

Minutes later, with fresh breath, presentable hair, and a chic Ankara top over denim shorts, Zaina slipped her feet into her slippers. She was headed to the resort's restaurant. Room service was an option, but she wanted to keep as low of a profile as possible. The boss already put her up in these luxurious accommodations; she didn't need any more attention. Deciding to give her contacts a break, she picked up her glasses. Reaching for her phone and keycard, she paused at the knock on the door.

Zaina stared at the door; she wasn't expecting anyone. When the second knock came, her feet moved. She stood on her toes to check the peephole. A gasp escaped her lips. *What was he doing here?* With her brows pinched in confusion, she opened the door and stepped back.

Mustafa's eyes roamed her body before settling on her face. "You didn't respond to my text." He answered her unasked question.

Zaina remembered the ding she heard while she was on the phone with her mother. Hunger didn't afford her the time to check it when they finished talking. Zaina swiped to the message icon.

Good. Do you need anything? His text said.

"Oh, I'm sorry. I was on the phone with my mother. Thank you I don't need any—" Her stomach growled, shattering that lie.

"It seems you need food. Let's go."

Zaina stared at him, her mouth agape. She didn't know what shocked her the most. The familiar arrogance of his tone, the presumption that she wanted to dine with him, or the fact that she was excited he still cared. She'd matured a lot, but that didn't change who she was at the core. Knowing Mustafa, if she didn't stand up for herself, he wouldn't respect her. She wouldn't even respect herself. She loved his take charge attitude. He was the most domineering man she had ever met, but she was Zaina Bakari.

Her hesitation and the way she crossed her arms over her bosom sent her message because the next words out of his mouth had her moving her feet.

He chuckled. "My apologies. Please dine with me."

"Sure."

CHAPTER 7

Mustafa shifted his gaze from his phone to the empty seat in front of him before landing on the hallway that led to the restroom where Zaina was. The restaurant he chose was a few miles from the resort. There would be enough time in the coming months to dine at the resort's restaurant, so he opted to take her to one offsite. The food was top tier, the customer service, ambience, and the privacy the place offered suited him.

What am I doing?

The question had plagued him since he saw her Friday evening. It wasn't lost on him that the path he was venturing on was a dangerous one; however, he couldn't seem to rein himself in. In a few days, he had already provided her access to his jet, drivers, and had given her premium accommodations. The lodges for consultants were at the opposite side of the resort. They were comfortable, but basic compared to her deluxe accommodation that was only a short distance from his.

Nothing good could come from pretending they didn't have a painful history between them. One that had him wound up in anger and regret at how he allowed her to make a fool of him.

She produced within him emotions that were comparable to the other horrible events that had taken place in his life.

On her approach, Mustafa stood to pull out her chair.

"Sorry, it took so long," she said, breathlessly.

"Don't worry about it. It gave me some time to answer emails and a few text messages."

"Still working around the clock, I see." She lifted her drink, wrapped her lips around her straw and drew a sip from the beverage.

"Apart from the resorts, I have other ventures that demand my attention. For me, time is a scarce commodity. One I don't give away freely."

"Hmm, I should consider myself lucky then." Her eyes sought his.

The Zaina he knew was trying to bait him, but he wouldn't bite. Instead, he grunted, ready to change the course of the conversation, when the waiter approached with their order. They sat in palpable silence as the waiter placed silver, covered dishes on the table and began to run down what they were.

"For you ma'am, *sewaa*, slow cooked goat, beef, and lamb meat with onions and peppers served with polenta. And for you sir, peppered steak, and a salad. Enjoy."

They expressed their gratitude to the waiter, said grace and settled down to eat. In the moments that followed, they remained in delicate semi silence as they enjoyed their meals. Zaina's moan caused him to lift his eyes. Her eyes were closed, head slightly lifted, and she was chewing slowly. She'd always enjoyed a good meal. He admired how expressive she used to be about their cuisine. The sounds she made then; he could do something about later in the bedroom. Now, not so much.

"Careful..."

Opening her eyes, she covered her mouth with her palm. "Oops."

They shared a brief smile.

"Tell me, why did you delay your dream?" He asked the question he'd been dying to know the answer to. According to her, it was the reason she had to go to Geneva. At least, that was what she'd told him then.

Zaina set down her fork and shrugged. "The truth?"

"It's always preferred."

"The opportunity lost its appeal."

"You're telling me your scheming didn't pay off?" Mustafa heard the trace of sarcasm in his voice, but at the moment, didn't care.

"I don't know how many times you want me to apologize. Do you want to finally have the conversation, or pretending nothing happened is better for you?"

"There is no pretense about it. Some things are not worth recollecting." He sneered.

Her brows rose. "Are you serious, Musa? Three years of our life isn't worth it? The pain isn't worth it?"

Ignoring her exasperation, Mustafa took another bite of his steak. When he made his way to her room earlier, arguing with her wasn't on his agenda. And it wouldn't be now. It was time to navigate this conversation away from its pending doom.

"You were speaking to your mother earlier. How is she?" he asked.

Zaina sucked her teeth and rolled her eyes. "Yeah, that's right, I forgot. Your MO is to act like the problem doesn't exist."

Mustafa dropped his fork and used his napkin to wipe the corners of his mouth. Steepling his fingers under his chin, he leaned back into the chair.

"I am a man of few words, this you know. If you want to argue, I will not engage. Your temper tantrum isn't going to force me to indulge in the unnecessary details of an unfortunate event. Now, I apologize for my earlier remarks. You're here to do a job—one I trust you'll do well. The last thing I want is for you to be bogged down with trivialities that'll cloud your mind."

Zaina stared at him with hard eyes. He noticed when they softened, marking her surrender. "You don't want to talk about it, fine! But you don't get to throw snide comments my way. We've gone seven years ignoring it. Six more months won't hurt." She lowered her eyes to her drink. "My mom is fine." She picked up her fork and resumed her meal.

After a few seconds, so did he. He was a man who maintained command over *everything* around him. His business, personal life, and family. The woman in front of him was the only person who could make him come undone at the seams. With what was at stake for his family's legacy, he couldn't afford to be wrapped in her web again.

Five a.m. Monday morning, Mustafa opened his eyes. Over the years, his body mastered no longer needing external stimuli to rise. As was routine, his feet touched the floor, bringing him to a sitting position. Head bowed, he said his prayers. Minutes later, he walked into his closet and changed into his workout attire. He stood in his workout room trying to decide on whether to do an upper body workout or go for a run.

Quickly deciding nothing indoors would cut it for the riot going on in his mind, he headed for the front door. An early morning run along the trail was exactly what he needed. The humid air hit his face when he opened the door. Most likely due to the weather from the previous night, the path was muddy, and the trees dripped with moisture. A few minutes later, he joined the few joggers already on the narrow trail.

Mustafa's thoughts raced as fast as his feet did. His problem was his underestimation of the effects Zaina still had on him. That was the only reason he risked taking her to dinner. In the end, he'd grossly miscalculated his immunity to her smell, laughter, and intellect. Following their awkward moment, they settled into an amicable discussion. After dinner, she declined his offer to escort her back to her villa. The headstrong, feisty woman who challenged him at every turn was back. Her refusal fell on deaf ears as he walked her back. Stubbornly, she didn't say much on the way; however, he made sure she got in okay. Her anger at his refusal to revisit her explanation about what ended their relationship years ago puzzled him. The voicemail she left him years ago, was clear enough. Encouraged by her friends, she concocted up a plan to manipulate him with a job she hadn't even been offered yet. Memories he'd pushed to the recess of his mind resurfaced as he recalled that fateful night.

They were at dinner, halfway into the meal he'd sat stunned as she ended their relationship. She'd explained that it was necessary because she didn't need any distractions. As the small velvet box containing an engagement ring burned a whole in his suit pocket, his head spun with the possibility of the second woman he loved leaving him. He'd known Geneva was where she'd applied to work under a famed interior designer. It was never his intention to stifle her dreams. How could she think he wouldn't do everything in his power to ensure she achieved them?

Before he could put his thoughts into words to tell her that, his phone rang. Omar had gotten into trouble with the law in America. Charged with getting his brother help, Mustafa had asked Zaina if they could pick up the conversation later. He'd watched in horror as she erupted in rage. His mistake was letting his anger get the best of him. He had jerked to his feet, almost knocking down the table causing her to flinch. The fear in her eyes was akin to her dousing him with cold water. Was he that angry that he drew fear from her? He had seen that look in his mother's eyes so many times. The fact that she took him to a place he'd sworn never to go, changed everything.

On the drive back to her apartment, she'd caught sight of the ring that had fallen out of his pocket. Right before she'd climbed out of the car, with teary eyes, she apologized. It was all a lie and she'd wanted to explain.

Zaina had brought them to that point, in public, as part of a test. Mustafa couldn't believe it then and he'd since let go of wanting to know the reason why. He couldn't trust her. It was a lesson she'd taught him, and one he'd do well to remember.

It took two laps around the trail to get his thoughts settled. Walking back into his villa, Mustafa made his way to the kitchen where the staff had delivered his breakfast, and his iPad had been set up. He was a creature of habit. He had the same meal most mornings—toast, poached eggs, a piece of some sort of meat, and tea. While he ate, he looked over his emails, browsed his itinerary and read the news highlights. He ruminated over his first meeting for the morning with Grand Amour legal counsel. He needed updates on the separation agreement or restitution from the former environmental company, and the case of the little girl who slipped on a wet spot in Tweede Kans Cove and her parents wanted compensation. The meeting with Zaina was after that.

Several minutes later, showered and dressed, he donned a grey suit over a black shirt and headed out. On his way, he decided to check in with his grandmother. The live-in physiotherapist reported that she was doing great with her exercises.

"Good morning, sir."

"Good morning, Assad. Bring me up to speed." Mustafa took the cup of coffee his assistant handed him. The young man only traveled with him if he was going to be gone from Tweede Kans Cove for an extended period.

Mustafa turned the corner to his office with Assad behind him, updating him about his full schedule and changes that had to be made. Mustafa settled in before inquiring about Zaina's temporary office. He'd found out that Safi Kijani had an office located in the capital city. That was where Zaina had worked out of for the last fifteen months. Just as her staying offsite wasn't satisfactory to him, neither was her working from Gaborone. Her office was down the hall on the other side. Assad gave confirmation that everything had been handled and began connecting the parties for his first call.

~

He was running late. The circumstance that led to his tardiness annoyed him. He and the lawyers didn't always agree and the meeting that just concluded had them on opposite sides. Mustafa agreed that it was ridiculous to claim that because the sign cautioning that the floor was wet wasn't in Arabic, the little girl's family ignored it. However, the girl sprained her wrist and Mustafa wanted the matter closed immediately. No more back and forth. Mustafa stood and gathered up what he needed for the next meeting. Entering the conference room minutes later, Mustafa's eyes scanned those present. The green director for Grand Amour, the resort's general manager, and two of his staff members. A frown formed on his face until his eyes traveled to the other side of the room.

There she was.

Zaina's back was to him. She was slightly bent over, talking to one of the administrative staff. From what he could see, they were testing the projector for her presentation. Her work attire was modest, yet sexy. Her silk black blouse was tucked into red, high waisted, wide legged dress pants. The outfit accentuated her curves he could trace with his eyes closed. He headed to his seat and noticed her jacket draped across the back of the chair next to his. Willing his eyes and mind to stay focused on the folder that was handed to him, he took a seat.

The surge of electricity that ran through his body at the sight of her was something he had to get under control. Now, she was a totally different person from the one he had dinner with the previous night. He admired the balance of business and casual aura she had.

The resort manager opened the meeting. After grounding everyone on the objectives of the gathering, formal introductions were made. When his eyes locked with Zaina, she gave him a faint smile and nodded. Kind of what she did with everyone else.

He didn't like it.

Mustafa wasn't sure what he expected after the way they parted after dinner. But this wasn't it. He didn't want or need her explanation, so why was he bothered by her indifference?

The floor was now hers. As Zaina strutted to the front of the room, his eyes followed her movement. Who was he kidding? He still wanted her. He just couldn't trust her. He was older and wiser now. A meaningless roll in the sack wasn't something that interested him. He wanted to settle down but couldn't imagine a world where he'd settle down with her.

After a few clicks of the clicker, she started to speak. "After reading the audit findings and going over the drawings, I was able to diagnose the problem and proffer a solution that will do two things. One, pass the upcoming audit and two, increase efficiencies if maintained correctly. Instead of relying on the rainfall and the inland river, this safari, because of where it's located, should be provided an additional source of water. This can come from the lake on the other side of the property. Like the former company, I suggest a recharge. But with indirect surfacing and not direct like they tried to do."

"Since the solution is still a recharge, why didn't that way work?" the general manager asked.

Zaina unscrewed the cap from the water bottle before her and took a sip. "The reason they weren't able to reach the deliverables is that, although this method had its good qualities, it is slow because it depends on other natural resources."

Zaina tried not to keep her eyes on him for too long,

Mustafa, on the other hand, kept his gaze on her. He was transfixed on the ease, intelligence, and articulate way in which she relayed the information. She took her time explaining how the indirect injection recharge which her company was offering was a much better solution. She answered each question with poise and patience.

Mustafa's eyes traveled to his green director. Something wasn't right if he didn't know the difference between the two methods. The man had sat in on every meeting they had along with some members of his staff. Mustafa made a mental note to speak with human resources. He couldn't pay people that weren't pulling their weight. This would've been avoided if he was paying attention. He was supposed to be the on-staff environmentalist.

The last slide was to go over the numbers. The general manager had already briefed him on what they were, but Mustafa wanted to hear Zaina's breakdown for each line item so he could understand them better. After several questions from him and some of the staff, the meeting wrapped up with Zaina providing a summary.

"Time is of the essence. My boss informed me of a final call which takes place after this. Once I get the go ahead, I'll have a meeting with my team from Gaborone at the site. To ensure we get this done in five months rather than six, I'll look for how we can adjust the existing model, rather than do a complete overhaul."

The meeting lasted a little under two hours. Mustafa was flanked by his managers as they discussed their thoughts. He observed as Zaina packed up her things. The decision to hire Safi Kijani had already been made, but he always wanted to hear other points of view. Even if in this case, the time to objectively listen to anybody's concerns had run out. Time wasn't something he had the luxury of now.

Zaina walked to the door. Her exit was halted by one of his

junior staff members. Mustafa couldn't hear their conversation, but from the pleasing smile on the gentleman's face, he knew it wasn't about business.

He didn't like it.

Mustafa saw the man reach for Zaina's hand and immediately excused himself and headed towards them.

"The lunch special for today is great. Would you like to join me?" the young man asked.

Zaina shook her head. "I'm sorry. I have a lot to get done today."

"But you have to eat. Or do you already have plans?"

Zaina turned her eyes to Mustafa. She probably felt his presence. Contemplation danced in her eyes. She turned to face the man in front of her but didn't provide an answer fast enough. He decided to do it for her.

"She has plans."

The staffer greeted him, but Mustafa kept his eyes on Zaina, watching as her eyes filled with confusion, asking for an explanation. Keeping his expression aplomb, Mustafa didn't offer her any. He didn't have one. He just wasn't comfortable with her having lunch with other men. She pursed her lips; defiance covered her expression. A beat passed with them deadlocked in a stare down.

Then Zaina smiled and turned to the gentleman who Mustafa was surprised was still standing there. She glanced down at her phone and up again.

"Would you look at that. My schedule just cleared up. Lunch is perfect, then you can tell me more about the Delta."

Without giving him a second glance, Zaina left the conference room, followed closely by her new buddy. Mustafa's jaw clenched. He put his hands in his pockets to hide his fists. He would allow her victory now; the consequences he would deliver later. Now he had a business to run.

CHAPTER 8

"*O*h wow, now I'm stuffed."

Zaina leaned back into the cushioned bamboo chair at the resort's restaurant. She winced as a fork scraped the plate of her lunch companion.

Tacky.

Mustafa would never have done that. He was always so poised and sleek. She chided herself...again. Since they sat down to eat, she'd been comparing the gentleman she now knew as Kabelo to Mustafa. It was an effort in futility. No one could be fairly compared to the insufferable, arrogant Mustafa DuBois-Arazi.

Her nose flared. He must think the sun rose and set at his demand. Granted, she was the reason they had this tension between them, but after he dismissed her yesterday, she was done trying. During the meeting, his intimidating gaze burned her skin, but she was determined not to give him the satisfaction of knowing he affected her. Then the nerve of him to try and regulate who she spent time with. Absurd.

"Zaina?"

Kabelo's voice jolted her from her wayward thoughts. He was easy on the eyes. Very easy. Dark chocolate skin, bald head with a small goatee.

"I'm sorry. What did you say?"

"Now that I've enjoyed a lovely meal with you, I'm ready for what comes next," he said.

Zaina raised her brows. "What do you mean?"

He chuckled. "Give it to me straight. How much trouble am I in?"

"With whom?"

"The boss man. I was almost convinced he was going to strangle me."

Zaina shifted in her seat and tittered. "I don't know what you're talking about."

Zaina's heart thudded against her ribcage. She was only in her first day and knew that the rumors of suspicion about her and Mustafa were about to start. Men gossiped too, so she knew Kabelo was about to whisper in some ears. She was already fighting for respect in her position at home. She couldn't lose respect here.

"Come on now, don't insult my intelligence. I won't mind risking—"

"Before you continue, I had a wonderful time at lunch. This, however, was nothing more than two people having a meal together."

"And a means to make the boss jealous. I get it; I was a willing accomplice."

Zaina stared at him for a moment, then broke out in a chuckle and shook her head. Leave it to Mustafa to stake his claim but swear he didn't want anything to do with her. Be that as it may, she wasn't looking for a relationship, especially not with anyone that worked for him.

Apart from this project, which was a priority, Zaina had

other projects she was a part of. The redevelopment project she'd just finished and the remediation one she worked on last year still needed her attention. She glanced at Kabelo, feeling a sharp pang of remorse for using him. In that moment, Mustafa infuriated her, and she didn't think straight.

"There isn't anything between your boss and me. So, you are safe."

The waiter brought over the check and Kabelo took it before she could get it. She twisted her lips at him. African men and their egos. He paid and the waiter left.

"I hope you don't believe that. For what it's worth, any time you want to use me to make the big man jealous, I'm available." He winked

Zaina rolled her eyes. She didn't know this man from Adam and here he was laying down his livelihood on her behalf. The Mustafa she knew *then* wouldn't take his job. She'd spent a lot of time on Google researching *this* Mustafa. He was wealthier and more powerful, two things that could change any man.

"I thank you, but that won't be necessary."

Zaina waited for the light entrée she'd ordered for later. If things went as she knew they would, she would be working late into the night. When her order arrived, she and Kabelo headed back to the offices via the elevator. When they arrived on the second floor, she headed to the office Mustafa's assistant had shown her earlier. Then, she had been too nervous to admire the space. Taking it all in now had her eyes widening.

The first thing she was drawn to was the large window that showcased the natural oasis that was the Delta. Three of the walls were painted in light cream color while the fourth one behind her chair was painted with a color that mirrored the beautiful sunrises she'd come to enjoy over the last couple of days. Somewhat left of center, was a medium-sized, white marble desk. Two paintings adorned the walls of the carpeted space, with a plant in the corner. The office was stunning. The only drawback was its proximity to Mustafa's. It wasn't that close, but close enough. She'd have to find a way to deal with it because a four-hour commute each day wasn't going to cut it.

With that in mind, she powered up her laptop and got to work. Zaina focused on the reward from completing this job successfully. That was what she needed to remember to move forward. Her why.

~

*L*ater that evening, Zaina stood up from the yoga mat she had laid out near the desk in her room. Surprisingly, the rest of the day was plain sailing. The most exciting thing that happened was when she thought her files were lost. The IT guy had come by to get her onto the Grand Amour network. She needed access to certain files that would be shared throughout the course of the project. During that first hour, her stomach was in knots waiting for Mustafa to pop up. The whole day, he never did. Zaina pushed him to the back of her mind and attended to the matters at hand.

She received a call from her boss informing her that the project was officially green lighted. Some hours later, she met with the resort manager and the green director and was introduced to the person that would be her liaison. Lastly, she had a meeting with her own team. The meeting ended with them scheduling a tour of the site in a few days.

Glancing at the time, she decided to call Ibiso. Other than a quick "landed" text when she first arrived, Zaina hadn't talked to her. Plopping down on the sofa, she tucked her feet underneath her and dialed. The phone rang unanswered, then rolled over to voicemail. Zaina clicked over to her Apple Music app and started her workout playlist. "Mama Africa" by Bracket blasted through the device as she got in her groove. About half an hour later, the music was interrupted by the ringing of her phone.

"Sam, *how now*? Sorry I missed your call. These kids will not drive me crazy. I refuse," Ibiso spilled out as soon as Zaina answered the phone.

Zaina laughed. "Leave my niece and nephew alone. That's their job."

"'Hance had all weekend to tell us he needed a book for his literature homework. All weekend. He didn't say anything. It's this evening, on the way back from school that he said something. See me, going from bookshop to bookshop looking for this book because the assignment is due tomorrow."

Zaina sometimes wondered what having a child would feel like. She didn't have any aversion to them but was scared she might turn out like her own mom. She never wanted her child to experience the neglect she felt growing up.

"Awww...*no vex*."

Ibiso chuckled at her attempt to speak pidgin English. It wasn't something she was exposed to growing up in London. Unlike other African households she knew where the parents instilled the culture in their Diaspora born kids, her parents didn't.

"Anyway, wassup? How is it going?" Ibiso asked.

Zaina bit her lower lip. "I'm still processing."

"Have you seen your man?"

Zaina sucked her teeth. "He's not my man, but I have seen him and girl—"

"*Oya* start from the beginning."

Zaina chuckled then began narrating everything that had happened since she'd arrived. From their impromptu meeting to the luxury, she was living in, to their disastrous dinner to the events of earlier. She finished with a sigh.

"*Na wa o.* Your life is now a movie. A weird 'godfather, you are mine' film. *Wahala dey o.* The attraction *sha.* Is it still there?"

"I'd be a total liar if I said no. I mean, intense, on my side. I don't know about him. He's bent on holding on to the past. I'm not going to keep paying for mistakes my Jesus has forgiven."

"My hubby is the meanest of all his brothers. But your guy has mine beat."

Zaina shook her head. "This is different. Mustafa and I have history. Bad blood. I broke his trust. I get it, but I won't keep begging him to hear me out."

"And I agree. There was a time in our relationship that I told Rasheed I won't go to war for him if he didn't deem me worthy enough to fight for. I hesitate to give advice because the heart wants what it wants. Only you two understand your situation. I agree, he can't have it both ways." Ibiso chuckled. "Imagine trying to monitor who you have lunch with."

Zaina laughed. "One thing a man will have, is an abundance of audacity. They can run out of everything else but that—audacity…they have plenty of," Zaina said.

The friends laughed and talked a little bit more before hanging up with promises to check in soon. No longer in the mood for a workout, Zaina prepared to utilize the outdoor shower. Not big on television, her evening plans involved watching the sun set with a nice, warm cup of tea until it was time to sleep.

Several minutes later, freshly showered with shorts and a nightshirt on, Zaina called down to the restaurant for some decaffeinated tea. She needed to wind down and what she had in the room would do the opposite of that. Moments later, she was stretched out on the hammock absorbing the view. Two rapid knocks interrupted her concentration. *That was fast.* She rose to answer.

She opened the door. "Oh, that was—"

The rest of her speech got caught in her throat when she

stared into a pair of sexy, dark eyes. Eyes that seemed to penetrate her soul. Without a word, Mustafa made his way in. Zaina locked the door and moved toward the living area. She needed to put enough space between them.

He was casually dressed in an all-black ensemble. A color that contrasted well with his olive skin. *Where had he been all day? Maybe he's been on a date?* All this time, she hadn't considered that possibility and now she felt stupid. Subconsciously, she crossed her arms over her bosom. She must look scruffy. Her curly hair was in a messy bun atop her head, and she had on a nightshirt for crying out loud. Granted she had shorts underneath, but with his piercing gaze, she felt exposed. He continued to stare at her. She knew the look all too well. It was the look he gave before he pounced. His stoic expression forced her to attempt to slice through the tension.

"Look Mustafa…I…"

Her words faltered as he stalked toward her. She retreated until her legs hit the back of the couch.

She was trapped.

Her heart raced.

Mustafa remained silent. She wasn't afraid of him, but his larger-than-life aura brought out emotions she was trying hard to contain. Her breath hitched as he entered her personal space. His scent filled her nostrils, jumbling her thoughts. Him being taller than her caused her to look up at him. His intimidating glare locked with her eyes. The tension between them was sucking the air she was desperately trying to fill her lungs with.

"Mustafa—"

"Don't do that again." His timbre caused her heart to skip a beat.

"Do…what?" Her voice was shaky.

"You feign ignorance? You do not know what I'm talking about?"

"I…don't." This time she couldn't recognize her own voice. She cleared her throat and repeated with authority. "I don't."

Zaina decided to create distance between them. She turned and tried to move away, but Mustafa grabbed her arm. He pulled her closer to him, a feat she didn't think was possible with how close they were already. Her eyes moved from their point of contact back up to his eyes.

He loosened the grip on her arm and bent toward her ear. It was only the two of them in the room, so he didn't need to whisper, but being so close to her neck was a power play.

He remembered her spot.

"Don't flirt with my staff to get a reaction out of me."

Zaina shook him off. "Then don't try to police who I can and cannot spend time with."

"You're not allowed to spend time with my staff outside of business." He shoved his hands into his pockets.

"Not allowed? Are you kidding me?"

"You know I don't kid."

"It must be something new for you because you can't be serious."

Mustafa stared at her for a few seconds then sauntered to the door. "It will be in your best interest to heed my warning," he threw over his shoulders.

She was so frustrated with this man that she wanted to scream. Of course, she wasn't going to date anyone while she was here. But what made him think he had a say in what she did? He didn't want her but was upset that somebody else did. This was part of their problem, communication. She wasn't going to go with the flow anymore. Mustafa placed his hand on the doorknob when Zaina decided to try one last time.

"Musa!"

He froze but didn't turn around.

She continued, "For the millionth time, I'm sorry. But this is where I draw the line. You can't have it both ways. It's clear you don't want me, but you can't dictate who does."

He turned but remained in place. His fiery eyes roamed her body before landing on her face. "People here have families to feed or people who depend on them. I'd hate for you to be the cause of them losing their jobs."

Her brows came together. "You wouldn't."

"Try me."

"Ugh!! I can't believe you."

"Believe it, *chérie*."

His eyes dared her to challenge him, but she was stuck on the French term of endearment he used for her. She was painfully aware that nothing about this moment was endearing, but to hear it come out of his mouth was something she longed many nights for. Zaina was tired of fighting with him. She had to think of a way that she could monitor the work from Gaborone and come to the resort once a week. This wasn't going to work for her. She had done a lot of work to get to where she was mentally and emotionally. Too bad he hadn't done the same.

"As to your earlier, unfounded claim, I do want you. But I know better than to satisfy that want. That doesn't mean you get to rattle the beast with your antics," he warned.

Stunned at his confession, Zaina was speechless. She had a response for the other stuff he said, but with him, she'd learned to pick her battles.

"I want you too," she whispered.

"I know you do," he smirked. "None of that matters. I don't trust you."

Zaina rolled her eyes at his arrogance. Once again, she reminded herself her goal was to win the war. This was progress. She might be getting the chance to do what she'd wanted to for seven years. Explain.

"I get that but let me explain."

Mustafa didn't respond. She rubbed her hands up and down her arms. She'd almost given up until he began walking toward her. Her eyes followed him as he passed by her, headed to the sofa, and sat. She wondered what he was doing. Her answer came when he leaned back into the sofa, crossed one leg over his other knee and looked up at her.

"Well, explain."

CHAPTER 9

$\mathcal{M}$ustafa started the day solid in his resolve to keep things strictly professional between Zaina and himself. She was here to do a job and be gone. It was a mantra he recited to himself repeatedly, but which vanished the moment he saw her walk out to lunch with another man. The desire to rip the man's head off washed over him like an ocean wave. However, he reined in his feral instinct and decided to tackle his day. Zaina was spoiled; she was used to getting her way but causing chaos in his business would not be tolerated. After a business dinner in Maun, he'd arrived back at the resort and his feet carried him to her room.

Now, what he wanted from her he wasn't even sure, but it didn't include watching her tuck loose tresses of her hair behind her ear and bite her lower lip as though she wanted to sever it. Patience was not his strong suit, but he decided to wait for her to gather herself and say what she desperately needed him to hear.

"The neglect from my parents did more damage than I was willing to accept," she murmured, her voice pensive.

"Neglect?"

"You know I'm the last of eight children. What you don't know, and I try to forget is, I'm the child that wasn't meant to be. My mom gave my dad his sons and they were content until I arrived eight years later. Neither of them had time for me." Zaina tittered.

Mustafa stared at her. Even though her laughter expressed her discomfort, he found nothing amusing in her pain. He had firsthand experience of the damage of childhood trauma. But he tried not to let it affect them, so he was curious to see where this was going.

"I didn't grow up in a two-parent household. My dad lives in Tanzania and my mother was there, but not present. I wanted so bad for my parents to acknowledge and affirm me. They took care of all my material needs but neglected what I needed most. Them. I walked around with a void. Like a part of me was missing. Then I met you." She stood and walked to the small kitchen area.

"You want something to drink?"

"No, thanks. I'm fine." Mustafa watched her mix a fruity drink. "Should you be drinking that?"

"Oh please, Musa. It's nonalcoholic." She took a sip of her drink and walked back to her seat.

"We happened so fast. One minute we were at a jazz concert and the next, I was spending weekends in your London apartment. We were wrapped up in the passionate cocoon of our bubble and that was my safe space. When we were out of that bubble, I didn't know how to handle your commitment to anything other than me. Your siblings or your family business. I know you told me that family was everything to you, but not having a sense of that myself, I didn't understand. I thought we would get to the place where it would be my parents all over again. Others would come before me. We talked of marriage, but when you started traveling more, cancelling, or postponing dates because you had to go to America or France to see about your siblings, I panicked."

Fire rose to his chest with every word she spoke. "Did I not show that I loved you?"

"You did. I've spent some time in therapy, and now I know that I needed more than your service. I needed your validation. Affirmation, that's my love language. Then, I was too immature to say I needed your words. Instead, I did what I'd always done to get my father's attention. I cooked up a scheme to jolt you into my desired action.

"Yes, the job in Geneva was real. I thought if I threatened the demise of our relationship, you'd fight for me. That the thought of losing me would get you to say more. I needed your words to assuage the insecurities I began having about us. Instead, you told me you were okay with me moving miles away from you. Omar calling you at that exact moment tipped me over. The things I said about your family, I regret 'til this day. What I did wasn't right, but there was a reason why. Over the years, I've realized I expected you to fill a void that wasn't meant for you to fill.

"It's not easy loving a man that hardly communicates his thoughts, is a tad bit controlling, and whose first instinct is to fix and not listen. Musa, you can be more of an enigma than a human. Being with you sometimes felt like being run over by a truck. Your intensity, passion, love, and compassion, mixed with the arrogant savagery you're capable of, can be overwhelming. My mistake was trying to get you to bend to my will instead of talking so we could strike a balance."

Zaina placed her forearms on her knees and bowed her head. He wanted so badly to go to her and comfort her but couldn't bring himself to do it. He understood her antics a little better, but that didn't ease the betrayal. And getting any closer to her would open the possibility of something deeper. He had never been one for a lot of words, and his family was still everything to him. That, he couldn't compromise on, so what was the point?

"I'm sorry you went through that. I'm even sorrier that you couldn't come to me. The first woman I loved left me broken when she didn't deem herself worthy enough to leave a toxic situation behind. I've seen what love can do, but like a fool, I handed my heart over to a second woman—you. You abused the power I gave you."

"I know—"

"My family will always mean everything to me. But they'll never take priority over the woman I choose to share my life with. I don't repeat myself, but I do remember the day I expressed my love for you. That day, I told you it meant you belonged to me. You were mine to care for, push forward to achieve all the goals you'd set for yourself, eliminate any obstacles that stood in your way. Nurture and protect your mind, body, and soul. If at any time I wasn't meeting those needs, my expectation was for you to voice your concerns."

She flung her hands up. Her frustration evident. "And I know that now. I can't change the past."

Mustafa stood and walked over to her. Her soft eyes were yearning for what he knew he couldn't give. Not without processing the information she had given him. He kissed the top of her head. The scent of her shampoo stirred his loins.

"Neither can I, *chérie*. Get some rest."

He had to leave. Their relationship wasn't a door he was willing to walk through again.

~

Friday evening, two weeks later, Mustafa scrolled through his phone as Salma went over the plans for their grandmother's celebration in a few months. He and Omar were in her villa. Mustafa had arrived in Tweede Kans Cove a couple of days ago. Using his thumb and index finger, he expanded the picture of the work site in Botswana. The amount of work that had been done by Zaina and her team in such a short time surprised him.

Zaina.

The day after they had their talk, he knew he couldn't stay in Botswana. He'd spent that night mulling over what she'd told him. He blamed himself for not reading her mood correctly. However, nothing exonerated her deception. He knew he had to forgive her. He wasn't sure he could do that objectively being so close to her. That night, back in his villa, he realized he hadn't forgiven her because he refused to deal with it. He had blocked their time together out and carried on with his life. Like he had done after another traumatic experience several years earlier. Now, to see her everyday would always remind him of the past and he had to figure out how he wanted to handle her before engaging. Even in a cordial, professional relationship.

The following day, Mustafa left for Gaborone for a meeting with the Minister of Tourism. Then he flew to Cape Town for a golf charity event, then the U.S before arriving home three days ago. He hadn't talked to Zaina since that night but received frequent updates on the progress.

"Musa, are you even listening?" Salma asked.

"No one listens to you," Omar said.

His brother had been back in Tweede Kans Cove running the resort with Salma in his absence.

"Leave me alone, O. I don't know why Yas didn't keep you there with her." Salma rolled her eyes at him.

"Enough with the bickering. *aikhti alsaghira*, I'm listening. A visit to her favorite charity on Saturday, after which we party all night. Church on Sunday. Correct?" Mustafa ran down the itinerary he'd heard numerous times before.

"Hmm, yes. Except that little sister you insist on calling me."

She closed the notebook that was on her lap and set it to the side. Omar laughed, soliciting an evil eye from their sister.

Mustafa grinned. "Even when you get to be a hundred, you'll always be my little sister."

"And mine too." Omar winked.

She pointed her index finger at him. "Don't you dare. Again, we're three minutes apart. Three!"

"Keyword, apart."

Mustafa ignored them. They could go on like this for several minutes. He missed Yasmine. She always helped balance everyone out. "If we're done here. I need to get on a conference call."

"It's Friday. Don't you have a date or something?" Salma asked. "All work and no play makes my brother a boring man."

Mustafa raised his brow. "You're using a cliché on me?"

"And I hate that it's true." She glanced over at Omar, shaking her head before turning back to him. "I can't believe I'm saying this, but look at O. He has a healthy balance of work and play."

Mustafa chuckled as Omar feigned choking on the water he was drinking. "When I need your help, I'll be sure to get it."

"*shaqiq*, I know we have a formal meeting on Monday to talk about the thing in Botswana, but how is it going?" Omar asked, making his way from Salma's kitchen.

With both of his siblings waiting for his response, Mustafa contemplated how much he wanted to tell them. The Christmas he'd brought Zaina home, his family loved her.

How could she question my love? Meeting my family cemented us.

Now, not so much. Especially Salma.

She designated herself as his protector. A trait he found adorable, but entirely unnecessary. Years ago, he was telling Yasmine of his breakup with Zaina, and Salma overheard. She hasn't had one good thing to say about her ever since.

"*hasan*...good. The company is exceeding my expectations. It's still early, but I'm thinking of signing them on for another project. Remember the shopping complex I want to develop? The land might need remediation and they do that well, as well as training our own environmental staff."

"*bahir*, anything that'll prevent this disaster from happening again," Omar said.

"I'm glad. I'm thinking of visiting. I need a change of scenery," Salma announced.

Mustafa studied her. This was news to him, but out of all his siblings, she was the most spontaneous. She could also be a brat.

"When you do, I expect you to behave," Mustafa warned.

She furrowed her brows. "Why wouldn't I?"

Mustafa released a cleansing breath and glanced at Omar who had confusion in the depth of his eyes. "Zaina is there."

"Get out of here! You and Zay got back together?" Omar shouted.

Salma sucked her teeth and rolled her eyes. "Please don't tell me you gave that woman another chance." She walked over to the counter and picked up her phone. "I need to call Yas. She needs to hear this. Oh, I'm definitely coming to Botswana now before she gets her claws into you."

"Enough." Mustafa growled, bringing her rambling to a halt. "I do not owe you an explanation about my personal life, but your misguided rant is understandable." A beat passed between them. Salma had her arms crossed over her chest. "Zaina happens to be the consultant sent from Safi Kijani. Everyone was referring to her as Sam Bakari. With everything else going on, I didn't connect the dots. I don't know how I missed it."

"Oh, okay. I'm sure if you knew, you would've requested someone else," Salma said.

"I didn't say that." He paused. "What happened between Zaina, and I is my business. No flames are being rekindled, but I demand she be respected."

"Wow. Bro, out of everyone in this entire world, she's the one that's sent to help you." Omar ran his hand through his hair.

His surprise was palpable. Mustafa was still getting over the coincidence.

"That's just luck. And she isn't helping him, she's doing her job," Salma corrected.

"I don't believe in luck. That's destiny," Omar replied.

"Coincidence, luck or destiny. She'll be around for the next six months." Mustafa narrowed his eyes at Salma. "Be nice."

She grunted her response. It was unfortunate her view of Zaina had been tainted, but he wouldn't tolerate any disrespect. Mustafa drew her close and kissed Salma's temple. She was spoiled and he accepted his culpability in it, but she would have to get over it. She hugged him for a few moments before releasing him. Omar approached him and he drew him in for a brotherly hug.

"Before I forget, send an invitation to Qadir and Qasim. They should be in Nigeria." He had met the brothers several years ago in the U.S when he visited Omar. They had remained good friends over the years.

Salma's eyes bugged, then danced around before she responded. "Why?"

Mustafa wondered what that was about. "Because I want them there."

He didn't have time to explore his sister's bizarre behavior. He thought she got along well with the brothers. Now, he had a call he needed to attend but he did intend to find out what had his sister rattled.

CHAPTER 10

They were two months in, and she was feeling good. Zaina squeezed the stress ball in her hand as she strolled the length of her office. She was on a routine weekly conference call with the Abuja office providing updates. The first few days after she arrived at Grand Amour, she was unsettled, but after talking to Mustafa and unloading the burden she had carried for years, she was at ease. Mustafa helped by staying away. They had a biweekly call which he attended from wherever he was. In the last eight weeks, she had seen him only twice. Initially, she was hurt by his blatant avoidance, but then again, she had given him a lot to process. She also wasn't in the mood to keep asking him to forgive her. The next move had to be his.

Her days consisted of various site visits, on and off the property. Vendor calls coordinating deliverables of key machinery. Making payments while staying within budgets for all the projects assigned to her. Collecting, analyzing, and reporting data from samples she got from the site. On top of that, she had to keep her Abuja office and Grand Amour management updated. At the end of each day, she had a relaxing shower, dinner and watched a movie, which most of the time, ended up watching her as she fell asleep. On the weekends, she toured some part of the resort and enjoyed the amenities it had to offer. The one thing she refused to do was go out on a safari.

Although Mustafa stayed away, his presence was felt. The staff catered to all her desires, spoken or implied. If she was late for lunch by as little as ten minutes, it would miraculously arrive some minutes later. There hadn't been one meal she didn't like. Another day, she was in the field and complained of a kink in her neck. The next evening, a female massage therapist appeared at her door, complete with her bench, oils, and scented candles. Zaina thought they were being nice. That illusion went up in flames when she overheard her name from two staff members and something about pleasing the boss. Mustafa might not have said anything about the conversation they had, but he heard her. Every time she reported the completion of a milestone in the last two months, the next day, she'd get fresh flowers sent to her office or villa. The message was always only two words.

Well, done.

MDA.

"Yes sir, we're making good progress. I'm still having an issue with the company that handled this project before we took over. I was told that as part of the separation agreement, I'd have complete access to the feasibility study and project designs, so I wouldn't have to start from scratch. We're at the stage where the injection pump needs to be installed, but they're giving me the run around," Zaina reported her status update.

"I thought this was handled last week?" her boss asked.

Zaina stopped pacing and walked back to her desk. Sitting in her seat, she moved her mouse to bring her laptop back to life. She browsed the email she had from the company.

"Yes, it was, and I was promised it would be taken care of. If it's not resolved this week, I'll make a trip to their head office in Maun."

"Ok, keep me updated."

With her projects all covered, Zaina muted herself and looked over her calendar in Outlook. She needed to find time to travel to Dar es Salaam. She hadn't been to her home country in over two years and hadn't seen her parents in about the same amount of time. Next month, her brother was officially taking over the reins of Bakari furniture since her dad wanted to lean into politics. There was a big celebration planned, and everyone was expected to be there. Her mom would be flying in from London, and she would meet her there. She'd run away from connecting enough. It was now time to face her fears.

Half an hour later, the meeting concluded. Zaina stepped out of her office heading straight to the restroom. All day she had been drinking water, teas and coffees and hadn't had the time to relieve herself. Moments later, she washed her hands and checked her makeup. Noting the time, she saw she had fifteen minutes before her final call of the day. The next day being Saturday, she vowed not to lift a finger. She and her bed were going to be inseparable.

Exiting the restroom, head bowed while scrolling through her social media pages, Zaina bumped into a soft body. Her eyes bugged when she recognized Salma DuBois-Arazi.

"Watch it."

The iciness in her tone was piercing, but Zaina decided to ignore it. She knew Mustafa never discussed them with his siblings, but there was no telling what could happen when a man was hurt. Out of Mustafa's sisters, she was the feistiest. Her lithe body was clad in white linen shorts and a cropped green top, displaying her dark olive skin. In her hand was a white clutch. Her manicured feet were dressed in green sandals. Her hair wasn't short anymore. Instead, she had a bob that rested on her shoulders. Back in the day, Zaina always teased her saying she belonged on somebody's magazine cover.

"Hey Salma, nice to see you." Zaina smiled at her.

"I wish I could say the same."

"Excuse me?"

Salma sneered, placing one hand on her waist. "I promised my brother I'd be cordial. That, however, doesn't mean I'll stand by and let you get your claws in him again. You won't have a second chance to hurt him."

Zaina remained stunned and before her brain could form a reply, Salma walked away. *What just happened? How is she here? Did Mustafa send her in his place?* From her extensive research, Zaina knew the siblings ran the resort together. Those questions rambled through her mind as her timer went off. It was time to join her meeting.

Several hours later, Zaina rubbed her palms across her face. The day was finally over. It was a good thing she didn't have to present on the last call. After her confrontation with Salma, her mind was everywhere. She stretched her back and rolled her shoulders. She attempted to stand when she was alerted to an incoming email. As she browsed it, her heart accelerated, and anger rose from her toes, jolting her to her feet. She didn't know how many times she had to tell Mustafa that she could solve her own problems. She closed her laptop and with urgent steps, made her way to his office. She wasn't sure if he was there or not, but with Salma prancing around, he might be. She approached his secretary.

"Is he in there?"

The woman's eyes widened. Zaina had never spoken with such a brazen tone to any of the staff, so the older lady could sense there was a problem.

"Yes, he is but he's in—"

Without waiting for a response, Zaina continued to Mustafa's office, with his secretary on her heels. She tapped on the door once and let herself in. Mustafa's eyes shot up to meet hers. He lifted an index finger because he was on the phone. She ignored him and stalked to the front of his desk. She placed both hands on her waist and glared down at him as she tapped her feet on the carpeted floor.

His eyes roamed her body. "Ben, I'll have to call you back. There seems to be something urgent that needs my immediate attention." After a couple of "okays" and "sures," Mustafa disconnected the call.

"It's okay, Brenda, thank you," he addressed his secretary.

The woman backed out of the office. Mustafa's eyes met Zaina's again. In silence, he stood and sauntered over to the small fridge in the corner of his office. He was too calm. Calmer than usual, so Zaina knew he had an idea why she was here.

"Hello, Zaina, do you want something to drink? Juice, water, soda?"

Her chest heaved causing her to fold her arms across her chest and frown. *I will not allow him to get to me.* "No."

Her terse tone didn't bother him. He retrieved a bottle of water and strolled over to the seating area of his office.

"Please have a seat." He gestured towards one of the black wingback chairs.

"I'd rather stand."

"Sit Zaina. Then tell me what's on your mind."

Ignoring him, she remained standing. "Mustafa, I'm here to do a job, and I prefer you let me do it." She sighed.

"And haven't I done that?" He leaned against one of the chairs.

"I already have a hard time looking these people in the face, considering all the extra stuff you do for me while you remain conspicuously absent. I can't have you stepping in and saving the day when it comes to my job."

The email that came through was her boss telling her she didn't need to travel to Maun on Monday. Between the time she told him of the problem earlier and now, Mustafa was brought in and of course, the issue disappeared. She didn't need Mustafa dousing any fires. Zaina didn't need her problems handled. She couldn't bear the baseless assumptions about her qualifications following her here. Her future and success with the company relied on the confidence her boss had in her. And possibly the key to kickstarting her own dreams.

Without saying a word, Mustafa gestured once again for her to sit. Zaina sighed and plopped down on the chair. *He must have his way.*

Mustafa took a seat opposite her. "Is the problem my absence or removing an obstacle?"

"Both…" She blurted out before she could catch herself. Clearing her throat, she clarified. "I mean, the *problem* is you solving problems I'm capable of resolving myself."

"My world consists of control. I may not have control over everything, but don't ask me to give up control over what I do. Your boss reported a problem that was hampering the project and I fixed it," he stated calmly.

"You're not listening. It wasn't your problem to fix."

"On the contrary—*my* resort runs the risk of losing its eco rating. Anything that hinders fixing that, is *my* problem, *chérie*,"

"Don't call me that. My name is Sam," she fussed.

She probably sounded ridiculous, but after her run in with Salma, his sudden reappearance and her boss not listening when she promised to handle it, she was at her wits end.

He snorted. "I'll never call you that." He took a sip of his water. "Now regarding your concern, I asked several times during the project updates if there was anything you needed assistance with. You said no." He lifted his hand to stroke his beard. "If you'd told me there was, but you were handling it, I would've backed down. For a moment at least."

Zaina shot to her feet and flung her hands up in the air. "I didn't tell you because I didn't need assistance!"

This wasn't her. Not anymore. She needed to get out of here. She walked toward the door and paused. She turned to him. "If you don't have confidence that I can do my job, save us both the hassle. Ask for someone else." Without giving him a chance to respond, she walked out.

~

The following morning, rays from the sun hit Zaina's eyelids, causing her to groan. Her temples thumped. It'd been a long time since she'd had to deal with a headache. She peeled her eyes open, lifting her hand to form a shield. After the day she had, using the room darkening blinds was the last thing on her mind. After a quick shower, she'd skipped dinner for a small tub of ice cream from one of the shops in the resort. While enjoying the strawberry vanilla decadence, she sobbed, asking God why He didn't keep Mustafa away. By the time she got to the end of the tub, she realized she was praying for the man not to return to his own business. Discarding the remnant, she brushed her teeth and headed to bed. With the aid of her lavender essential oil and a meditation app, she was able to get some semblance of a restful slumber.

Presently, the reality of her situation came flooding back. During her years of active therapy and as her relationship with Christ became stronger, she was able to come to the realization that she had to be mindful of the words she allowed to settle in her spirit. Her therapist brought to light that the same words she needed for validation could cause damage through destructive internal dialogue and absorbing negative opinion of others. More than she wanted to admit, she had allowed Salma's words to throw her off kilter. Words were important, but she had to know whose to listen to and remember that what God said about her was what mattered most.

Zaina reached for her phone and clicked on her Bible app.

She went to the notes section where she pasted important passages.

Romans 15:7 Christ accepted you, so you should accept each other, which will bring glory to God. I am accepted. **2 Cor 5:17 Therefore, if anyone is in Christ, the new creation has come. The old has gone, the new is here!** I am a new creation.

Zaina closed her eyes and said a prayer. A few moments later, she swung her legs over the bed. She needed pain relievers. Standing, she reached for her robe at the foot of the bed when she heard a knock on the door. Wincing in pain, and praying it wasn't Mustafa, she put on her robe and strolled to the door.

It wasn't Mustafa, but his representative, Assad. He had in his hand a bouquet of white roses. "Good morning, Ms. Bakari."

"Good morning, Assad." She opened the door wider for him to enter.

"These are from the boss. Where should I put them?"

"Erm, over here." She pointed to the coffee table in the small living area. He walked over and set the vase down before handing her a note.

"Have a good day, ma'am."

Zaina nodded and he opened the door and left.

She walked over to the bouquet. White roses…new beginnings. She opened the note in her hand.

Good morning, *chérie*

Clear your schedule for me. Please.

Be ready in an hour.

MDA

Excitement coursed through her body. He was the most infuriating man she'd ever met, but there was no denying she still loved him. She sadly came to that realization when he was away. She chided herself for being presumptuous. Him asking for her time could mean several things. Instead of him confessing his feelings for her, it could just mean he was going to be nicer. Nothing more.

She had nothing planned but wondered if she wanted to be in his presence now that she was still so raw with emotion. After an eight-week Mustafa detox, he'd reappeared and sent her back to ground zero. Knowing there was no denying him, especially since she stayed in his resort, she went to get ready.

Exactly an hour later, there was a rap on her door. She checked herself out in the full-length mirror... again. She had no idea where they were going, but since it was barely nine, she assumed it wasn't anywhere fancy. So, the unbuttoned white linen dress shirt she had over a floral asymmetrical dress would have to do. She fluffed her ponytail and tugged on the tresses she let fall to the side of her face. The knock came again.

"Coming..." she yelled.

Zaina smacked her lips together, evening out her lip gloss and hung her leather crossbody across her shoulders. With her sunglasses tucked in her bosom, she headed for the door. When she opened it, Mustafa stood on the other side in full confidence, wearing brown linen knee length shorts and a white linen shirt. His sunglasses were perched on his head. As usual, his eyes traveled her body before landing on her face. As his dark eyes pinned her in place, hers were fixated on his full lips encased by his moustache and full beard. The gray that was sprinkled on his hair and beard made him look sexier than should be lawful.

After a few seconds of pregnant tension, Zaina cleared her throat and wiped her sweaty palms down her dress.

"Hello, Zaina."

His voice washed over her, sending a tingling sensation down to her toes. "Hi, Mustafa. Thank you for the flowers."

"I hope they are to your liking." His brow raised in anticipation of her answer.

"Yes, thank you."

Mustafa reached for her hand and out of instinct, Zaina placed hers in his. The familiar feel caused her breath to hitch. *Get it together, girl. He's being nice, that's all.* After she locked up, they walked hand in hand down the small pathway from her villa. She tried to sever their connection, but he held her hand tighter.

"Er...you might wanna let my hand go," she whispered.

Mustafa looked down at her, drawing his brows together. "Do I make you uncomfortable?"

"No."

"Do you feel ashamed holding my hand?"

"Of course not."

He stopped walking. "Then I'm not sure I understand the problem."

"I don't want any rumors started. I'm sure they have, but I don't want to fuel the fire. Besides I don't want to have more words with your sister."

When Zaina remembered the incident the previous day, she'd kicked herself for not having a good comeback for Salma. Then again, the woman was only protecting her brother. Apart from the occasional times her brothers called to check on her, Zaina didn't know what it felt like for someone to look out for another. Until she met Mustafa.

"Zaina?"

"Huh? Yes."

He stared at her. "Where did your mind wander off to?"

She waved him off. "Nowhere. Where are you taking me?"

He ignored her, instead he asked, "You and Salma exchanged words?"

She shrugged. "Not really. More like her telling me I won't have another chance to get my claws in you."

Mustafa gave an irritated grunt. It was a sound she was familiar with. They approached the Mercedes Benz GLS Class she knew was his. It was the same car that took her to the airstrip that first night. His driver got out.

'Good morning, sir. Morning, madam." He bowed his head in respect.

"Hello, Edward, I'm sure you're familiar with Ms. Bakari." Mustafa said, scrolling through his phone.

"Yes sir. How are you today, madam?"

Zaina smiled at him. "I'm fine thank you. Please call me Sam."

Mustafa let out a disapproving mumble before helping her into the truck. He went around to the other side and got in.

"Are you going to tell me where we are going?"

"Yes, but first…"

Mustafa placed his phone on his lap. Zaina's eyes bugged when she saw who he was calling. She shook her head, trying to get him to disconnect the call. He looked right at her but ignored her unspoken plea. Zaina took in a deep breath and sighed. She couldn't deal with this. She was distant from her family and didn't want to be the cause of a rift between the DuBois-Arazis.

"Hey Musa, wassup?" Salma's cheery voice came through the phone he had on speaker.

"I'm fine *aikhti alsaghira*. Did you make it back okay?"

"Yes, I did." She exhaled. "I needed those three days."

Zaina glanced over at him. They had been around for three days, and Mustafa didn't bother to reach out to her. Zaina didn't know how she should process that.

"You owe someone an apology. I have you on speaker." His voice had changed from the caring older brother to the authoritarian leader. Zaina shook her head.

"To whom?" Salma asked.

"Zaina."

She sucked her teeth.

"Salma!" Mustafa growled.

Salma let out an exaggerated sigh. "Is she there?"

"Yes," Mustafa responded.

"Look, I'm not sorry for what I said. I am sorry for how I said it. For that, I apologize."

Mustafa turned to Zaina; his brow raised awaiting her response. What did he expect her to say? He should've left well enough alone. Not wanting the matter to drag on any further, she nodded her head.

"Apology accepted," Zaina responded.

Mustafa said a few more stern words to his sister in Arabic and disconnected the call.

"You shouldn't have done that. Now she'll think I came whining to you."

"What she thinks is of no consequence. But she counted on you not telling me which you almost didn't." Displeasure laced his voice.

"Because I didn't want it to be a big deal. I kind of understand where she was coming from."

"I'm going to make a request," he said.

"What's that?"

"Stop keeping things from me."

It sounded more like a demand than a request. Mustafa didn't need to know everything, but that wasn't a hill she was willing to die on now. So, she nodded and looked out the window. Edward had been driving for a few minutes.

"Where are we going?"

Mustafa looked up from his phone. "I heard you haven't been on a safari yet."

She placed her hand on her chest. "Oh my gosh Musa, for good reason!"

"Are you scared?"

"Er…yes!"

Mustafa smiled, something he almost never did. Then he

raised her head with his index finger. "While I draw breath, no harm will come to you. But first, I'll feed you."

His phone rang and he answered. While he was engaged in his conversation, Zaina gaped at him for a few moments. Probably feeling her eyes on him, Mustafa turned and grinned at her before resuming his CEO spiel.

Zaina lifted her eyes. *Father, God, if You give me a second chance with this man. I'll behave. I promise.* Zaina blew out a low breath to get her heart rate back to normal. She was in for an adventure.

CHAPTER 11

"Assad, I'm off the grid for the rest of the day. My family is the only emergency. And I do mean emergency."

After an acknowledgement from his assistant, Mustafa powered off his phone. He didn't find pleasure in having his attention divided, but the calls he'd been on were things that couldn't wait. Now that they were done, he'd be able to give his guest his full attention. When Zaina walked out of his office the previous day with flared nostrils and her chest heaving, he knew she'd reached her wits end. Regardless of their history, her distress was his failure and needed to be fixed. When they were apart, he'd given up responsibility for her. But now that she was under his radar, that responsibility resumed. In what exact capacity was still a question he grappled with.

"How will he reach you if you turn off your phone?" she asked

"He'll get in touch with the driver who has our itinerary and knows how to reach us." Mustafa opened the door. "Ready?"

He climbed out of the truck and walked over to her side to help her out. He opened the door and extended his hand for support. Once she was out of the car, Mustafa used the opportunity to give her a once over. Her light floral fragrance awakened his desire. Her dress clung to her curves before falling loosely. With her hand firmly in his, he walked them to the jet he had chartered for the day's activities. Upon boarding, a hostess greeted them. After ensuring Zaina was comfortable, Mustafa strolled to the cockpit.

"Good morning, Mr. Dubois-Arazi," another hostess said.

Mustafa nodded, returning the greeting. "Everything set?"

"Yes, sir. We'll fly the expanse of the inlands. Then we'll end at the concession where Cliff will be waiting," the pilot said.

"Perfect."

Mustafa had flown over the Delta numerous times. He wanted Zaina to experience the same euphoria he had. By the time they finished, Cliff, who was their safari guide, would be ready for them.

"Your assistant said the plans for dinner are still fluid. Have you decided, sir?" the pilot asked.

"He's making the arrangements and will get a message across." Mustafa turned to the hostess. "Once we're in the air and steady, serve breakfast. Thank you."

Mustafa walked back to his seat near Zaina and buckled himself in. The pilot's voice came over the speakers, welcoming them and informing them of what to expect. Soon the jet was in the air.

"If you told me we were flying, I would've been better prepared," Zaina whispered.

"Telling you would've ruined the surprise."

"You hate surprises. At least you used to." Her tone was low.

"I still do. That's why this isn't *my* surprise."

Zaina nudged his shoulder with hers. "Smartie."

He found pleasure in her playful side. "Anything you need should be at the back of the jet."

A few minutes later, the spread of the breakfast foods he had the resort restaurant prepare arrived. He looked over at Zaina and she had her smart phone angled so she could take a picture of the oasis below. He reached over her and took the phone out of her hand.

"Hey, I wanted to get that beautiful shot," she whined.

"There'll be plenty of time for that. Now you eat. I heard your stomach protesting the whole drive here." He put the phone in the front pocket of his shirt.

She laughed. "That's not true."

"It sounded like a marching band in there." He chuckled.

"Yeah, whatever. Hmm, this smells good." She lifted her eyes to the hostess. "Thank you."

"My pleasure. Call if you need anything." The hostess headed back to the front of the plane.

Zaina placed her hand on his and said grace. Mustafa reached across the table set before them and uncovered the dishes.

"I wasn't sure what you wanted, so we have an English breakfast and a traditional Botswanan breakfast."

"It all looks so good." Zaina surveyed the array of crème cheese bagels, French toast, eggs, sausages, bogobe and diphaphata. "Wait, what is this?" She pointed to the hot bowl of bogobe.

Mustafa picked up a spoon and scooped a little of the hot porridge from the side. He raised the spoon to his mouth, blew on it and turned to feed her. Zaina's soft eyes questioned him. He urged her on until she parted her full glossed lips to take in the spoon. Her moaned satisfaction sent his body into a frenzy.

"It's porridge, made from the sorghum grains."

"Oh, I know what it is. But I ate it as dinner, and it looked different."

He nodded and quickly described the different ways of preparing the meal. He then picked up a clean plate. "So, what do you want?"

"How do you know so much?" Zaina pointed to the food she

wanted to eat while Mustafa prepared her plate. Moments later, he set the plate down in front of her.

"Any resort we open, Omar who's a chef, comes—"

"I saw that, so he finally became a chef. On the site it says he's a two-time Michelin star chef. Now that's fancy," she squealed.

Mustafa smirked as he observed her. The elation in her voice appeared genuine.

"They are not babies for goodness' sake. Are you the only man with younger siblings? You're always running to their aid like some super-hero. You are nobody's superhero."

The words she'd spoken so harshly at dinner that night seared him. His brother was in trouble with American immigration and the woman he wanted to spend his life with didn't even care. The call he received at dinner was to inform him of Omar's status at the detention center. It was late, but he'd insisted he be informed of any changes. His grandfather was sick, and his grandmother was losing her mind over her grandson being locked up in a foreign country.

"Musa, are you okay?"

He blinked his eyes and shook his head, trying to wave off the bad memories. It'd been seven years. He loosened his clenched teeth.

"Yes, I am *chérie*."

"You were telling me about Omar." She cut a piece of her eggs and put it in her mouth.

"Ah yes. He attained that status some years ago. I'm told it's a big deal," Mustafa said.

"Yes, it is. That's huge. So, Omar goes to all the resorts and prepares the meals?"

"Not exactly. He works with local chefs, adjust the recipes, but not so much that they lose their originality. He also trains the kitchen and restaurant staff. We're his guinea pigs while he's creating."

Zaina laughed—a sound that was pleasing to his ears. They ate in comfortable silence. Although Mustafa was occupied by his thoughts, he was able to periodically answer her questions. He had none of his own. Not yet anyway. He had spent the last two months away from her. That gave him time to accept that he couldn't hold all the misgivings of the past against her alone. He had some culpability. The time away was to give him clarity on what he wanted. Was he on the hunt again, or had their time run its course? Those answers he still didn't have. What he did know which was also solidified when he saw her the previous day was that he'd missed her terribly. Anger and all, he'd missed her.

He suspected that last week when he had dinner with Monica when he was in Tweede Kans Cove. He spent the evening comparing her every move to Zaina. Monica could comfortably pass for a model. She was built as though a factory put her together. Her proportions were excellent with a face that could bend any man to her will. Therein lay the problem; she was stiff. Her laughter was robotic, and conversation stilted. He'd taken her to a quiet restaurant near the mountains. The evening was going well until their waiter mistakenly put lime in her water when she'd asked for it plain. She was rude and crass, complaining about everything from that point on. That evening, Mustafa told her that there wasn't any likelihood of them being anything more than acquaintances.

When Zaina barged into his office with her hands on her voluptuous hips telling him off, he came alive. That's when he knew he had to call a truce or risk running her off. They were bound together, at least for the next four months of her contract. It would be in his best interest to wave the white flag.

After about forty-five minutes, breakfast was done. The hostess walked over and handed Mustafa two new pairs of headsets. He handed one to Zaina.

Zaina lifted her juice glass to her lips, draining the remnants. "What's this for?"

"These are so you can hear the tour guide." He stood, extending his hand to her. "We're going to move to a different part of the plane so you can get a good view." He returned her phone to her.

When the pair was settled in their new seats, Mustafa signaled to the hostess that they were ready. He observed as Zaina's face lit up when the pilot started to speak. He grinned. To see her happy settled his heart.

"Welcome to the Okavango Delta. This massive, fan-shaped wetland is the crown jewel of Botswana. The wetland provides one of the most pristine habitats for wildlife on the planet. We are now flying over the Okavango River which feeds the Delta. The river begins in the highland of the neighboring Angola and ends in the Kalahari Desert. Fun fact, the name Kalahari is derived from Kgala which means 'the great thirst.'"

Zaina leaned toward Mustafa. "Why do they call it that?"

"The desert gets a lot of rainfall, unusual for a normal desert. But the rain filters through the sand very quickly and you barely see anything at the surface."

"Wow. Got it." Nodding, she returned her focus to the area below.

"Because of its scale and significance, the Okavango Delta is a UNESCO World Heritage site," the pilot continued.

Next, they flew over a few private concession sites. The sites were home to other lodges and offered other safari experiences. To end the aerial tour, they flew over the northern side of the Delta. Zaina commented on how breathtaking Grand Amour looked from above. The pilot explained that unlike other lodges, Grand Amour provided a combination of wet and dry activities. This allowed for a diverse habitat that made hosting an incredible array of wildlife possible.

When the pilot announced that they were headed for the

Grand Amour concession to start on their safari, Mustafa felt Zaina's eyes on him.

"I get it now," she whispered.

"Get what?" He searched her eyes for answers.

"My job in relation to the exclusivity Grand Amour enjoys. Now I understand how everything fits together." She glanced out the window then faced him again. "I promise if I have any issues that need your bulldozing prowess to get a solution, I'll tell you." She smiled.

Mustafa clasped his hands together. "I appreciate your cooperation."

Soon after, they landed and made their way to the 4WD Land-Cruiser. They were greeted by the guide who gave them each a pair of binoculars. After ensuring Zaina was buckled in safely, Mustafa secured his own seat belt. Cliff gave them a brief introduction on what to expect. The expanse of the dry land would enable them to sight predators like lions, cheetahs, elephants and if lucky, they'd see an African Wild Dog.

Fear danced in Zaina's eyes when she turned toward him. Mustafa took her hand and used his thumb to massage her wrist in a circular, calming motion.

"You'll be fine. If at any time you want to stop, say the word." He drew her near and kissed her temple. Mustafa noticed her wide-eyed surprise at his gesture. He was equally surprised at the impulsive act, so he didn't have an answer to the question he knew she wanted to ask.

~

She was happy. Tired, but happy.

Zaina leaned her head on Mustafa's shoulder as he roasted their s'mores over an open flame. Their day was winding down and it pleased him that Zaina seemed satisfied. During the land activity earlier, they sighted a few lions, cheetahs, and elephants, but unfortunately the African Wild Dog didn't make an appearance. Even though they were at a safe distance, Zaina clung to him as the guide ran down information about the various species. Later, they took a break and enjoyed a picnic the staff set up in a secluded area of the concession.

Next were the water activities. Her favorite of them all was the mokoro ride. Mustafa found her resistance at first amusing. Especially when she saw the unique canoe dug out of traditional wood. After threatening to do him bodily harm if she fell into the water, and he agreeing to surrender himself to her mercy, she got in. They rode through the maze of clear channels and opaque lagoons of the Delta. The guide told them to expect some hippopotamus sightings. During the ride, the disappointment on Zaina's face deepened when no hippopotamuses appeared. Right as they were to climb out of the canoe, one appeared. Mustafa smiled at her delight.

Currently, they were both stuffed from the bush dinner they had under the stars. For dessert, Zaina had requested s'mores that she was about to have. Throughout the day, they had kept the conversation light. She educated him on the environmental issues not only facing the wetlands of the world but other environmental issues. She asked a lot of questions about the hospitality industry as well.

From their discussion, he knew that although she'd been in Botswana for fifteen months, she didn't know much about it. She made frequent trips back to Nigeria, so never stayed to enjoy the country. The prospect of her moving back to Nigeria at the end of the contract ruffled his insides. He ignored the feeling. Allowing passion to get the best of him wasn't an option. Mustafa wasn't aware of how much power Zaina had over him until their demise. Entering that space with her would mean him relinquishing the control he'd regained. He reminded himself why he couldn't do that. The last time brought him to his knees.

"Here."

Mustafa removed the cooled s'more from the skewer and placed it in a small plate. Zaina sat up, adjusting the blanket that was draped over their shoulders. Instead of taking the plate, she opened her mouth. His mesmerized gaze narrowed on her lips. He once again took in how beautiful she was. He hadn't encountered her type of beauty again over the years. The rush of emotions he held at bay came rushing to the surface. He slipped the confectionery into her mouth. She set her smoldering gaze on him while she moaned and licked her lips.

My chérie is flirting.

"Don't do that," he warned.

Her eyes fastened to his. "Do what?"

"Lick your lips and make that sound."

"You mean this sound?" She moaned again.

His chest tightened at her mischief. With one swoop, Mustafa picked her up and had her straddling him. His hands went into her hair and loosened the bun she had it in. He massaged her scalp, and another moan escaped her lips. She closed her eyes.

"Look at me," he demanded.

Zaina opened her eyes. They were fiery with desire. He struggled to control the force between them. Chemistry had never been their problem.

His hand went around her neck. "Don't needle the beast."

She placed her hand over his and leaned in, her lips brushing his ear. Her breath was warm and inviting. "Supposing it needs needling."

Mustafa leaned back. Her lips were slightly parted. He felt her breath hitch. His need for her rose. He'd done everything in his power to starve what he knew was his growing need for her. He did nothing halfway. He wanted her but giving into that desire without a conversation would be a disaster. That didn't mean he couldn't...

Zaina's eyes narrowed on his lips, tempting him to throw caution to the wind. Her low audible pants were driving him crazy. They were in a secluded area, but her reputation was his utmost concern.

"Mustafa…"

Her lustful whimper did him in. It made him weak and subdued him to her will. His feral need to give her what she wanted could no longer be tamed.

"Can I kiss you, *chérie?*"

She nodded. "Yes…please."

A slow smile eased to his lips. He cupped her face, keeping it steady as their lips made impact. The kiss was rough and aggressive. Her moan sent him into primal mode as he tried to punish her for the heartache they'd endured. Zaina wrapped her hands around his neck, stroking his nape with her thumb. He recognized her intention was to calm the beast rising within him.

She remembers her secret weapon. Their tongues continued to explore as he pulled her closer. The sweetness of the chocolate she enjoyed earlier teased his senses. He felt himself swell, signaling his need to bring this to an end. He pulled away, but Zaina refused to meet his eyes. Instead, she buried her head in the crook of his neck. Her energy was raw. He sensed her vulnerability. He rubbed her back in a circular motion to help bring her breathing back to normal. They remained in silence, but a few seconds later, he heard sniffling and felt the wetness on his neck. He tried to get her to look at him, but she refused.

"I love you. I never stopped," she whispered.

Mustafa exhaled as the meaning of what she said settled. She lifted her head, allowing him to study her as he thumbed away her tears. He pecked her lips a few times.

"I got what I thought I needed, but I was wrong. It was horrible," she confessed.

Mustafa's chest tightened at her reference to another man.

He knew he shouldn't ask for more details. However, the need-to-know overpowered sensibility.

"How many were there?"

"Huh?" A deep frown appeared on her forehead.

"After me, how many?"

She rolled her eyes. "One Mustafa. One."

"Name?"

She wrinkled her nose at him. "I'm not giving you, his name."

"Tell me." He no longer had a real desire to know of any lover other than him. The implication that her entanglement wasn't as idyllic as she expected made him want to know if she had a deranged or scorned man out there. Again, her safety was his number one concern.

CHAPTER 12

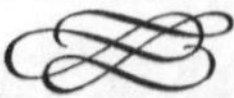

Zaina moved from Mustafa's lap to reclaim her seat. She silently winced at the absence of his warmth. The realization that she'd just confessed her truth settled in her belly. It was something she'd avoided admitting to herself. At her age, and through what she'd learned over the years, one thing she no longer had the desire for was games. She'd laid out her cards. Mustafa had to make the next move.

"Zaina, tell me."

She noticed the shift in his tone. He was giving her one last chance to be open, or he'd start digging himself. Zaina glanced at him, then returned her gaze to the firepit in front of them.

"You wouldn't take my calls, nor return my voicemails. I spiraled, but the world still turned, so I had to get a grip on my life. The last thing I wanted to do after declaring my independence was ask my parents for money while I wallowed in self-pity. So, I had to work. I got the formal offer letter and left for Geneva a couple of weeks later." A beat passed between them. "After a while, I started dating. Nothing serious until I met him. At first, I enjoyed being with him. He wasn't like you—"

"Spare me," he grunted.

She tittered.

"I won't give gory details, but you need to hear this. A few months in, I found out the extreme side of those affirming words I wanted so badly." She chuckled. "He became so clingy, always wanted to know where I was, what I was doing. He claimed I was his compass. It was cute until it wasn't. When I didn't respond the way he wanted, those same words turned nasty. It was verbal torture mixed with guilt tripping."

"Name?"

She heard his growl and turned to him. "No."

Zaina quickly learned that most Arab men had the "normal" possessive man beat. To make it worse, *her* Arab was also an incommunicado alpha. Being raised by his grandparents, schooling in France, then working in London for a bit mellowed his traditional outlook. However, his jealous streak was something she always found contradictory to the poise he always maintained. He never stifled her or stopped her from going out with coworkers without him. Majority of the time, he footed the bill. But he never failed to remind her that the fate of any man she entertained for longer than necessary lay in her hands. He had no problem stepping in. She remembered the one time he did and almost got her banned from a club.

"You do know I can find out," he said.

"I know. But it's nothing to worry about."

"The emotion I feel isn't worry..."

Zaina rolled her eyes. "After leaving Geneva, I moved back to London and started working for Safi. About a year in, I'd had enough of Europe and took a role in their Abuja office."

"Has he ever contacted you again?"

"No. Can we move on?"

"Continue."

"Moving to Abuja was good for me. I reconnected with an old friend who after a while, invited me to her church. There I found my self-worth, focusing on how God sees me. Affirmation will always be my love language, but not getting it from people shouldn't turn me into something I can't recognize."

Zaina let out a cleansing breath. Confronting her own deceitfulness, anger and self-sabotaging tendencies had been raw and painful. She was better for it and wanted him to see that. She *needed* him to trust she was different. She wrung her fingers through Mustafa's silence. She knew him well enough to know he was processing. More than likely figuring out where he had failed. Moments later, he pulled her close and planted a kiss on her forehead.

"Musa—"

"It pleases me that you got to this place of revelation. I want nothing more than for you to be the highest level of yourself," he said.

Her shoulders slumped. Although comforting, those weren't the words she wanted to hear. She knew she needed to give him time, but still, she didn't like it. Another thought crossed her mind.

"How many have there been for you?" she asked.

He chuckled. "None worth remembering."

"Come on. None?" She raised her brow.

"Worth remembering..." he emphasized.

Knowing he wasn't going to elaborate; she tried another approach. "Anyone now?"

"No."

"Worth remembering or...?" She was fishing and failing at it.

"None, at all." Mustafa stood, ending the conversation. He checked the phone Assad returned to him during lunch. "I should get you back. It's late and although I enjoy your company, you need your rest. I hope you had fun."

Zaina stood on the tip of her toes and placed a soft kiss on his lips. His hand rested on her waist. "It was the best day ever. Thank you."

"You're welcome. Thank you for spending the day with me."

Mustafa put out the fire then excused himself to make a call. While he did that, she folded up their blanket. Then she searched the bigger bag she got at one of the shops for their things. Her crossbody purse, their sunglasses, souvenirs, and her cell phone. She had so many pictures, and she couldn't wait to load them on her computer. She turned her head to Mustafa, who was still on the phone, and smiled. There was nothing he didn't think of. There was a time she was upset at missing the shot of an elephant. He told her not to worry, that he was sure his photographer got it. It was then she noticed a photographer trailing them.

"Ready?" He took the bag from her and grabbed her hand.

They walked a small distance before getting to his truck. Mustafa had let his driver go home earlier so he was the one driving them back. Mustafa placed the stuff in the back seat and helped her in. Once they were in motion, he glanced at her.

"Assad will email my schedule to you. I leave tomorrow night for Kenya, but only for a day before heading to Accra. After that, I have some business in London. Before returning here, I'll stop by in Tweedes."

"Wow, that's a lot," she gasped.

"The nature of the job. I'm trying to travel less, but to do that I need to have things run seamlessly."

He had shared more about his responsibilities for the resort and his personal ventures, so his travel made sense. Her heart ached at the thoughts of the days ahead without him. Even when he was cold and distant, she'd missed him. Now that they were in a better place, his absence would for sure evoke melancholy.

"How long will you be gone?"

"Is that your way of saying you'll miss me?"

"Without a doubt," she answered truthfully.

He glanced over at her, then returned his attention to the

road. He gave her hand a gentle squeeze. "Two weeks. If I can shorten it, I will."

"Please don't hurry back on my account. Complete what you need to. Besides, I have to go to Nigeria for—"

"Why?"

"It's only for a few days. I'll remain connected to ensure all deliverables are met in my absence."

"That's not my concern."

"Remember the Danjuma project I told you about? It's time for its annual observation—"

"Can't someone else do it?"

"Don't start. And stop cutting me off. Yes, someone else can, but it's my project..." She smiled when he raised one hand in surrender. "While we're at it, I might as well tell you I'm also scheduled to go to Dar es Salaam to see my family."

She felt his eyes on her, but he said nothing as he pulled into the underground parking garage of the resort. He turned off the engine and got out. He opened her door and helped her out but pinned her against it.

"Do you need me to go with you?" His face searched her eyes.

She desperately wanted him there. Someone who she knew understood her. But this was the first time she would be with her whole family in years, so it was something she had to do by herself.

"No, I'll be okay."

He cupped her face. "Family is important, but not to your detriment. I told you before, I'll share mine with you."

Remembering that conversation years ago, Zaina gave him a weary smile and nodded.

"I'll protect you from anything and anyone. If at any time you need anything, I should be your first call," he said.

She understood the unspoken threat behind his words. She also knew he wasn't making a request, but rather a demand.

Still, if anything was to go wrong, she didn't plan on having Mustafa and her family at war.

"Zaina!"

"Okaaay, Musa. I got it." She sighed.

He observed her for a bit, searching for her sincerity. He must have seen what he was looking for because he kissed her forehead. "Good. Assad will contact you in the morning."

Mustafa stepped back from her, grabbed their things and her hand, and moved toward the entrance door that led to the villas.

~

A few days after Mustafa left, Zaina embarked on her trip to Abuja. She was there for only three days and had returned to Botswana as scheduled. There were no surprises, and things were going as planned. Everything going according to plan had taken on a new sense of importance to her.

She placed the back of her hand over her mouth and let out a yawn. She was tired, but this trip to Tanzania was one she couldn't back out of. Sitting in the back seat of one of her father's cars, Zaina took in the city's scenery. The driver weaved through traffic headed to her father's estate. She noticed a couple of changes since she'd been here last. When she landed two days ago, her father had been in Zimbabwe, and the rest of the family had yet to arrive. She used the free day she had to explore the city. One thing was for sure, the tourism industry was booming. The abundance of beaches in Tanzania was something she knew and learned about growing up. Now it was as if the whole world knew about it too. With the popularity of Zanzibar, she shouldn't have been surprised, but nothing could prepare her for the heightened level of activity.

The previous day, her mother arrived from London. By then, the whole family began trickling into the estate where Zaina had spent many summers. Her sisters, who all lived in Tanzania with their families, arrived first, then her stepmom, who had several boutiques around the country, came in from a business trip to Dubai. Next to arrive were her brothers. Hashim had relocated from London with his family a few years ago. He'd been working with her father and was taking over the role of CEO of the company. Her other brother, who lived with his family in America, was the last to arrive.

Zaina wasn't sure how her mother and stepmom got along, but they did. They both served at the pleasure of Chief Bakari. With them and several servants cooking furiously in the kitchen, the family sat down to a dinner feast. It was weird sitting with people that were her blood but felt like strangers. Everyone seemed to know a little of everyone's business and she barely knew any. Her anxiety turned to melancholy as it dawned on her that she had really exiled herself. Her mother must've seen her discomfort because she latched on to Zaina, drawing her into conversation she had no clue how to navigate. As time went on, Zaina relaxed and got to know her nieces and nephews, most of whom she'd only seen pictures of.

The handover ceremony concluded about half an hour ago and the ride home was the only time she'd had to herself all day. Her ringtone rang through the air and Zaina ransacked her bag looking for her phone.

If it's him, I can't miss his call.

Her shoulders slumped, once she registered the caller ID. Letting out a sigh, she answered the call. "Hello."

Ibiso chuckled. "He still hasn't called?"

Zaina knew her friend meant well, but her amusement irritated her soul. "It's not funny."

"*Abeg*...allow me to laugh *jare*. Do you remember when you were like, men are not worth it. Besides Jesus is my husband..."

Zaina chuckled. She remembered the statement she made when lamenting to Ibiso about a failed blind date. She'd recently surrendered her life to Christ and decided to allow her mother to convince her to go on a date with her friend's son who also lived in Abuja.

Ten days.

It had been ten days since she'd seen him. His checking in on her morning and evening assuaged her longing for him. But all his communication was via text. He hadn't called her once. She ached to hear his voice.

"The man is busy. Besides he checks on you. Cut him some slack. You do know you can call him instead," Ibiso said.

"I told you why I don't want to call."

She had been as raw as she could be the day they spent together. The next morning, he had breakfast delivered to her with a note telling her he was on his way to the airport. Zaina tried to squelch the unpleasant feeling that rose within her when she rolled back the tape of their day. They had fun and she could've sworn they shared a moment. But that still didn't make him open to her, at least to give her an inkling of where his mind was.

Didn't he hear anything I said? Work stopped her from obsessing over it and strengthened her resolve to allow him to make the next move.

"Okay then, and I agree with you. The man is busy, so chill out."

"How do you do it with your husband? These long absences..."

"I stay busy with my restaurants, kids, family and community obligations, and I have my sisters-in-law. We make it up when he gets back, but sometimes, I have to hijack his schedule to get time in." Ibiso giggled. "Rasheed complains that he pays his staff, but they answer to me."

Zaina exhaled. *It must be nice. Mustafa's family hates me, and I'm not close to mine...*

"You guys will sort yourselves out. Don't let it weigh you down. I called to check on how it's going with your family."

"I haven't talked to my father yet. My mom and I had a long talk. Like you said, I'm learning to meet her where she is and let the other stuff go. It's either that or keep holding her to a standard she can no longer do anything about. It's in the past."

"Exactly. When my mom and I talked, she insisted everything she'd done was for my good. I was tired of fighting with her," Ibiso said.

"But you had your husband there for support," Zaina said.

"Yeah, but not when we talked," Ibiso said. "Besides, do you really want Mustafa there when you talk to your father?"

Zaina smiled. "I guess not."

"Then there, you can do this. Just remember he's an African, old-school parent. Don't expect an apology."

"If I haven't told you before, I'm glad we reconnected. I'm so grateful for your friendship."

"You have and right back at ya. Love you, girl. Keep me posted."

They disconnected right as the driver pulled into the compound. To Zaina's surprise, her father opened the door for her.

He extended his hand to help her out. *"Binti yangu."*

"Baba…" Zaina took her father's hand and stepped out of the car.

At seventy, her father's dark skin was now kind of wrinkled, but he was still strikingly handsome. His low-cut hair no longer showed signs of once being black. His once salt and pepper look was now completely taken over by gray. His keen dark eyes now showed signs of being placid, making her wonder why he wouldn't outright retire instead of going into politics. Dressed in a simple dashiki, he led the way to the garden area of the compound.

"We haven't had our time together and your mother tells me you leave in the morning," he said.

She looked toward the mansion. There were already some cars parked. "Yes *baba*, but isn't there supposed to be a party going on?"

"Yes, and they'll wait. Come."

They sat on the bench in the garden. The landscaper kept the space pristine. Even the small fountain in the middle of the area had not one dead leaf floating in it. After an awkward silence, her father asked her about her job. She could still tell he didn't like her working for others when she could work for the family business, but he didn't voice his opinion *this* time. They laughed at a few memories before her father cleared his throat.

Here we go.

"So, tell me why you don't come and see your old man or answer when I call. Your mother told me, but I want to hear it from you," her father said.

Zaina shrugged as her brain gathered the words to say in the right order. Her father had always been strict, but not overbearingly so. "I didn't know what to say."

"But I am your father."

"That may be the case, but we really don't have a relationship."

"I don't understand. I made sure you were well taken care of. A sound education in the best schools in Europe, holidays to anywhere in the world, birthd—"

"Your money did that *Baba*, not you. I didn't have you. I was an inconvenience you and my mother had to put up with. I felt left out. Any time you came to London, or my brothers and I visited, you only spent time with them."

"I was grooming them—"

"But what about me?"

"That was your mother's job...your older sisters were all nurtured by their mother," her father stressed.

"That might have worked for them, but it didn't work for me. You rarely gave me the time of day. Never told me you loved me or that you were proud of me. Much less have more than a ten-minute conversation with me." Tears slipped from her eyes. She'd tried not to let them fall, but she could no longer hold them back. "I needed support from my parents. Mother was busy travelling with you or sitting on one charity board or the other. I know you guys had me late, but I was still your child, not a project to be managed."

Zaina placed her elbows on her thighs and covered her face with both hands. She cried. *I'm too old for this. I can't believe it's still affecting me.* She felt an arm around her shoulder. Her father drew her nearer.

"You were never a project to me. I thought I was doing what a father should, provide. I cannot undo what has been done, but I'm your father. I do not enjoy having my youngest child estranged from me. We have time to make this right."

This was as close to an African parent apology as she was going to get. He asked, she talked, at least he listened. What happened next would take an effort on both their sides.

"Okay *Binti yangu?*"

"Okay *Baba.*"

"Good. Now let's go join the party." As they walked hand in hand towards the house, her father spoke again. "I haven't heard news of a husband. Don't worry my daughter, some of my mentees are here. I'll introduce you."

Let me survive this night without telling somebody's son off.

Her mother had hinted the same thing, so she knew that her parents had talked. And their plan was to showcase her all evening.

~

*B*y mid-morning the next day, Zaina was packed and ready to go. Her father and brothers had left for a meeting while her mother was currently fussing about her not forgetting anything.

"Mother, stop fussing. If I forget anything, I can replace it, or have it sent to me." Zaina wheeled her luggage out of her room.

"Okay, I'm done." Her mother raised her hands to the sky. "My happiness is complete. You and your father finally talked."

Zaina giggled at her mother's dramatics. "Yes, I am too."

A few minutes after they'd rejoined the party, Zaina began the game of "dodge men." It was as though every member of her family was playing the "let's get Zaina married" game. The men she was introduced to were not bad. They were all handsome and oozed money, but they weren't her type.

At bedtime, her mother entered her room under the guise of checking on her, but she really wanted to know how her conversation with her father went. Zaina obliged her but skipped the part about him basically blaming her mother for the disconnect. Before her brothers left, Zaina spent some time with them, promising to communicate more.

"We've agreed, you'll come visit me when your contract ends. Right?"

Zaina laughed. "Do you need me to swear by something?" Her goal was to move back to London permanently, but she didn't want to get her mother's hopes up too soon.

"No, let your yes be yes." Her mother turned towards a member of the house staff. "Is the driver ready?"

"Yes, madam." The man took her luggage and carried it outside.

Zaina and her mother linked their arms and followed behind him. After she opened the front door, Zaina's eyes widened, and she squealed before taking off down the steps. She flew into the arms of her Arabian knight. Mustafa, who was leaned against the car door, enveloped her in his arms and squeezed her to him. In her peripheral, she saw the driver take her luggage.

"*Chérie* ..."

Leaning back to see his face, Zaina smiled and brushed her lips against his in a sweet kiss. The sound of a throat clearing caused her to turn, remembering they weren't alone. Her mother...

"So, this is why you avoided those men." Her mother smiled. She gave Mustafa a once over and nodded in approval.

"What men?" Mustafa stared down at her.

Zaina waved him off. "Nobody. Mom this is Mustafa DuBois-Arazi. Mustafa, this is my mother."

During their time together, Zaina never took Mustafa to meet her mother. Not because he didn't ask, but because she wanted to wait until she could say they were engaged. It made no sense now, but then it made a lot of sense to her.

Mustafa took her mother's hand and kissed the back of it. "Nice to meet you, Mrs. Bakari. I'm pleased to see her beauty will be enhanced with time."

Her mother beamed. "A charmer. I like him."

Zaina squeezed Mustafa's hand. She was ready to be alone with him. He looked down at her.

"Ready?" he asked.

"Yes." Zaina hugged her mother and said her goodbyes.

Mustafa opened the door for Zaina before turning to her mother. "It was nice meeting you."

After Zaina was settled, he closed it and went around the other side to get in. Before the driver could even put the car in gear, Mustafa turned toward her.

"Men?"

She rolled her eyes and rested her head on his shoulder. His familiar scent tingled her nerve endings and at the same time, provided the comfort she'd been missing. Not even he could spoil her joy. Last night, it was like he'd discerned her mood.

After talking to her father, she was raw and emotional. To her surprise, she received a text from Mustafa. He inquired about her day. Not thinking things through, she sent a one-word response. **Okay.** Followed by a crying emoji. She didn't get a response from him. All night, so many narratives ran through her mind as to why. What never came up was that he was making his way to her.

CHAPTER 13

The following evening, peering up from his phone, Mustafa watched as Zaina emerged from the turquoise waters of the swimming pool. She tilted her head to the side and squeezed her hair to get rid of excess water. Her skin glistened, glowing where the emerging twilight hit her at a perfect angle. Her carefree smile enticed the deepest parts of his being. His eyes remained pinned on her as she strutted toward him.

Stretched out in a lounge chair on the terrace of his beach-front cottage, Mustafa used his index finger to gesture for her to turn around. She laughed and twirled, modelling the black, two-piece bikini that clung to her curves as though it was painted on. Zaina moved toward him and plucked his phone out of his hand. She powered it off and placed it face down on the other side of her lounge chair.

"Hey, woman."

She picked up her terry bikini cover and stood over him. "You do know it's okay to take time out for rest?"

"I'm aware." He leaned his face up and she bent to kiss him before taking the lounge seat next to his.

"Then act like it. You come to my father's house, whisk me away and bring me to Zanzibar, but still, you can't completely unwind."

Mustafa gazed out into the water. When he received her crying emoji, his heart thumped against his chest at a rate he didn't even know was possible. When their lips met that night, all the feelings of old resurfaced. As he'd prepared for bed, an array of emotion overtook him. His lingering mistrust cautioned him to measure their interaction. The distance allowed him to do exactly that. While away, he made sure she was okay and didn't want for anything, but that text had been his undoing. He needed to get to her. Moving some things around, he boarded his jet. However, those things he left uncompleted still needed to be tended to.

Mustafa turned his head to her. "How are you feeling?"

A wry smile graced her lips. "I'm perfect. Thank you."

Mustafa looked away. "You're welcome."

Her fingers moved against the surface of her phone and seconds later the melodic chords of a familiar jazz tune began to play.

"Musa…, can I ask you a question?"

He faced her. He's never known her to be shy. Most of the time, she was cheery to a nauseating degree. Now, he noticed trepidation in her eyes.

"Sure."

"Your world consists of control and thrives on routine. You take care of everyone, but find it hard to take compliments, or let others take care of you—"

"Is there a question there somewhere?"

"Erm…yes. In an ideal world, if you could just be, what would be your ideal activity? Her eyes remained on him. "Those traits make you who you are. But it must be tiring to be on all the time."

"I'm a man, Zaina. It's my responsibility." He kept his tone even.

She sighed. "Your gender is not a point of contention. Who takes care of you?"

Mustafa set his drink down and sat up. He stretched his hand into the portfolio next to him and retrieved a long velvet box. During his trip, he saw a 14K white gold, diamond solitaire necklace he thought would look perfect on her.

"I have something for you."

Zaina gazed at him for a few moments. She took the box and opened it. Her mouth opened in awe. The smile on her face warmed his heart but was short lived when she closed the box and set it on the table.

A frown covered his face. "If you don't like it, I can change it."

She shook her head. "No, no, that's not it. It's beautiful."

"Then what's the problem? Let me put it on." He reached for the box, but she stopped him, placing her hand over his.

"Musa, answer my question."

This time he recognized the plea in her voice. "Where are you going with this?"

Zaina ran her hands through her semi dry hair. "I'm trying to get you to talk to me."

Mustafa chuckled. "*Chérie*, we've been here for two days, and have done nothing but talk."

"Me asking about your trip, updating you about the project, talking about the island's history or telling you about what happened with my family... is me talking to you. I want you to talk to me!" Her nose flared.

He stared at her. Their eyes were at war. He relented. "What do you want to know?"

"I want you to trust me enough to let your guard down. You're not telling me anything. Not even about Grandma Olly and I've asked about her many times."

Mustafa heard the frustration in her voice. She wasn't wrong, but he struggled with giving her what she wanted. His family was sacred to him. He told her about them once and when it came down to the wire, she couldn't handle it. His hesitancy to hand over his heart to her extended to his family as well. They'd been reconnected for close to three months now. She had bared herself to him, maybe it was time to reciprocate. Even if it was only a little.

"Grandma Olly is doing fine. She'll be eighty soon." Mustafa smiled, thinking about his grandmother. He intentionally didn't tell her about Zaina. However, when she called to give him an earful about Salma's hurt feelings, he knew she was aware. Surprisingly, she kept her opinion about Zaina to herself.

"We're planning a big celebration for her. Yasmine and her family are in Accra, while Salma and Omar are back in Tweedes." He shrugged. "There's nothing much to it."

"So, back to my original question."

"Which is?"

"You're a busy man; that I know. You are also in a position where you can hire people to do some of the things you travel for. Grand Amour runs—"

His impatience at her ramblings rose. "Get to it, Zaina."

"I'm curious about what's lurking behind your busyness." She raised her hands to silence his speech. "When I was acting out, it was because I was running from the pain of neglect in my childhood. You told me your mom died at the hands of your father, so I've been thinking—"

"I wasn't aware you became a psychologist." Her desired topic of discussion infuriated him.

"Huh?"

"Are you trying to psychoanalyze me?" He tossed his head back, throwing the remnants of his drink down his throat. Slamming the glass on the table, he turned to her. "Me spilling dirty memories of my parents…are those the words you need to feel loved?"

"What? No! How dare you say that to me?" she screamed at him.

The hurt in her voice chilled his spine. Mustafa covered his face with his palms. Moments later, he lifted his head. Her eyes glistened with tears she didn't let fall.

"Your tears break me, *chérie*. I'm sorry."

Her eyes widened and he knew instantly what she was about to say. "Don't."

"But I have to. Your apologies are becoming a thing."

He chuckled, a grin resting upon his face. She used to complain about him never expressing his apology in words. Instead, he'd buy gifts, take her to fancy dinners, or spontaneous trips.

"You said the words. I can't believe it." She clasped her hands together before placing one on her chest. "I'm so proud."

Her declaration solicited hearty laughter from him which she joined in on. After their laughter died down, he drew in a deep breath, then exhaled.

"My mother was a beautiful woman, several years younger than my Papa. As a young boy, I could tell she loved him deeply, but I wasn't sure he loved her back. Even though we suspected she favored Omar over all of us, she never failed to tell us she loved us. After she died, over the years, I've questioned the sincerity of her declarations."

"Why?"

"How could she love us and not protect us from him? How could she love us and not care enough for us to leave the situation she was in?"

"That doesn't mean she didn't love you. We're not sure what she was going through," she said.

"That's what I thought too until my grandparents took us to Tweede Kans Cove after her death. She was an only child that came from wealth. She wanted for nothing. But she deliberately ran away with a man who didn't mean her well. She didn't consider what she was doing to her parents then, or the consequences for her future kids."

Zaina stood and walked to him. He didn't need her pity. That was the reason he kept his baggage to himself. He didn't have time to expose the demons that haunted him. The emotions they had the potential to produce were potent enough to send his world crumbling. A risk he wasn't willing to accept.

"Musa, I'm sure your mom did the best she could. Yeah, she made mistakes, but I'm positive she loved you." She snapped her fingers. "Remember that weekend that Salma, Yasmine, and I went to watch a play in Marrakech?"

Mustafa grunted, remembering the only Christmas she spent in Tweedes. His sisters were so ecstatic he brough someone home that they hoarded her all weekend. He allowed her to leave his side only because she promised to make it up, which she did.

"Wipe that smirk off your face and focus."

He grunted again.

"Anyway, when we were there, your sisters shared a lot of fun, goofy stories of you guys growing up. Trust me, your mom loved you. She might've been scared to go back home."

Mustafa no longer wished to dwell on what ifs he'd never get the answers to. "Is there something else you wanted to know?"

Zaina narrowed her eyes at him, but he'd indulged her enough. "Hmm, I was wondering when you were gonna shut me down."

"Are you saying I'm predictable?"

She gasped. "How dare I?"

Her playful mischief amused him.

"Okay, you never answered my initial question."

"What was it?"

"If you had a day to just be, what would be your activity of choice?"

"I have no time to deal in idyllic fantasies," he said.

Zaina rolled her eyes at him. "Humor me."

"Painting, maybe fishing. My grandfather used to take me."

"Painting! How could I forget that? You used to take classes in the evenings. You stopped?" Her eyes fell.

"The real world called."

"You don't always have to answer, Musa."

"Yes, I do." Mustafa stood and reached for her hand. "Now my stomach calls. Since you made me dismiss my chef for the night, let's see what you can do in the kitchen."

The six-bedroom, beach bungalow came with a two-room staff quarters to the side. There, a resident chef, and house staff stayed and maintained the grounds. Since they'd arrived, the chef provided their meals, but earlier, Zaina gave him the day off.

"Are you going to help me?" she asked as they walked through the sliding back door into the house.

"No. But I promise to watch the sway of your hips as you move graciously around my kitchen."

She whipped her neck around to face him. Her now dry tresses covered her wide eyes. He brushed the loose locks from her face. Their eyes locked and he leaned in for a kiss, but she turned her head away.

"No kisses for those who don't help in the kitchen." She laughed and started to walk away. She didn't get far because Mustafa caught her arm and pulled her back. He gripped her waist with one hand while the other slipped in her hair.

"You deny me?" He brushed his lips against her neck. Her pulse raced with each breath she drew. "Answer me."

"You…you're not being fair." Her voice shook.

"Answer the question, *chérie*."

Mustafa felt her resolve to maintain her composure melt

against him. He fought against the desire to have her share his bed. Sex between them had complicated things in the past. Moreover, he respected her new relationship with God. And the one he was building with the Big Guy himself. That knowledge, however, did nothing for his present state of arousal. But he needed her submission.

"No…"

He kissed her before letting her go. "Good girl."

~

"I promise I'll find a way to make the money up," his mother said.

Mustafa paused his steps on his way to the kitchen to get a glass of water. The whole family had just arrived home from visiting one of his father's friends. It was a few days before the Christmas holiday, but their father had announced earlier they didn't have money to celebrate. It was the second year in a row. Mustafa turned his head to the bedroom he shared with his siblings. He didn't want them to hear the noise.

"How? I told you not to touch that money!" his father roared.

"Omar was sick. You weren't here. I had to take him to the hospital. Please don't raise your voice."

Mustafa's jaw tightened at the familiar sound of fear in his mother's voice. He wanted to enter the living room, but the last time he got in between their fight, he ended up with welts on his back. Handed down by his father. So instead, Mustafa headed for his room. He'd been saving the allowance he got from doing odd chores for Mrs. Badawi, who lived across the street. The widow was blind in one eye and had no one to help her do simple chores in and around her house. After school, eating dinner and settling his siblings, Mustafa went over to help her with what she needed. The money he had should be enough for his father. Anything to ensure his mother didn't get hit. As he opened the door, Yasmine ran out.

"Yas, where are you going?" he asked.

"To tell mama I don't want to eat chicken for dinner. I want lamb."

"No Yas, stop..." His sister frowned at him and ran off.

Mustafa turned to follow her but didn't catch up with her before she entered the living room.

"Mama, can we have lamb for dinner tonight?"

Mustafa entered the room to find his father standing over his mother, who now had Yasmine on her lap.

"No. You will eat what we have," his father thundered.

Mustafa frowned, walking over to his mother. His sister had tears rolling down her cheeks.

"It's okay, baby. I will make it—"

"No, you won't! That's the problem now. You're always using money for the wrong things."

His mother stood. "Ahmed, it's not the wrong thing. Feeding our kids is not the wrong thing."

"Are you saying I am a bad father?"

Mustafa moved toward his sister and drew her close. The vein in his father's neck was protruding and that was always a bad sign. He consoled his sister and walked her out of the living room. He needed to get her away.

"Why are you always trying to put words in my mouth? I don't have time to argue with you," his mother said.

Mustafa assumed she attempted to walk away because the next thing he heard was his father's roar.

"Are you walking away from me? I rescued you from your miserable existence as a spoiled only child."

"Yas, please stay here. Do not come into the living room. I'll be right back," Mustafa begged. He looked over at the double beds in the corner and his twin siblings were taking a nap. He looked back at Yasmine. "Okay, Yas?"

His sister nodded her understanding and Mustafa left the room. Before he got back to the living room, he heard glass shattering. He dashed down the hall, entering the living room as his father's hand was *lifted to strike. Mustafa lunged to where his mother was on the floor, fragments of glass around her. He tried to help her up.*

"Move, boy." His father growled. "Have I not told you not to interfere with I and your mother's business?"

"But Papa…"

He was not able to finish his sentence before his father lifted him from his mother and flung him across the room. The pain in his ribs traveled to his brain. He winced but had to get up. His father continued to curse at his mother although he didn't hit her again. He pulled himself to his feet and made his way back to his crying mother.

"Stop crying before I really beat you. You're trying to make these kids think I am a bad father." In one swift move, his father pushed his mother. She landed on the coffee table. Mustafa watched her head bounce before she slumped to the floor.

Mustafa ran to her. "Mama!! Mama!! Please wake up." He shook her. "Papa, help her. Mama!" He looked over at his father whose hands were on his head as he slid down the opposite wall. His eyes expanded at the realization of what he'd just done.

A dip in the bed caused Mustafa to jerk upright. His heart raced as his lungs heaved for air. His skin was clammy with sweat. Swinging his arms, he aimed for the intruder.

"Musa, it's me. Please stop…stop. You're scaring me," a soft voice murmured.

His eyes darted across the room looking for the source. They landed on Zaina. She was on the other side of his king-sized bed, sitting on her haunches. Her voice was laden with fear and apprehension. She moved closer to him. The slightly open curtain allowed the moonlight to illuminate her worried expression. She reached out her hands.

"Can I touch you?"

He stared at her, swallowing hard to ease the ache in his throat. He must've been shouting. Mustafa hung his head. He never wanted her to see him this way. He hadn't had this dream in a few years. *What triggered it?*

"What are you doing here?" he growled.

"I was in my room, headed for the bathroom when I heard shouting. I thought it was coming from the staff quarters, but it was you. I rushed over and found you thrashing on the bed." Her voice regulated his raging heart.

"I'm sorry," he mumbled. "I didn't mean to wake you."

"I was already awake. I'm going to touch you now, okay?"

Mustafa nodded as he struggled to shake off the images that had haunted him since he was twelve. Zaina eased behind him. With her back against the headboard, she adjusted her legs to both sides of him and drew him towards her chest. He went still for a moment. One of her hands remained over his chest while she used the other to gently stroke his hair. The tension in his body began melting away.

"It's over," she reassured repeatedly.

Mustafa remained silent. He didn't trust himself to speak. If he did, he would fall apart and that was a sign of weakness. That weakness caused his mother's death. He should've been able to fight harder.

"Baby, I don't know what the dream was about, but I'm going to pray, okay?"

Mustafa tried to get up, but she held him tighter.

"Please babe, close your eyes. Please."

Her plea took the fight out of him. He relaxed and closed his eyes.

"Dear Heavenly Father, we come before your throne boldly. Your power is perfected in our weakness. Grant Mustafa peace of mind and calm his soul as only You can. With a couple of words, You calmed the raging sea..."

Mustafa drifted at the sound of her voice and the warmth of her arms. He needed her and he wanted her to know it. He had to find a way to give her what she wanted. His trust.

CHAPTER 14

The sound of a lawn mower roused Zaina from sleep. She peeled open her eyes and lifted a hand to shield them from the morning rays that spilled into the room. She stretched her body, moving her legs to free them from the tangled, black satin sheets. A yawn escaped her mouth as she pulled herself to an upright position. The events of the previous night flooded her mind. She was in Mustafa's bed. Alone. Her eyes darted toward the door. She frowned at the stack of packed luggage. They weren't supposed to leave until the next day. Why was he packed? Where was he?

Zaina got out of bed, rolled her shoulders before pulling her robe over the cotton pajama shorts set, she had on. She left the room and walked the short distance down the hall to her room. After brushing her teeth and washing her face, she went in search of Mustafa. Following the aroma of freshly brewed coffee, she headed to the kitchen. She leaned against the door frame and observed Mustafa. He was dressed in a tailored black suit with his phone to his ear. He had a half-eaten plate of food in front of him.

"Good morning Ms. Bakari," the chef greeted, entering the

kitchen from where she knew was the pantry. He had a few things in his hand which he sat down on the counter.

"Erm…good morning," she replied, causing Mustafa to turn around.

Their eyes connected for a few seconds before he broke contact and continued talking to whoever was on the phone. No smile, no wink, no head nod, or the other gestures of acknowledgement she was used to. His expression was stoic. *Did I miss something?*

"What can I get for you this morning?" the chef asked.

"Nothing right now, thank you." She tightened the sash of her robe. "Chef, can you give us a moment?"

Her ask caught Mustafa's attention. The chef nodded and exited the kitchen while Mustafa wrapped up his call. Her stomach clenched in anger. How dare he try to shut her out after the connection they made the night before? Whatever mask he thought he was going to put on now, she was bringing that sucker down. If he didn't cooperate, she was done. She was no longer going to overextend herself for someone who couldn't meet her halfway. She'd gone on with it long enough, but after last night…

"Good morning, Zaina. We—" His glacier tone seared her.

"What's going on?"

"We'll be leaving in the next hour." Mustafa stood and walked around the island to the sink.

Zaina walked into the kitchen and stood opposite him. She searched for his eyes, but he wouldn't make contact. "Why? What's happening? We weren't scheduled to leave until tomorrow."

"I have some business to take care of. I need to get you back and head to Tweedes."

"Musa, last night—"

"Is over." His harsh tone stumped her.

"No, it's not!" She clasped her palms in front of her face and took in a deep breath. "You will not do this again. Something happened yesterday and we're going to talk about it."

He glanced at her, then continued doing something with his phone. "People have bad dreams Zaina. What is it you want to hear?" He was annoyed.

"I'm Zaina now?" She ran her hand through her hair. This man frustrated her to no end.

His eyes stayed on her for the first time that morning. They held a blank expression; she couldn't read him. However, his body language told her she was losing him. Her heart raced. Mustafa returned to the table and closed his iPad. Tension engulfed the space, threatening the air her lungs needed.

"What do you want from me?"

"For you to see me. To talk to me. I'm in love with you, for goodness' sake. Can't you see that!" she screamed. "I've exposed my soul to you. How else can I get you to see that you're safe with me!"

"Why would I want to expose demons I'm trying hard to suppress?" Mustafa bellowed.

Zaina recoiled at his thunderous tone but was glad he was displaying any kind of emotion.

"If you don't, then how do you expect to conquer them? Last night, your shouts were gut wrenching. When I came into your bed, you almost punched me."

Regret filled his eyes.

"No, no please, I'm not saying it to make you feel bad. I'm saying whatever you were battling had you in pain. I want to carry your burdens with you. You helped me with mine, so why is it so hard for you to let me do the same?"

Mustafa remained silent, his calm veneer resurfacing. He opened his mouth to speak when his phone rang. Zaina folded her arms across her chest as she watched him talk to the driver. When he disconnected the call, his regard fell on her, and he walked towards her. He cupped her face in his hands.

"Your concern for me warms my heart, but I'm fine. Let's get you breakfast so we can leave." He sauntered to the table, grabbed his briefcase, and started out of the kitchen.

That's it!

"Mustafa DuBois-Arazi…"

Mustafa stilled, but he didn't turn around to look at her.

She continued. "If you walk out that door, I'm done. You do not get to wine and dine me, buy me expensive gifts, then shut me out of the things that are most important. I'm not an escort. I will finish your job and you will never hear from me again. This time, I'd be content that I gave it all I got."

Mustafa turned. "Are you threatening me?"

"Nope. I'm advising you on the consequences of your next move. You decide whether you can live with it or not."

Their eyes battled in a war of wills. She had to stand her ground, or Mustafa would never see her as his equal. She had no problem yielding to his alpha except where their emotional and mental relationship was concerned. They were going to have an equal partnership, anything else was settling, and she was done with that. He broke eye contact and advanced toward her. He glowered at her, his eyes piercing her resolve. Grabbing her hand, he exited the kitchen, dragging her along.

~

Minutes later, Zaina sat on the ottoman opposite Mustafa. His suit jacket hung on the side of the sofa. He'd just narrated what his dream was about. As he told the story, her heart ached, watching him struggle to keep his voice steady. They currently sat in silence as she waited for him to gather his emotions. In times past, she would've enabled him to continue faking normalcy. But like she'd learned, sooner or later, it all came crashing down.

Not wanting to disturb his process, she waited. A few more

minutes passed, then he lifted his head and pushed out a shaky breath.

"I grew up with uncertainty. There was no telling what mood my father would be in when he returned home for the day. When I was younger, I made it my responsibility to get my siblings to be on their best behavior, so nothing rattled him. Some days I succeeded, some days I failed. When it counted the most, I failed. I couldn't save her. For years after my mother died, I continued to relive the moment she slumped before my eyes. Over the years, I suppressed the memory by distracting myself with work and routine. If I don't have control, I sink into depressive episodes and anxiety."

"Have you seen anyone?" The haunted look in his eyes made her heart ache.

He shook his head. "When we went to live with my grandparents, I started having the dream. The one I had last night. My grandmother would stay and pray over me until I fell asleep. But then I thought, they'd taken the four of us in, and I didn't want to be a burden so they wouldn't change their minds. So, I started to avoid sleep. Anything so I didn't fall asleep and relive that moment."

"How did you do that? Did you—" Her chest tightened as the thought of him being on drugs flashed before her eyes.

"No. I would watch over my siblings. We'd lost both parents and I feared losing them too."

Her throat clogged with emotion. "Were any of them sick?"

"No." He pointed to his head. "Up here, I knew they were safe and loved, but anxious thoughts gripped me with fear. I tried seeing someone years ago, but my schedule became busier. I've been fine—"

"Baby, your success has been built on your trauma, but you have to stop and deal with this. See someone. I know the stigma surrounding mental health, especially in Africa. But no one has to know. Anxiety has bullied you into control, and I know part of it is your innate nature, but the nightmares aren't something you have to deal with." Tears rolled down her cheeks.

Zaina shed tears for the little boy who still shouldered responsibility he shouldn't. She shed tears for all the time she wasted because she wasn't aware of the real reason, he felt so responsible for his siblings. Like all African firstborns, there was that expectation, but she always thought he went overboard. She knew his father accidentally killed his mom. But she never knew he watched it happen. Never knew he tried to save her while keeping his siblings protected. She fell to her knees before him. She palmed his face, forcing his eyes to connect with hers.

"You're the strongest man I know. My wish is for you to be whole, mind, body, and soul. Please let me help you."

Mustafa remained silent, his hands moving to her waist.

"Please…"

His lips brushed against her forehead. "*Chérie…*"

"Think about it. Promise me."

"You know I hate to deny you—"

"Then don't start now. Promise me."

"I'll think about—"

"Fair enough." Zaina planted a series of kisses on his lips.

Mustafa stood, lifting her to her full height as he did. "Now let's get something straight."

Her brows came together. "What?"

His arms tightened around her waist. "Don't ever threaten me with your absence again."

Zaina laughed; a fine tremor ran through her body. She snaked her arms around his neck. "I use all tools in my arsenal to get alphas to come to their senses."

His brow hiked. "As in more than one?"

She brushed her lips against his. "My alpha. Feel better?"

"Watch it, woman." He kissed her passionately. "Go get dressed so we can see this spice farm you wanted to see."

She turned and he smacked her on her bottom. Zaina giggled as she made her way to the room she occupied. She had gotten Mustafa to talk to her. Her joy couldn't be contained. The next step was to contact her former therapist and ask for any recommendations for uber wealthy folks. For right now, they had a full day of paradise to cover. They already had a late start, but it was time well spent.

~

*L*ater that night, Mustafa's palm held her body close while they swayed to the soft sounds of "Surrender." The melodic tune by Natalie Taylor that filtered through the saxophone expressed her sentiments in a way she couldn't verbalize, infusing serenity into her soul. Zaina's head fell to Mustafa's chest, allowing him to guide their bodies across the dimly lit room.

A smile she had no desire to suppress crept up her lips as she brought the memories of the day they'd had to the forefront of her mind. After the emotionally draining conversation, they had earlier, they embarked on a tour of the island. Zanzibar offered sights she didn't even know existed. They started with the interactive experience of a spice farm. They had a very immersive experience, smelling about fifty different spices, tasting exotic fruits with names she'd never heard of.

To Zaina, their personal tour guide was very funny and friendly. But when Mustafa grunted a time or two, she knew the man's excessive touchy feely behavior ruffled his feathers. She'd just finished calming him down when the farm hand, who was clearly smitten with her, climbed a coconut tree so Zaina could taste fresh coconut water. His gallantry was met with stern eyes. She knew Mustafa was content seeing her happy, but she teased him about his serious expression, to which he responded something about enjoying the experience through her.

Next, they walked through Stone Town, after which they headed to Prison Island, their final destination. After lunch and sometime resting by the pool, they decided on a night out on the town.

The jazz club they were currently in provided the perfect ambience for them to end their day. After a dinner of salmon croquettes and house rice, she stood and pulled Mustafa to his feet for a dance. They continued to sway in silent bliss until the tickle of Mustafa's beard against her temple, and the vibration in his chest caused her to look up at him.

"Did you say something?" she asked.

"I was asking if the day was to your satisfaction?"

"Beyond."

He kissed her temple. "I'm glad."

"I've been wondering, why did you buy a second home here of all places?"

Since they arrived on the island, she wanted to know why he bought a house in her home country. When they visited here years ago, they rented a home for their weekend stay. It was here he told her he loved her. If he hated her so much, why did he come back here to buy property?

If this were a fairytale, the answer would be because he wanted to hold on to a piece of her. But this wasn't a fairytale. Her prince charming hadn't come to swoop her up with a declaration of undying love. She was fighting for her fairytale. Her apprehension of what his answer would be stopped her inquiry, but they had an emotional breakthrough earlier, so it was worth a try. Mustafa stared off into the distance while their bodies continued to move. Her eyes remained on him until his regard found hers.

"Here, I met the happy version of me. I found love and hope. I didn't want to completely let go of that."

Her heart raced as the meaning of his words settled in her spirit. She stopped moving. Even though there was a saxophonist in the corner and the wait staff stood in the distance, the only person that existed was the man in front of her. Tears pooled her eyes, blurring her vision. Mustafa thumbed away the tears rolling down her cheeks.

"Your tears, joyful or otherwise, cause me pain," he whispered.

Zaina let out a wry chuckle. "I can't help it. You're so sweet."

Mustafa groaned. "Sweet is for babies."

She laughed as he ushered them back to their seats. He sat and pulled her down to his lap.

"Oh, trust me. I know you're far from a baby. To the world you might be 'I am king, hear me roar', but you're my baby." She winked. "Sweet, slightly overbearing, kind, compassionate, sometimes mean. Yeah, let's not forget mean—"

Mustafa's lips landed on her, causing her to swallow the litany of adjectives she had left. After searching and massaging the depths of her mouth, he broke the kiss.

His smoldering dark eyes expressed his desire. "As long as you remember I'm the baby that runs the show."

CHAPTER 15

ustafa raised a hand to summon their waiter over. He glanced down at the empty, used plates on the table before his eyes traveled to his phone. He stared at the reminder on his phone. Turning to confirm his lunch partner, Ben Moseki, was still off to the side on a call, he checked the rest of his calendar for the day. The reminder dinged again, notifying him of a forty-five-minute window.

Video call with Pastor Mensah.

On return from Zanzibar, he and Zaina resumed their busy schedules. There was no denying that the trip produced a deeper connection between them. His need for self-preservation was waning but he was still cautious. He couldn't afford to get this wrong. He could no longer deny that Zaina wasn't the same woman from several years ago. She was whole, healthy, sexier, and more passionate than before. He'd accepted some responsibility for their demise. And as such, after the time they spent together, he understood how important it was to work on himself.

Inasmuch as he liked to lean on her deception as the cause of their demise, his unresolved trauma was at the root of his response. After operating under the guise of "I am fine" for so many years, he decided to give it a shot. He was still haunted by the fear in Zaina's eyes when she entered his bed that night. So, he reached out to his sister's husband, Kojo. One night a while ago, Kojo mentioned he'd been a client of the pastor that wedded them. Mustafa being acquainted with the pastor, had Assad get him an appointment which he now had forty minutes to get to.

"Yes sir," the waiter said.

"Can I have a malva pudding to go?"

The waiter nodded and retreated to prepare the order.

He and Ben were together in France, then met up again some years later when Mustafa was in London. Ben was there when Mustafa met Zaina and was one of the few people who knew details about their past.

"I know that sweet tooth isn't yours." Ben placed his phone in his jacket.

Mustafa studied his friend. "Is there a question somewhere?"

A few hours ago, the men concluded a meeting at the ministry, after which they decided to have lunch. Mustafa had to give an update on the progress of the recharge and guarantee it would be complete by the deadline given. Although Ben ran the ministry, he wasn't the only one Mustafa had to convince of Grand Amour's commitment to the conservation of natural resources needed for wildlife survival. The previous day, he'd been in a meeting with Zaina and some members of his staff for hours, poring over the details to ensure the ministry's satisfaction.

"Well, since you're so stingy with information, I'll ask." Ben leaned back in his chair and raised his glass to drink. "The Sam Bakari on the slide you presented today, is that who I think it is?"

"I don't know, who do you think it is? "Mustafa raised his brow.

"It's like pulling teeth with you. Is that my Sam?"

Mustafa folded his napkin and placed it on the table before looking at his friend. "You don't have a Sam. That's *my* Zaina."

Ben laughed. "So, I had to claim possession for you to admit it."

Mustafa observed the security men that surrounded them adjust their stance. They perhaps hadn't seen their boss that jovial.

"She was the one sent from the new firm I hired and as you said yourself, she's doing a great job."

"When I recommended that firm, I didn't even know she worked there. They just did some work for a friend of mine. But out of the billions of people in the world, she was sent to you," Ben shook his head, expressing his shock.

"You sound like Omar."

Ben raised his index finger. "Omar has a good head on his shoulders."

Mustafa narrowed his eyes at him. He loved his brother, but he was a wild card. He'd been that way since they were children. Omar spoke his mind and danced to the tune of his own drum, an admirable trait Mustafa sometimes envied. Then he'd remember that someone had to be the one to bail his brother out of sticky situations he got himself in.

"Are you going to make it work this time? And don't tell me you feel nothing for her. I can see it in your eyes, my friend."

"I didn't destroy it the last time."

"She may have done the deed, but you need to own up to your part in it."

"Which is?" Mustafa folded his arms across his chest and leaned back.

"Being so unforgiving and stubborn. Everyone longed for what you guys had. One mistake and you let it all go."

Mustafa snickered. "That was not a mistake."

"Whatever it was, I knew how much you loved her—"

Mustafa pinned his gaze on him. "Sometimes love is not enough."

Ben raised his hands in surrender. "Okay man, I'm gonna stop trying to rewrite history. I will say this, give yourself permission to be free. Those walls will eventually have to come down. There's no use for all this…" Ben gestured around them, alluding to wealth and power. "…without someone whom you get to go home to. Someone whose intimate connection centers you."

Mustafa's attention was interrupted by the approach of the waiter. He acknowledged him with the nod of his head, grateful for the reprieve. He had never been one for extended loquacious utterances, especially about his feelings. He had to do it in a few minutes so had no desire to do it here now. Mustafa peeked inside the bag that had been set before him. Satisfied, he took the tablet to sign the invoice. He could sense Ben's eyes on him, but he refused to engage in any further discourse about him and Zaina. Once the waiter left, Mustafa's eyes returned to his friend.

"You're right, my friend, this is for Zaina. I'll take your words under advisement."

For the remaining of the time, they moved the conversation to family and other hassles of his job with the government. After Ben reminded him about the annual banquet the ministry held for foreign companies based in Botswana, the men said their goodbyes and parted ways.

Minutes later, headed to the airstrip, Mustafa picked up his phone that buzzed a little earlier.

Zaina: Thank you for lunch. I miss you.

A smile spread across his face. He hadn't had time to see her before leaving the resort. He learned earlier on, of her propensity to work through lunch and made sure to put an end to it.

Her workload often annoyed him, although he knew better than to voice the sentiment. He was all for her working, but when he found out how many projects apart from his she had to manage, he wondered when she had time to relax. He texted back.

You're welcome, *chérie*. And not more than I. Save room for dessert.

Zaina: Yum. Hurry back. Wait, are we talking you or real dessert?

She accompanied the text with a wink emoji. Mustafa's brows furrowed at how forward she could be on occasion. They were not sharing a bed, but Zaina got her amusement from needling him sometimes. If he were being honest, the ability to speak her mind was one of the things he admired about her. It was also why he was so taken aback by her deception. He thought he'd read her correctly. Another failing on his part.

Zaina!

Zaina: Oops, the first name. Okay, have a safe flight, grumpy.

Mustafa started to type out his response when the car came to a stop. Focusing his attention on exiting the car and boarding his plane, he set his phone in his pocket. Returning the crew's greeting, Mustafa walked to his seat in the private room at the back of the plane to settle in for the ninety-minute flight. His phone buzzed again. This time it wasn't Zaina. It was another woman who was itching to give him an earful.

"Musa, really?"

Mustafa chuckled. He knew what she was referring to but chose to let her tell him. "Yasmine, what has you riled up?"

"Is this how you want to play it? Because if you haven't said a word to me, that means Grandma Olly is also in the dark. Do you want to gamble on me hanging up and updating her on the latest in your life?"

"I thought you just insinuated *you* were in the dark," Mustafa teased.

"I'll embellish the stuff Salma told me and make your life look like one of those American Hallmark movies," she threatened.

Mustafa chuckled. "And I thought you were the sensible one." His eyes went to the laptop he'd set up to connect with the Pastor.

"Spill it."

"For clarification, you threatened to get our grandmother on me. You seem to forget I helped with Kojo?"

"Stop telling that fib. You conspired with Kojo, so I'd listen to him. I, on the other hand, have minded my business—"

"Until now."

"Musa—"

Mustafa laughed. "What do you want to hear, Yas? I'm sure Sal has given you the background of—"

His sister's loud sigh cut him off. "This is me you're talking to Musa, not the twins. I know how bad she hurt you. How are you really?"

After a few moments of silence, allowing her implied meaning to sink in, Mustafa responded. "I've gone through a number of emotions. Anger, disappointment, desire, mostly struggling with uncertainty."

"Why are you uncertain? I can tell you still love Zay—"

"And you know that how?"

"Your voice. You can deny it to yourself, but I can tell. Especially after the way Salma told me you had her apologize to Zay."

Mustafa groaned at the memory. His baby sister stayed mad at him for a week after that. She strongly defended her stance, then decided to give him the cold shoulder. Not before telling him that if she couldn't protect him, he couldn't protect her either. He laughed at her, which further vexed her. He'd sent her a basket of her favorite things as a peace offering, reiterating his position of his demand of respect for Zaina.

"Hey man, is this chick bothering you?" Kojo's voice brought him out of his musing.

Mustafa chuckled. "Yes, she's trying to lecture me on love."

"KJ, give me back the phone. I'm trying to get him to happily ever after," Yasmine scolded from the background.

"Good luck with that man. She's been on some super emotional stuff lately."

"Wanting him to find love is not emotional. For that, better see if our son has space for you in his room."

"Why?" Kojo asked, the disbelief in his tone evident.

Mustafa didn't mind being entertained by the couple's playful bickering, but he had other things to do.

"I've told you before, but I guess it's worth repeating. Same roof, same bed."

"She's kicking you out of the room?" Mustafa asked.

Kojo laughed. "So, she thinks. I still might need to grovel."

"I meet with your pastor in a few minutes. Keep this—"

"Your business is safe with me. I know the stigma around therapy, but it helps," Kojo advised.

"My love to Yas and the kids."

"I'mma need your love and mine to get back on her good side after this stunt." Kojo laughed and Mustafa joined in.

His brother-in-law walked right into that one. Even he knew not to taunt and call a pregnant woman emotional. They said their goodbyes, then disconnected the call.

~

"How does this work exactly? I've been to these kinds of sessions before, but stopped," Mustafa said.

The men had spent the first five minutes greeting and reestablishing a rapport. The pastor then went over the questionnaire Mustafa had filled out earlier in the week.

"Why did you stop?" Pastor Mensah asked.

"I was fine."

"Are you fine?"

Mustafa paused, raking his fingers through his beard. The hope that adulthood would provide an escape slowly waned over the years. The reoccurrence of his dream was a reminder that despite the new life he tried to create, he was still a prisoner of his past.

"The dream is back."

"From your questionnaire, I'm assuming you mean the one where you relive the day your mother died."

"Was killed," Mustafa corrected. Intentional or not, his father killed his mother. She didn't just die.

Pastor Mensah nodded. "I help you understand your emotions, so you become aware of what you're feeling or what you're trying to avoid feeling. Once you can establish authority over your demons, then you can get to the real purpose of your time on earth. The reason God has you here."

"No magic wand?"

"None. We're a sum of our experiences, good, bad, and ugly. I can't erase your history, but I can give you techniques coupled with biblical principles to ensure a shift in perspective and a more meaningful life."

"Proceed."

"Tell me about the dream."

For the next few minutes, Mustafa went over the dream the same way he'd done with Zaina a few weeks ago.

"When you wake up, how do you feel?"

Feelings.

Mustafa hated talking about them. "*Being in touch with your emotions is courageous and sexy. Emphasis on the sexy.*" The words Zaina had spoken to him some nights ago came flooding back to his memory.

"Anger, disappointment and sorrow," he responded.

"Toward?"

"Myself…my mama. But mainly myself."

"I noticed you didn't mention your father. But before we dig into that, why you?"

"I should have been able to save her."

"How could you?"

Mustafa's jaw clenched. "I could've fought harder. I'm a man. It's my job!"

"You are a man, but you were a boy. A twelve-year-old boy. That's toxic patriarchy we must get away from. It wasn't your job to be the adult." Mensah paused. "What about your mother?"

"How could she keep us in those conditions?" Mustafa growled. No matter what his grandmother said, he still grappled with how his mother didn't get them back to the safety of Tweede Kans Cove.

"We can't begin to dissect what your mother's state of mind was, but I've counselled a number of people in abusive relationships. The shame of the situation can often overpower the knowledge of love. In your case, the love of your grandparents. There's also fear. Fear of judgement."

Mustafa struggled with the logic of the truth and the rage he'd had to deal with since that night. The failed sense of justice that burned his soul.

"Why don't you feel any of those emotions toward your father?"

"I do."

"But it's not as strong?"

"We visited the place my papa was from in Rabat. He comes from poverty. From the moment I could discern him better, I knew he used my mother as a meal ticket. I guess you can say, I learned not to expect much from him, so he was not a disappointment. I feel anger, but the disappointment isn't there because I had no great expectations."

"So, because you found out your mother came from wealth,

your disappointment is in her failure to meet *your* expectation of being able to make better choices?"

The weight of the pastor's words fell to the pit of his stomach. He grunted in confirmation.

"Our time is almost up, but I want to leave you with a thought. Nothing excuses accountability. Making the right party accountable is the first step to absolving the twelve-year-old you from misplaced blame."

"The second?"

"Shifting perspectives by censoring your inner critic. The—"

A knock on the door paused the conversation.

"Enter," Mustafa said.

"Sir, we're a few minutes from making our descent," a cabin crew member informed him.

"Thank you. Please retrieve the bag I gave you from the fridge, so I don't forget. I'll be up there soon to prepare for landing."

"Yes, sir."

After the man left, Mustafa turned his attention back to the screen in front of him. "That's my cue, Pastor."

"Mine as well. Until next time. I want you to practice getting out of survival mode."

"How?"

"Any time you have triggering thoughts, acknowledge and release."

An announcement came over the intercom and Mustafa opted for non-verbal acquiescence instead of dragging the conversation on. He had a lot to think about and another meeting to attend once he got back to his office. He needed some time to get his thoughts together. After a promise of ensuring he'd keep his next appointment, the call ended. Mustafa made his way to the front of the plane, buckled in, and gazed out of the window.

Release.

Something he hadn't done in twenty-seven years. He wondered if he even knew how.

CHAPTER 16

From the Earth.

She was going to take a chance. She had to take a chance. It was time, wasn't it? Zaina stared at the two words dancing on her screen. She looked over at the business card on her exposed lap. The chirping birds caused her to lift her eyes. She took in the golden sun that had peaked over the horizon, making way for blue skies to replace its retreating dark counterpart. The smell of fresh precipitation lined the air. The greenery dripped with moisture showing evidence of the previous day's rainfall. Zaina filled her lungs with the fresh smell of the new dawn. The old was giving way for the new and it was time for her to do the same.

Kutoka Duniani

The words translated in Swahili was the name she'd chosen over ten years ago for her business. The environment became her passion since a girl in her high school class almost died while they were on a school excursion. They were in a park where deadly nightshade was growing. The exposure almost killed her. The incident sparked Zaina's curiosity and passion to do something that would contribute to the safety of humans while preserving the environment.

The décor of her childhood home was expensive, but cold. She'd decided a long time ago that would never be the case when she had a family of her own. In the meantime, she wanted to provide others with warm, welcoming décor pieces. Pieces that illustrated the importance of sustainability and regenerative practices. Her mission was upscaling and contributing to the circular economy.

Once her love life fell apart, she chucked that dream and decided to pursue a more traditional career path. After all, if she no longer had security in her personal life, she had to make sure her professional one remained intact.

Currently, in the early hours of the morning, she was seated on the terrace of her villa, looking at the logo design she wanted to send to a graphic artist. Zaina was still reeling from the news Ibiso gave her when she was in Tanzania. A little over two years ago, Ibiso asked her to design the VIP part of her restaurant, Bisso Bites. The woman was sweet, but pushy. Zaina did it. It was a small area, so it wasn't too daunting. She would never have imagined that years later, the CEO of one of Africa's leading progressive furniture brands, Irek Designs, happened to have lunch in Bisso Bites, loved the decor and wanted to meet the designer.

Intimidated by the possibility of her dreams becoming a reality, she tucked the information deep down in the recesses of her mind. Mustafa showing up and them being in Zanzibar made it easy to avoid thinking about it. It'd been a month. The injection pump for the lake recharge was operational. She was in the transfer and monitoring stage. Her two other projects were moving along nicely. With everything running smoothly, including her love life, she had time to think about what she wanted to do.

Thinking of her love life, her thoughts traveled to Mustafa.

They'd settled into a comfortable routine. Dinner together every evening when he was on the resort. When he was away, he checked in on her frequently, sometimes obsessively. Things between them were familiar, yet different. She knew he was supposed to start therapy, but he hadn't shared anything, and she didn't want to pry. It was harder, however, to silence the voice reminding her that Mustafa hadn't declared his love or lack thereof for her. She'd be lying if she said she didn't feel his love. But assumptions led them to doom the first time, and she wasn't ready to go down that road again.

Something that also bothered her was how he still shielded his family from her. When they talked, he skillfully navigated around the topic of family. Armed with the knowledge that culturally, introducing her to his family was a big deal, she couldn't help but shift a little into self-preservation mode.

Personally, things were better between her and her family. She also didn't slack when it came to nurturing her relationship with God. But somehow, she still felt empty. She loved her job, but it was never meant to be her end game. Reconnecting with the love of her life strengthened and gave her the courage to believe she could do more.

Glancing at the photo of her and Mustafa in Zanzibar, she felt a pang of guilt in her stomach. She hadn't shared Irek Designs' demand for her portfolio, or the leap she was thinking of making. His happiness and pride in her weren't in question. This was something she wanted to do on her own. She hadn't even shared her potential move to London when the project was done. At first, she didn't because he wasn't around. Now so much time had passed that she was afraid to. He assumed she was going back to Abuja, and she hadn't corrected him. She had eight more weeks in her contract and Kutoka Duniani might be the way to prevent her fairytale from blowing up in her face.

Zaina's eyes darted to the toolbar at the bottom of her device. Six fifteen. The sun had made its full appearance She needed to get ready. It was Friday, the day for her biweekly trip to the lake and pond sites to get measurements and samples. When she first started working for Safi, she learned to never rely solely on the measurements provided by the site workers. She looked at the screen again; satisfied with the email and the sample logo she'd put together, she hit send. Her design portfolio was almost done. Once she had a website and official business cards, she'd reach out to Irek Designs.

Leaving the terrace where she'd been for the past hour, Zaina walked through the double doors into her lodge. "Thank You Lord" by Called Out Music was still playing in a loop. The track she'd put on after her prayers relayed the depths of her heart. Things her mind couldn't form the words to express when it came to her gratitude for God's grace.

She walked into the kitchen. The relaxing smell of the pink roses Mustafa had delivered two days ago permeated the room. She opened the small fridge and got out the jam for her toast. A few minutes later, with toast and tea set before her, Zaina scrolled through her social media pages. She liked and commented on various accounts she followed. She jotted accounts she could use as inspiration on a small notebook.

"I can do this."

"God didn't give me the spirit of fear but that of a sound mind."

"Everything I need God has already given to me."

Zaina continued to chant her affirmations on the way to the shower.

~

Hours later, Zaina listened to the site leader update her on his discussion with the lab manager. They were backed up on their work, so the samples of soil and water collected the previous week hadn't been tested yet. The site leader failed to share that detail until right before she had to present to her boss earlier. Now she was at the site to collect samples herself for the current week and was being told they weren't any closer to providing the results from the previous week. When the golf cart came to a stop, she and the site leader climbed out. She picked up her backpack, and they made their way down the small pathway leading to the lake.

"Still no hope of having last week's result?"

"That's what they said, ma'am."

"I've told you to call me Sam." She shook her head. She'd been working with Hamid and his guys since she'd been in Botswana and had been telling him the same thing for just as long.

"You should have told me this earlier."

"I'm sorry. I thought my connection there would be back in the office and help me move our samples to the front."

Zaina squatted before the body of water. "And?"

"My guy is still on leave…"

Zaina already knew what that meant. She would probably have to put on a fake smile, pretend to be timid and helpless to hurry things along. The heavy lifting had been done, but monitoring was crucial. Apart from the water being of sound level, the quality of the water also had a standard to meet. If the quality of the water wasn't optimal for the survival of the wildlife and plants, Grand Amour would still fail the audit.

Next week, she'd meet with Grand Amour to provide an update. The last thing she wanted was to have to stumble through the data. She didn't want Mustafa troubleshooting her problem again, so she'd have to take the samples to the lab in Maun herself. She removed her phone from the pocket of her khaki capris to check the time. It was a few minutes 'til noon. She'd be back from the two-hour round-trip way before dark.

Over the next several minutes, Zaina got to work with her team collecting the day's water and soil samples, measuring the lake depth, ensuring the continued integrity of its structure. She packed up her beakers and equipment before heading to the ponds and doing the same thing.

Once they were done and headed back to the resort, she instructed Hamid to secure a taxi for her. She was going to try groveling on the phone one last time. If that didn't work, she wanted to have transportation on standby. Not seeing the need, she didn't bring her car with her to the resort. An official Grand Amour resort car was always there to take her to where she wanted to go. For this trip, she didn't want to draw any attention to herself. Mustafa was away, and she knew that if she asked for a car, he'd be notified. He was in Tweedes attending a security assessment meeting and she didn't want to distract him.

Minutes later, with hurried steps, Zaina headed towards the entrance of Grand Amour, ransacking her purse. She was in search of the card for the lab's address. In her haste to leave her office, she'd just thrown it in there. Hamid, who had the briefcase that contained the samples, was outside waiting on the car.

"Ah, I've fou—" Zaina muttered to herself. The card fell to the floor as she collided with a hard body. Her eyes followed the direction of the card before she looked at the person who halted her steps.

"Hello, Sam," Kabelo greeted her, bending down to pick up the card.

He glanced at the card before handing it to her. She hadn't really seen him around since the day they had lunch together a while ago. Occasionally, he'd pop up at their meetings via conference call. She thought it was strange since he told her he worked out of the Botswana office. But after that little stint with Mustafa, she didn't ask any questions.

"Hey, Kabelo. How are you? It's been a while."

"I'm good. Busy, busy, busy." He glanced down at the card

again before his eyes returned to her. "Where are you off to in such a hurry?"

"I need to get to the lab in Maun."

His brows came together. He looked at his watch. "At this time?"

"Yeah, I really need to get there as soon as possible. It's almost lunch time, so if I head out now, I should be able to get what I need done." Zaina looked past him to the door, trying to give an indication that he needed to get out of the way so she could continue with her mission.

"How are you getting there?"

"My site lead is supposed to be waiting outside with a rental." She made steps to move past him. "It was nice see—"

"I'll walk you outside," he offered.

"That's not necessary. I'm fine…" She continued to walk and noticed he was following her. Unwilling to engage in further discussion, Zaina exited the building. She located Hamid in the corner.

"Where's the car?" she asked.

"I had one, but when the guy arrived, a few minutes later, he got a call about a family emergency. The rental company is sending another car," Hamid explained.

Zaina ran her hand through her hair. The thump against her temple was growing louder. She'd been experiencing the simmering onset of a stress headache for the past couple of hours. The day had started off perfect. She should've known it was a little too perfect.

"How long ago was this?" she asked.

"About five minutes or so."

"But the rental place is not that far. They should've been here by now." Her eyes darted toward the stretch of road leading up to the entrance of the resort. No car seemed to be coming toward them.

"I'll take you." Kabelo walked up from behind her.

Until then, Zaina had completely forgotten he was still there with them. She turned to face him, then looked at Hamid.

"You don't have to do that," she said.

"I know. I want to help."

Zaina shifted her weight from one foot to the other. Having lunch with someone she just met in a public environment was far different from entering a car with the person. She would have Hamid with her, but still…

"From the sound of it, you need the results urgently. So, you'd rather stay here and keep wasting time than to take me up on my offer to drive you there?"

"And I appreciate it. I just don't want to inconvenience you."

"It's not that much of an inconvenience. If it was, I wouldn't have offered. So, what's it going to be?"

Zaina looked at Hamid with a silent request for his input. Reading him correctly, she gave a slight nod.

"Okay, thank you very much. Where are you parked?"

"Come on."

In silence, the three of them made the short trek to Kabelo's jeep. She would've felt more comfortable sitting at the back of the car and letting Hamid take the front seat. However, she didn't want to seem snobbish when Kabelo insisted. After the man had gone out of his way to help her, it was the least she could do. She said a silent prayer as Kabelo backed out of the parking lot.

Sometime later, in the lobby of the laboratory, Zaina frowned at Kabelo as she tossed some peanuts in her mouth. "You cannot possibly think that Rocky III was better than Rocky IV," Zaina said.

Kabelo took a piece of biscuit from the packet they were sharing and brought it up to his lips.

"No matter how many roundabout ways you ask me that question, my answer remains the same." He bit into the biscuit and laughed when she rolled her eyes.

It was a true blessing that Kabelo had inserted himself into her mission. When they arrived about four hours ago, she went from scolding and sharing her utter disappointment, to anger and threatening to report the lab to their governing body, then back to groveling and appealing to their sensibilities. Nothing worked. Their power lines were down and so they had been working with a generator. Because of the price of fuel, they couldn't keep it on all the time, so they fell behind. She had initially told Kabelo to stay out of it and he did. When she started to tremble in frustration at their blatant stance, he stepped to her again and asked to help. This time, she let him.

He spoke to them in the native tongue. Whatever he said, which he refused to share, seemed to get the ball rolling. She no longer cared what he said if both weeks' samples were being processed. Since they were promised delivery soon, she didn't want to leave and risk them getting sidetracked. It had been a long wait and they had about another hour to go.

Zaina had asked Kabelo to leave, promising to find her way back, but he refused. He was actually a nice guy. During lunch that day, Mustafa had her so rattled that she barely listened to anything he said. Now she was and he was a well-versed conversationalist. Zaina took a sip of her Coca Cola and they continued to talk pop culture when the door chimed.

Zaina felt him before she saw him. Her eyes searched for the source of his pull. Her legs propelled forward causing her to stand. In quick strides, she was standing before Mustafa. Without thinking of the audience, they had, she flung her arms around his neck.

"What are you doing here? I didn't know you were coming back today," she said.

His hands went around her waist, but his body was stiff to her touch. Zaina pulled back and followed the direction of his narrowed stare. They were pinned on Kabelo.

"Musa..." she whispered.

"I didn't think I needed permission to surprise you." He turned his eyes to her.

"You don't." She kissed his lips. "Now, stop being grouchy, I missed you."

"Good to know I wasn't alone."

Zaina pulled him toward the area she'd vacated. She glanced back at him. "Behave."

CHAPTER 17

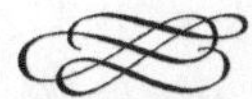

The time away from her was torture. By the third day, he'd asked Assad to double up his appointments where he could. Still Mustafa couldn't make it back in time for their date two days ago. Their calls and texts kept him in good spirits, but it was barely enough. The meeting that would have kept him until the next day had been rescheduled, allowing him to fly back to Botswana.

During the flight, his longing to see her blazed like an unquenchable fire. The feel of her lips on his, her fingers threading through his beard, her laughter that sent sweet vibrations through his chest, her essence. After ten days away, his anticipation to have her in his arms crash landed when he got to the resort, and she wasn't there.

Mustafa immediately pulled out his phone. Maybe she'd left him a message he missed. She hadn't, and to fuel his panic, no one seemed to know where she was. He called her phone, but his call immediately rolled over to her voicemail. When he remembered, she was supposed to go to the lake earlier, his world threatened to collapse. His heart raced with worry of her being harmed.

Edward rushed to him several minutes later, informing him that one of the clerks in the lobby heard Zaina talking about a lab and Maun. Mustafa knew where that was and headed to her. His heart rate returned to normal, given that her "disappearance" was work related. What he hadn't expected was to see her laughing and carefree with Kabelo while he'd been worried to death. In his present state, Zaina's warning that he behaved wasn't something he could adhere to.

Which was the reason she was now seated far away from him as Edward drove them back to the resort. Mustafa glanced over at her. Her arms were folded across her chest and her body turned away from him as she stared out the window. This wasn't the homecoming he'd envisioned. He needed to fix it. He slipped his phone into the inner pocket of his blazer.

"Do you want to have dinner at the resort, or do you want to get something along the way?" he asked.

"Oh, I get an opinion?" Her tone was terse, but she didn't look at him. That burned him.

"Don't be ridiculous."

She turned to him. Her eyes were fiery, her lips swollen a bit. She had the tendency to bite her lower lip when upset. All he wanted to do was kiss her, but she wanted to argue about trivialities.

"Me? I'm not the one who was rude for no reason at all."

He waved her off. "I wasn't rude."

Zaina scoffed. "It took you almost a minute before you accepted the hand he offered in a handshake. The whole time, you kept staring him down like you were in a duel of some sort."

"Enough already."

Her hand went flying, trying to buttress her point. "No, not enough. That man works for you. I don't want everyone that tries to help me to feel threatened by what you will do to them."

Mustafa raised a brow. "Did he tell you I did anything to him?"

"No, but when I think about it, after our lunch, I've rarely seen him."

Mustafa snorted. "Did you want to see him?"

"That's not the point."

"It is now."

"Musa, that man doesn't want me. He was only trying to help—"

"Why didn't you come to me if you were having a problem?"

"For the last time, because it's my job and I want to do it myself."

"And I want a kiss from my woman, but we all can't get what we want."

She tilted her head toward him. "Huh?"

Mustafa reached over and drew her closer to him, before lifting her to his lap. "Kiss me."

Zaina cupped his face and stared into his soul. She brushed her lips against his forehead, both of his eyes, then she peppered kisses along his neck. Lifting her head, she placed her soft lips against his and gave him a passionate kiss.

Their foreheads met as they struggled to catch their breaths. "When I couldn't get in contact with you, I panicked. Then when I did find you, you were with another man, and you seemed to be enjoying yourself. I didn't like it," he confessed.

She lifted her head while her arms circled his neck. "I only have eyes for you."

"That pleases me. Now, what do you want to eat?"

"We can get something at the resort and eat on the floating firepit. Tell me about your trip."

Mustafa brushed his lips against her temple. "I will. Let me make a call first."

~

*M*ustafa absently ran his fingers through Zaina's hair as they gazed into the lagoon before them. When they arrived, they separated to get freshened up for dinner. As instructed, Assad had a part of the floating pit partitioned off for privacy. Mustafa didn't care who saw them together, but he understood Zaina's need for caution since she was here on assignment. He wanted her comfortable, so anything she wanted, he'd give. When she had emerged in an African print top that exposed her shoulder which she paired with ripped jeans and some kind of strappy sandals, he was in a trance. Her giggle and light tug of his beard grounded him. He ushered her to their table on the circular deck, amid the standing tiki lamps and cushioned wingback bamboo chairs. Both famished from their day, they ate in relative silence.

After dinner, they moved to a wide cushioned chair in the corner. Zaina was snuggled up next to Mustafa under a light blanket as he slowly massaged her scalp. The burnt-orange sun was slipping below the horizon and some wildlife performed their chorus.

"I'm proud of you but worry you're going to get busier..." Zaina's soft whisper pulled him from his reverie.

Mustafa brushed his lips against her hair. "Why do you say that?"

"You just bought an apartment building and shopping complex that's going to need some work. In addition to running Grand Amour—"

"Running the resort doesn't fall solely in my lap."

"Stop being coy. Your siblings have their departments, but you oversee everything. You'll be busier."

Mustafa didn't speak immediately as he digested her concern. There was no way around it now but explaining his goal might ease her fears.

"My father stifled my mother. His insecurities were threatened by her potential. Funny thing is, she didn't have money since she was cut off after a while. She used her hands to make money. She loved to weave straw baskets. Different sizes and designs which she sold to the neighbors. Soon word spread, and people sought her out. My father always complained about her not cooking on time, taking care of us and whatever he could complain about until she stopped. I often lay awake at night and wondered what would've happened if she were allowed to be all that she could be. I want to provide that opportunity for women with business ideas. A percentage of the total capacity of the complex and apartments will go to women with small businesses at a subsidized rate."

"I'm in awe right now. That's so admirable. Musa, she would be proud." She exhaled. "Promise me you won't drown in work. Hire the right people so—"

"In the beginning, I need to be hands on. It's important that things run exactly as I want them to."

She sighed. "How did I know you'd say that?"

Mustafa chuckled. "You should come work for me."

Zaina sat up straight. "Umm, no, but as what?"

Mustafa shrugged. "Consult with the construction crew. Ensure we're in line with the environmental standards. You can also design pieces for the common areas."

"There's so much that can be done to help the environment. Discontinue the use of lead-based paint, ventilation, the use of greenery to clean the air, appliances that are energy efficient, acoustics to down noise…so much can be done. But no, sir. You can hire anyone else."

"Why?"

Zaina laughed. "I can barely get you out of my business now. Working with you every day is bound to drive me crazy."

"*Cherie*, your business is my business. You belong to me… all of you. Don't ever forget that. Besides, you like when I drive you crazy." He squeezed her tighter causing her to squeal.

"If you say so, but still no. How will I know if you're hiring me because you don't want me out of your sight or because I'm actually doing a good job?"

"I don't need to hire you to keep you by my side. Nigeria is only a four-and-a-half-hour flight away."

Previously, he hadn't given much thought to their future after the project was done. He was determined to stay unattached. As the days crept by, he knew he wanted her with him. The better deal would be for her to relocate to Tweede Kans Cove, but he recognized that she loved her job. So, for now, that discussion could wait.

"Cocky much?"

"With a lot of things, yes. With you, no."

She stared at him, then returned her head to his chest. He could feel her shift. He waited for her to say what was on her mind while they sat in silence.

"Your thinking is hurting my chest," he whispered.

She let out a cleansing breath. "Musa, about earlier…"

The shakiness in her voice told him she was searching for the right words.

"What about earlier?"

"I don't want to be another problem for you to solve."

"What are you talking about?"

"Everyone relies on you for something. You have the whole world on your shoulder, and I don't want to add to that."

Mustafa grunted, expressing his displeasure at her insistence on revisiting this issue. "It is my job to shoulder anything that bothers you."

"But I don't want that to be our thing. I'm no damsel in distress," she said.

"I never said you were. You're smart, sexy, bold, and brave. That doesn't mean you shouldn't ask for help."

She sat up straight. "When I need—"

"You never do!" His chest tightened.

The rage he felt when he saw her earlier with Kabelo resurfaced. Mustafa knew the owner of the lab. He could have easily gotten her what she needed. Instead, she got another person to help her.

She caressed his cheek. "Remember when we were in London?"

He grunted. He wasn't sure where she was going with this. Of course, he remembered. The good, the bad and the ugly times.

"We both had big dreams. You've done so well, while I, on the other hand, have spent my life scared to take chances."

"It's not a competition," he said.

"I know. You inspire me to get things done. I want to do them, but on my own. You can't get mad any time you feel I should've asked but I didn't."

"Understood," Mustafa murmured.

"I promise, if I need your help, I'll ask."

He was tired of arguing with her and didn't want their evening ruined. So, he didn't respond, but instead pulled her closer.

"Will you accompany me for my grandmother's surprise birthday celebration in a few weeks?"

The way her body stilled against his and the sound of her breath hitching were the only signs he had that she'd heard him. Zaina remained silent. Mustafa had been having weekly sessions with the pastor. In his last session, they'd talked about Zaina's reentrance into his world. They dissected the reason he hadn't given her full access to it. Especially when it came to his family, which was an integral part of his makeup.

The reason for his hesitancy and guarded state still had to do with trust. Despite his need for her, he kept her on a level he could afford to lose. Subconsciously, he had maintained his walls while giving her the illusion of vulnerability. If he wanted them to have a chance, he had to be willing to share her with the people that mattered to him most. It was time to reintroduce her to his family.

"Zaina?"

"I heard you."

"And?"

"I'm processing. All this time, you rarely talk about them to me. You keep that part of you from me. So, I'm trying to figure out what changed."

"You're important to me. It's time for both of my worlds to connect."

She attempted to get up, but he held her closer. Scared of what the loss would mean. Selfish though it may be, he wasn't giving her an opportunity to be rid of his scent, offering her a clear mind. He needed everything in his arsenal. The thought of her refusal rumbled his soul.

She turned to face him instead. "Why?"

He shrugged. "Because it's time."

"I'm asking what makes this the time? What has shifted?"

With a crease in his forehead, he studied her. Her stance was foreign to him. "Does this mean you don't want to accompany me?"

Her finger stroked his beard. "Why do you have to be so stubborn? Tell me what changed."

"The pastor recommends I begin to confront those things I've suppressed over the years. If I don't, they will continue to rob me."

"And I'm one of those things?"

"Not you, *per se*. The thought of letting down my guard, allowing myself to be cared for and loved."

Her lips turned up in a smile. One that settled his heart with satisfaction. "I'm liking this pastor..."

"Careful."

Zaina leaned her head back and laughed. Mustafa took the opportunity to brush his lips against his favorite place; her neck. She moaned and threaded her fingers through his hair. She kissed him lightly, but his soul demanded more. Before he could satisfy his need, her palms rested on his chest, pushing away.

She cupped his face, her thumb caressing the small scar next to his ear. The raised skin was one of his battle wounds from his father.

"You are worthy of love. You are enough. You don't have to constantly prove it by doing. God is committed to you being free, so babe, … just be."

Mustafa nodded.

"Some days ago, I was reading Psalm 106, and verse eight struck me. The Psalm was talking about how Israel rebelled, but the Lord still delivered them. That verse said, "Nevertheless, He saved them for the sake of His name, that His power might be known." Despite everything they did, God still dried up the sea so the Israelites could pass to the other side. It amazed me how committed He was to their freedom, so He could get the glory. Babe, you went through what you went through, but God will still get the glory for your life. When He leads you to a storm, He'll also lead you through it. If we settle in it, we can miss God. Like the Israelites, we have to be willing to walk through on dry land."

"Storm?" he asked.

"Yeah, storm. My childhood, your childhood. In my rebellion, I couldn't see what God was trying to teach me. You didn't act out—instead you decided to recreate your world by pretending your pain didn't exist. It's time to be free, babe. And I'm so happy the pastor is helping you through that."

Mustafa cleared his throat, trying to dispel the sting of its rawness. He couldn't boast of the most intimate relationship with God. He did what he needed to do, but truthfully didn't totally rely on his Creator. The words Zaina spoke, however, sent a shudder up his spine, piercing through his bones, providing clarity to the thoughts he had been struggling with. In silence, he allowed the revelation to settle in his spirit.

"Is that all?" Zaina asked.

"Huh?"

"Is that all you need to confront, the tearing down of the wall between your family and me? Is that all?"

Mustafa took in a deep breath, then exhaled. "He wants me to revisit my childhood home."

Her eyes bugged. The rise and fall of her chest showed her apprehensions for him. "Where it happened?"

Mustafa nodded.

When the pastor suggested it, Mustafa gave him a resounding, no. Why would he do that? But days later, he took inventory of how it might do him good. It could help him separate that, that was then, and this is now. Or make him see that it was impossible for him to have done anything more for his mother. Release the shame of failing to protect her.

That conversation was a week ago and he hadn't even looked at his schedule for an available opening. Looking in Zaina's eyes now, he acknowledged that he was afraid to relive the experience alone.

"I think it's a good idea. I don't say this lightly because the situations are far from the same. But for me, even though I'd forgiven my parents, I didn't release them. Not until I talked to them." She twisted her lips. "Did it fix the past? No. But it allowed me to rewrite the story I'd been telling myself."

Depleted by the depth of the conversation they'd been having, Mustafa decided to get them back to happier discourse. "You've not answered my question."

She chuckled. "I see you deflecting. Anyway, yes. I'd love to go to Tweedes, and I'm just putting this out there. If you decided to go to Rabat, I can go with you."

Mustafa drew her close by her chin and brushed his lips against hers. "Thank you."

"You're welcome." She stretched out her arms, examining them. "I've got to double up on my gym time before we go."

"Why?"

"I need muscles in case Salma and Yasmine try to take me out. Hopefully, Omar and Grandma Olly still like me a little."

Zaina chuckled, but Mustafa didn't join in. The idea of her enduring any pain, even if it was totally farfetched, annoyed him.

"That will never happen. But if you did need to fight, you can use my muscles." He displayed his arms.

"You'll fight *for* me? Against your family?"

"As long as I draw breath."

Before he could form his next thought, Zaina had her arms around his neck, drawing him into a hug that threatened to cut off his airflow. His arms wrapped around her waist. Seconds later, he noticed her giggles turned into sniffles. He tried to lift her head, but she refused, holding him tighter.

"You don't know how much it means to hear you say that."

In her ear, he whispered, "Your safety is always my priority."

CHAPTER 18

Zaina tapped a pencil against her palm as she paced the length of her office. She wanted to continue basking in the perfection that was her weekend, but alas, it was Monday morning. The meeting to explain the absence of timely data, and report on her analysis was in a few minutes.

Friday night after dinner, she and Mustafa remained on the floating fire pit, talking, and laughing until she fell asleep in his arms. It wasn't until she felt herself being lifted that she noticed Mustafa had her in his arms, bridal style, and was making his way to her room.

The next morning, she went to his villa where they decided to spend the day indoors. They enjoyed breakfast, played cards, watched movies, and talked some more. Zaina was in shock when he surrendered his phone to her. The day was pure bliss and after dinner, she retired to her room.

Since she had prevented him from working on Saturday, she didn't expect to hear from or see him much on Sunday. The pure shock on her face when he arrived at her door solicited a deep chuckle from him. He brought breakfast from the resort's restaurant and a bag of ingredients for something he was going to prepare for lunch. Sunday must've been the day for surprises because he asked to watch service with her. Zaina had so many questions but kept them to herself so as not to cause any awkwardness.

The Holy Spirit was surely on the job because she couldn't have thought up a more fitting message than the one Pastor Mensah preached. The message was titled "Sacred Torment." In it, he drew a contrast between being a practicing Christian that's still being tormented by ghosts of the past. There was one part that struck Zaina straight in the heart.

"Your past doesn't disappear because you've accepted the salvation of Christ," he'd said. "The difference is, now you have the power to shine the light on it. Trying to outrun it or keeping it hidden is what gives it power, but if they're exposed—your guilt, offence, shame, anxiety, anything you live with—they're powerless when you elevate above it. Through His Word and worship. Flip the script. Your guilt...look at it as a chance for grace. Your offence, as an opening for forgiveness."

When service was over, they both sat in silence for a few minutes. She could tell the message impacted Mustafa as well. She decided to give him space to process, excusing herself to call her parents. The offence statement was meant for her. She'd enjoyed the victimhood of offence for so long that even now, she often struggled to prevent it from overtaking her.

By the time she got back, Mustafa was in the kitchen prepping for lunch while a smooth jazz medley flowed through the air. Some hours later, they enjoyed his delicacy which was roasted salmon over zucchini ribbons with saffron couscous. He left soon after, citing work he had to do.

The ding of the Outlook reminder interrupted her musings. She walked back to her seat and glanced over at her presentation on the second monitor. It was looking good. Hopefully, her boss wouldn't dwell on the late results. She wanted to ask him what she'd spent the past couple of weeks ruminating over. The possibility of reversing her previous request. The one she'd spent the last three years positioning herself for, assistant director in the London office. That job was practically hers after this project.

She tapped her nails on the desk. She loved her job and was in no position to quit if her request was denied. Her business was the ultimate dream, but she needed capital for that to even happen. She had some money saved, but not enough to live on and start a new business at the same time. Being an assistant director for Safi Kijani was a huge opportunity. Even if she was going to eventually venture out on her own, the position would give her an added edge. But she no longer wanted to leave the continent.

Her heart was here.

"Sir, I know that for the last few years, my goal has been to move back to London, an opportunity that awaits me once this project is complete. But I don't want to pursue that route anymore…" Zaina murmured her rehearsed speech to herself.

She shook her head. *That's so weak.* The height of unseriousness. *Who does that?* Apparently, she did. She browsed the screen again to make sure everything was in place. After saying a short prayer, she put on her headset and started the call. Moments after Mustafa's grand entry into the lab last week, she was given the results. Luckily, they were favorable. Her plan was to give her boss the good news, buttering him up for her request.

～

"I should've known he'd say no," Zaina murmured to herself.

God chose me
With God all things are possible
God has given me everything I need to succeed
I am victorious in Christ

I am God's masterpiece

With her legs folded beneath her, and journal on her lap, Zaina lifted her eyes toward the ceiling. Returning her eyes to the open page, she wrote another biblical affirmation. After the day she'd had, she needed to pull on everything at her disposal to hold captive the self-deprecating thoughts that roamed her mind.

A muted Nollywood series played on Netflix while she sat in silence. Earlier, her boss had flat out denied her request. He reminded her of how she had insinuated nepotism, favoritism and all the other 'isms'— his words not hers—when she'd been passed up for the promotion before. At the present, even if he wanted to, he couldn't. After emphasizing he didn't want to, he told her that the current assistant director was retiring, and things had been set in motion for her to take over. Now she understood how the company suddenly had the position open. Still, it was exactly what she said she wanted. It was also too late to hire and train someone new since the director was slated to go on personal leave soon.

Zaina felt worse for even asking, and the remainder of the day went downhill from there. Nothing bad happened, but her mood crashed further into despair. Mustafa had stopped in to check on her before heading out and she didn't feel any better. She feigned having to get on a call for him to believe she was okay. She knew he would've pushed further if he didn't have to leave for Gaborone.

Her mood finally tanked when she got back to her room and checked her email. She had two messages, one from Ibiso with more angles and professional shots of the Bisso Bites design. The second from the designer with her logo and a few mockup graphics. They were absolutely beautiful, but panic set in. Could she even do this thing that she felt would be the answer to all her problems? Supposing Irek Designs decided to pass on her after she had done all this work? Was it worth risking her steady job for?

Her phone buzzed on the table. Zaina stared at the device. She didn't know who it was but talking wasn't something she wanted to do right now. Wallowing in the emotions that had her at the brink of tears was the more desirable option. After a few more seconds, the phone stopped ringing. Zaina picked it up and saw Ibiso's missed call. She made a mental note to call her back in the morning, but before she could completely form the thought, Ibiso called again. Zaina was going to ignore it until something her mother said when they talked the previous week flashed in her mind.

"The enemy counts on your isolation when he wants to run havoc on your mind. God intended for us to have relationships of all kinds."

Zaina's regard fell on the phone again before she answered the call.

"*Na wa o.* Is everything okay?" Ibiso asked.

Zaina's brows creased. "SoSo, *how now?* Yes, it is. Why?"

"*I dey.* You don't sound convincing. Also, the person I talked to some days ago was eager to get the additional pictures. It's been almost ten hours since I emailed them, and you didn't respond."

Zaina sighed.

"What's wrong? Is it your *Oga?* Do I need to fly to Botswana?"

Zaina hadn't intended to, but Ibiso's reference to Mustafa and flying over to fight her battles drew a hearty chuckle from her. One she hadn't afforded herself all day.

"You know Rasheed isn't letting that happen. And no, this time Mustafa doesn't have anything to do with my funk." Zaina thought about her answer then amended it. "Well, not directly."

"Rasheed is not the boss of me...well not all the time." Ibiso giggled and Zaina joined her. After a few moments, she thanked her friend for the pictures and spilled her troubles. When she was done, Ibiso didn't speak immediately.

"Sam, are you telling me that Mustafa still doesn't know you're moving back to London once this contract is over?"

"Erm, no." Zaina felt the onset of a headache.

"Why?"

"I should've told him in the beginning, but I didn't, and time just kept passing." Zaina scratched her head. "And don't forget, the man hated me then. He disappeared for two months, sending everybody but the disciples to me instead of talking to me directly."

"That was four and a half months ago! You guys have been good—"

Zaina tugged on her hair and yelled, "I know!"

"Don't yell at me. I'm trying to understand because it's not making sense."

"I know, I'm sorry. I'm frustrated. Everything was finally lining up. I was excited to start my business and my personal life is moving along nicely and I'm stuck." Zaina exhaled. "Who am I kidding? I knew this was too good to be true."

"If you want help beating yourself up, I'm the wrong friend. So, just stop." A beat passed between them, and Ibiso continued, "Has he proposed?"

"Huh? No. Why would you ask that?"

"Because I want to know where he thinks you'll be when it's all said and done. He does know this is a contract job. Or is he planning to make you a housewife?"

Zaina laughed. "SoSo, shut up. Do I even look like a housewife? Nothing against them. That is a serious ministry, but I know I'm not set up to be with children twenty-four seven. I don't even know if I want children."

"You used to want children. What happened? No don't answer that. One crisis at a time. Back to the matter. What does he think will happen in six weeks?"

"He knows I'm getting a promotion, but he thinks it's in Nigeria, not in London."

"So again, why didn't you clarify?"

"We broke up because I used a job opportunity to manipulate him…well among other things. Some weeks ago, I told him I loved him, and he hasn't said it back. I'm not trying to push him, but I've been dropping hints. He's smart. I know he's picked up on it but decided to ignore it. I can feel that on some level, he's still struggling with trusting me. Now, if I tell him that I'm leaving for London, not Abuja, it will be exactly like the Geneva situation. The same thing all over again, but this time it's true." Zaina used her finger to wipe the tear at the corner of her eye.

Ibiso let out a breath. "Now, I get it. But why not just tell him what you just told me?"

Zaina shook her head. The tangled web she'd weaved was becoming more complicated as she talked about it. *Don't keep anything from me.* The words he'd uttered some time ago, fluttered like a butterfly through the room. She'd been asking him to trust her and all this while, she hadn't said anything. As each day passed, she no longer knew how. The fear that everything would come crashing down had her in a chokehold.

"I was going to but was too scared to disturb the still waters. Then you mentioned the Irek folks and I saw the possibility. Ask my boss to stay in Abuja, then I'll work on my business and eventually quit."

"Still, tell him. He can help. It'll be okay."

"I don't want his help. This is something I want to do on my own. With what you told me about your restaurant, you should know exactly what I mean." Zaina held the phone in place with her shoulder and picked up her now cold, raspberry tea. She picked up the remote and clicked telling Netflix to continue playing without asking again, then headed to the kitchen.

"True, but you forget I and hubby don't have the same

history as you and your man. *Las, las*, you do the long-distance thing."

Zaina ran water into her cup and groaned. "That's not for me. Mustafa being away from me like that will drive me crazy. Now *sef*, the way women look at me when we go out, you'd think I stole their property."

Ibiso cackled.

"You're laughing. He doesn't even live here full time. I can only imagine what will happen when we go to Tweedes."

"Wait what? You're going to meet the family?" Ibiso squealed.

"Yeah. He asked me to be his date for his grandmother's surprise party."

Ibiso yelped. "That's fantastic. These African men and their families. In fact, all men…hmm let me not say all. Because some collude with their family to call you 'our wife' then turn around and call the side chick 'our wife' all in the same breath."

Zaina laughed and opened the fridge, trying to decide between warming her leftovers or placing a fresh order from the restaurant.

"Don't laugh. You know I'm speaking truth. But what I'm saying is, if he's willing to take you to the family, then this thing between you guys is so much more to him. So, tell him. Let this not blow up in your face."

Opting to warm her leftovers, Zaina removed them from the fridge and got out a plate from the cupboard. "Yeah, I know. Emma told me the same thing years ba—"

"Girl, don't compare me to that spawn of the devil that encouraged you to play games."

Zaina choked on the cold piece of food she'd put in her mouth. "Something is seriously wrong with you. I'm not com—"

Ibiso giggled. "Anyway…all I'm saying is, tell him now."

Zaina put the food on a plate, placed it in the microwave and set the timer. She leaned against the counter and took the phone in her hand. "I will. In the meantime, I'll send the stuff to Irek Designs. Let the chips fall where they may.

"You see, problem solved."

"I still have to tell him, but at the end of the day, he's just going to have to trust me." The microwave dinged and Zaina turned to face it.

"It'll be fine. Let's not keep dissecting a situation that may or may not play out the way we think. That's unnecessary stress," Ibiso said.

Zaina took her food and a bottle of water with her. She was glad she had answered Ibiso's call. "I agree. Give me recent Yohance gist. I know it'll be far better than this series playing on TV." Stories from Ibiso's motherhood diaries were always entertaining, especially when it came to her fourteen-year-old son.

Chuckling Ibiso asked, "What series is that?"

Zaina looked at the television. "No idea."

"Anyway, it's not 'Hance that's my issue this week. It's Jummi."

Zaina sat and placed the phone on speaker. "Not my sweet niece. What did she do?"

For the rest of the call, Zaina couldn't even get her food in from laughing so hard. The little lady showed up at the table for Sunday dinner with a Rolex dangling from her tiny hand. The whole family was gathered and when they joined hands to say grace, one of the cousins shouted. Apparently, a new boy in her class had been giving her expensive gifts for a week. She tried to give them back, but he said that he'd stop talking to her because that meant she didn't love him. When she was asked to show all she'd taken, her dad and uncle went on a tirade when they saw what she had. What sent the men completely over the edge was the name on the Visa card she had in her possession. It was one of Rasheed's business competitors. They were supposed to meet the boy's parents and school officials in two days, and Ibiso was dreading the event.

As Zaina prepared for bed later that night, the sulk she had on her face was replaced with a broad smile. Her joy was complete when Mustafa sent his regular goodnight text. She declared to herself that God didn't do things halfway, and He'd complete what He started with her. All she had to do was do her part and leave the rest to Him.

Trust Zaina.

Trust, she thought to herself as she closed her eyes and faded into a restful sleep.

CHAPTER 19

"The perks of technology can't be entirely underestimated. However, I hesitate to convolute the process of navigating the app for our customers."

Two weeks later, Mustafa leaned back into the leather seat with his forefingers steepled under his lower lip. He glanced at the documents before him, then lifted his eyes again to the screen in front of him. Yasmine and the Grand Amour Head of Security, who were both in the Tweede Kans Cove office, nodded in agreement.

Minutes earlier, they'd concluded a meeting with the owners of RoMac Technologies for the development of an advanced layer firewall for the Grand Amour app. The resort had always had its exclusivity and intimacy as its key selling points. With the changes in the world, the DuBois-Arazis decided to update its accessibility through technology. Their app allowed accessibility for booking, but also for guests already lodged in the resort. There was an upgrade done several months ago that led to a hack. Those were the three most torturous days he'd experienced in a while, trying to get everything back under control. What turned out to be a huge selling point for the upgrade—connectivity of all locations—ended up being a nightmare.

"Sir, I don't think it will be too bad. It's better than what we've gotten so far. The quote they gave was fair," the head of security said.

"I agree. Our customers come to us for the personal touch. They also come to us for the luxury we provide. Nothing says luxury like technological advancement," Yasmine added.

"What he's proposing seems like things we already do," Mustafa argued.

"Not all. Not by a long shot. We still rely heavily on manual abilities. We need to get on board with the rest of the world and start using artificial intelligence."

"Hmm," Mustafa grunted. He looked back down at the numbers.

Yasmine, as Director of Operations, and the head of security would work directly with the RoMac team, however, he wanted to confirm the financial strain would be worth it. They were coming to the end of the fiscal year and with the unexpected expense of the lake recharge, they were dangling toward tipping the scale. The recharge was three times the amount allocated for conservation because of its complexity and speed.

"Okay. Yasmine work with the accountant to see if the money is available and depending on how that meeting goes, you can mix and match the packages." Mustafa turned to the head of security. "Work with the general manager, I want to make sure the ROI supports the app as well as customer satisfaction."

The trio discussed a few more things before the head of security left the call. Yasmine decided to stay on and immediately, Mustafa knew she had something on her mind. Most likely something that had nothing to do with her.

"You look happy," Yasmine grinned.

"Do not start. How are the kids?"

"They're good. Missing their uncle 'Stafa."

Mustafa let out a low laugh. "I'll be there before they know it. How are you doing?"

She and the kids were in Tweede Kans Cove. They'd arrived from Accra the day before for their grandmother's party happening in a few days. He knew she probably wasn't well rested, but he needed to clear as much as he could from his schedule.

"I'm fine. Depending on what I wear, no one can tell I'm pregnant." Yasmine chuckled. "My statement was, you're happier."

"That's an observation."

Yasmine rolled her eyes. "Why am I wasting time with you? If you're bringing Zay to the party, I'll get the scoop from her."

Mustafa deadpanned her. "She will not be bothered."

"Are you telling me or are you asking?" Yasmine raised her brows.

Mustafa absently twirled the pen in his hand. "Both."

"That's not how this works, big brother." She shrugged. "But since you claim there's nothing between you two, then why are you worried?"

"I didn't claim anything, and I'm far from worried."

"Good. Besides if you were worried, I'm not who you should be worried about," Yasmine goaded him, her eyes dancing with excitement.

"Keep Salma away from her," he said.

"Don't order me around, besides, why? If she's going to be in your life, she has to know how to handle herself."

"Yasmine!" Mustafa pulled on his beard. His sisters knew how to push his buttons.

"Yes, brother." She blinked her eyes.

"I'm serious."

"So am I. But since there's nothing between you two or

anything to worry about, Salma won't care one way or the other."

"Yasmine, I—"

"You do know that your growl only works on the twins and your employees. No matter how many times you call my name, my position is the same."

Mustafa shook his head and grinned. He opened his mouth to speak when his desk phone rang. He lifted a finger to ask Yasmine to hold on and pressed the button to answer the call.

"Hello, Brenda," Mustafa greeted.

"Hello Sir, I have Ms. Bakari here for you. Also, Assad called. He's on his way back from the city."

"Thank you. Send her in."

Once the call was disconnected, Mustafa returned his focus to his snickering sister. "I have to—"

"I want to say hiiiiii," Yasmine whined.

"tatasaraf binafsik."

"I always behave." Yasmine winked.

Mustafa wanted to say more. What he really wanted was to get his sister off his screen, but she was right. If Zaina was going to be around, she'd have to earn his family's respect. Although, he'd never allow her discomfort.

After a light tap on his door, Zaina walked in. Mustafa's eyes roamed her body, making the trip from the vibrant curls on her head which she left free flowing, to her black, open toe heels. The blueish gray, African print, short sleeve jumpsuit she had on clung to her curves perfectly. A grin snaked up her lips as she strutted towards him. Without looking at his laptop, she moved it slightly to the side, and bent over to press her lips against his. Her fingers threaded through his beard, something he knew she enjoyed.

Yasmine cleared her throat and Mustafa let out a chuckle at Zaina's startled expression. She swatted him on his shoulder, letting out a harsh whisper. "Why didn't you tell me you were on a video call?"

"Hey, Zaina. Don't be shy. Carry on, I couldn't see the whole show," Yasmine joked.

The pressure in his heart released at his sister's tone. Yasmine was milder mannered than Salma. That didn't mean she was predictable. Mustafa moved his hand to Zaina's waist and positioned her between his legs. She sat on his lap and positioned the laptop properly.

"Hi, Yasmine. I didn't mean for you to see that."

Yasmine giggled. "I know. Which makes it better. How have you been?"

"Good, I can't complain. I heard you got married. Congratulations. Where's the lucky man?"

"Yeah, thanks. He should be arriving soon. I couldn't get anything out of your man here, but I trust I'll see you this weekend."

Zaina turned her eyes to Mustafa, her bottom lip caught between her teeth. He observed her nerves but waited for her answer. He squeezed her thigh, and she returned her eyes to Yasmine.

"Yes, I'll be there."

"Good. I'll get the full gist then," Yasmine said.

"Yasmine," he warned.

"Mustafa," she echoed.

Zaina looked between the two of them. Something between a smirk and confusion laced her expression.

"I got to go. You look really good, Zay. See you soon." Yasmine disconnected the call.

Zaina stared at him. "Are you going to tell me what that was about?"

He played with her hair. "It was nothing."

A crease formed on her forehead. "Don't let me walk into anywhere blind, Musa."

He narrowed his eyes, palmed her chin to draw her face closer, their noses almost making contact. "Do you think I'd ever do that?"

Mustafa heard her breath hitch, the rise and fall of her chest increased. He loved the effect he had on her. It mirrored the one she had on him, which she wasn't aware of yet. She remained silent and tried to get her lips to touch his. Mustafa leaned back.

"Answer me."

"No," she whispered.

"Then don't teach me how to protect you." He cupped the back of her head. Steadying her, his lips found hers and his tongue forced entrance into her mouth. The need to possess her suddenly overtook him when she questioned his ability to keep her safe. The explosion of their battling tongues sent his heart racing. Zaina tried to break their contact, but he wouldn't allow it until he got his fill. Her hands pushed slightly against his chest, prompting him to let her go. Her eyes blazed through him. They locked eyes in an unspoken battle of wills.

"You made your point," she whispered.

"Good. Don't let it happen again."

Zaina rolled her eyes. Mustafa snickered and tucked a loose tress behind her ear.

"To what do I owe the honor of your visit?" he asked.

"Can't I just want to see you?"

"Any time you want." He tapped the tip of her nose. "But I also know that you don't want my staff to know how special you are to me."

Zaina waved him off. "That ship sailed when you came to the lab like King Kong. Now people move to the side when they see me coming."

He shrugged. "It could be worse. How was your meeting?"

"I don't even want to know what worse will look like." She giggled. "Anyway, that's what I came to tell you. It was fantastic. I've been working with this land developer for the past eight months and every time I think we've gotten rid of the asbestos on his land, we find another patch. Well, as you know I've been trying this new mixture treatment for a few months. We've been monitoring at intervals and finally, for three straight months, we've got it."

She pumped her fist in the air and Mustafa chuckled at her delight. She'd been worried about this last month of testing and potentially having to give a bad report to the customer. He was happy for her. Her joy gave him pleasure.

"Good job, *chérie*, I am so proud of you."

She stared at him, her eyes blurry. He knew that sometimes she thought he didn't understand her love language. He wasn't a talker but was trying to change his habits for her.

"You better not cry," he warned.

She lifted her hand to the corner of her eye. "I won't." She sniffled. "Thank you for saying that."

He didn't want to somber the mood any further, but he had something else to tell her. They'd previously discussed his charge to visit his childhood home in Rabat. For the first week, he'd pushed the thought to the abyss of his mind. Then he had the dream again. He didn't tell her, but it made him rethink his decision. He felt her soft palm on his cheek.

"Hey…what's wrong?" she whispered.

"I found the apartment." He looked up at her.

"Oh my God. In Rabat?"

He nodded.

"Are you going?"

"Will you come with me?"

She leaned closer so her forehead rested on his. "Yes, baby, I will. When do you want to go?"

"Tomorrow. I want to get it out of the way before the weekend."

Her brows hiked. Skepticism filled her eyes. "Musa, I'm not

sure this is something to get over like that. It was a traumatic time in your life."

"No one knows that better than me. But it is also something I need to deal with if I have any chance of moving on."

"I know that. I don't want it to be something that you don't have enough time to process before you have to face your family."

"I understand your concern, but I'll be fine."

He knew she wasn't assured by his words, but he didn't want to dwell on it any longer. "Have you had lunch?"

"I guess that means we're done discussing it."

"You're a fast learner."

"Yeah, well whatever. No, I haven't, but if we are to leave tomorrow, I need to move some things around." She stood from his lap and smoothed down her attire.

Mustafa looked at his watch. He picked up the receiver to the phone on his desk. When Brenda answered, he asked her to connect him to the chef on duty. While he waited, he faced Zaina. "Local or continental?"

"Musa, I don't have time to eat now. I have to adjust my schedule and pack and—"

"All of which can be done later. But it is time to eat."

"Bossy much?"

"You call it bossy. I call it taking care of my woman."

~

Two days later, Mustafa stood in front of a door that no longer looked familiar. He held on to Zaina's hand with a vice-like grip. She anchored his unsteady state. The grey paint had been replaced by blue. The number 1209 and the indentation at the top left corner of the door were the only indication that he was in the right place. Zaina's thumb caressed the back of his hand in a circular motion. The movement he'd always found calming did nothing to loosen the pressure in his chest. He felt her questioning eyes bore a hole into his temple, but he was thankful for her silence.

"Sir, as I told you over the phone, the apartment is currently vacant. It's furnished so you can see what it looks like with furniture in it." The caretaker looked through the bunch of keys in his hand for the right one.

The man was under the impression that Mustafa was in the market for an apartment. He didn't bother to correct him.

The caretaker found the key. "Are you ready to go in?"

His eyes must've followed Mustafa's gaze because he lifted his hand to the mark in the corner. The one that Mustafa was intently focused on. Zaina tried to slip her hand out of his, but he squeezed it tighter. She lifted her other hand to his chest and his eyes met hers. Mustafa understood her silent request. He released her hand and she moved closer to the caretaker.

"Sir, can I ask you for a little favor?" she asked.

"Of course."

Zaina cleared her throat. "Will it be okay if we explored the apartment on our own? I promise we'll have the place locked up and the keys returned in no time."

The man's eyes darted from Zaina to Mustafa, then he scratched his head. "The building owner won't like that."

"We won't be long. I promise."

The plea in her voice snapped Mustafa out of his trance. His woman begged no one. He narrowed his eyes, giving the man a deep frown. Left to him, he would have gone directly to the owner of the property. It was Zaina who insisted he not, in her words, throw his weight around. Especially since the DuBois-Arazi name was well recognized and he didn't want his siblings to know he was here. At least not yet.

"Um…okay. Here, I'll be in the lobby area downstairs." He took the key off the ring and handed it to Zaina. She thanked him and he scurried away.

"I was handling that," she scolded.

Mustafa ignored her and turned back to the door. He lifted his hand to the dent he'd been so focused on.

"I can't believe this is still here. Omar and I were late one afternoon because we were playing. My papa came to find us. He was so angry. Omar, forever the jokester said something, and our papa threw his shoe. We were near the door. I don't know if he intended to hit us or just frighten us...and it's still here."

Mustafa flinched when Zaina caressed his back. Her touch, which always had a calming effect, now felt like thorns against him. The concern in her eyes stabbed him in the chest. He wanted to reach out to pull her close, but he didn't want to touch or be touched right now.

"Are you ready to go in?" she asked.

"Yes."

Zaina unlocked the door then shifted to the side making way for him to enter. For a few moments, Mustafa remained rooted just beyond the door frame. Overwhelming terror pierced his heart, paralyzing him from moving as he surveyed the room. Not much had changed. The walls were the same disturbing ugly orange. The biting smell that attacked his nostrils was evidence of a recent fresh coat. The ceiling fan rotated at a low speed.

He stepped in and Zaina shut the door. She moved to the side, pretending to study a cheap piece of artwork that hung on the wall. It was her attempt to give him space and he appreciated it. The television which was still a plasma panel sat on a wooden table with a record player next to it. They couldn't have been the same ones from twenty plus years ago but were vaguely familiar. He wondered if there had been any other tenants here, or did the stigma of what happened here prevent it from being marketable? Turning his head, he stared down the now lifeless hallway that led to the bedrooms. Mustafa stumbled as the vision of pleading with Yasmine to go back to the room that day flooded his memory. He'd never forget it.

"Please Yasmine, just go in the room. I'll be there soon."

The curdling sound of their mother's scream sliced his heart. Torn between his sister and his mother, he tucked Yasmine's hair behind her ear, kissed her forehead then darted out of the room.

His heart thudded against his chest. He closed his eyes to keep the tears that began to well at bay. He opened his eyes, and his lips began to quiver as they landed on the chair to his right. It wasn't the same chair, but it was in the same spot. At that moment, all attempts to keep his emotions in check failed. Mustafa fell to his knees. His heart caved, forcing him to draw deep breaths. The struggle clogged his throat, and he belted out a deep roar. The anguish he had held in for so long shredded his heart to pieces, causing him physical pain.

Why didn't she leave? Why did this have to happen? Mama, I'm sorry I wasn't stronger.

The more he fought back the tears, the more they poured. Tears he hadn't shed when he was told his mother had died at the hospital. Tears he hadn't shed at her burial. Tears he hadn't shed when his father died in prison.

Mustafa felt Zaina's presence. She was on her knees beside him, her soft hand on his back. At first her touch was unsure, probably testing his reaction. He had none. She drew him closer, rubbing his back as he cried in her bosom.

Mustafa wasn't sure how long they remained in that position. What he did know was that with each passing moment, his torment eased, allowing him to receive comfort from the woman who held his heart in her hand. The woman who'd helped him see that letting himself feel by thawing the ice around his heart wasn't weakness, but courage.

He wanted to be free.

He longed to be free.

Mustafa clung to Zaina. In this space where he'd been dealt

his worst pain, he was embracing the potential of his greatest happiness. Zaina was his past, present, and future. Since she had been back in his life, she consumed his days and dominated his nights. Her presence steadied him. Things were different now. They were different now. They could have, no, they would have another chance at once in a lifetime. She was his destiny.

CHAPTER 20

The following morning, with measured steps, Zaina moved into the living area in search of Mustafa. The day before, they sat in silence for almost an hour in that apartment. The weight of the atmosphere was tangible. Zaina fought the need to tell him it would be okay. He needed space to grieve. From what she saw, he never had. Immediately they left, he wanted to get out of Rabat. The city held too many painful memories. The initial plan was to head to Tweede Kans Cove, but she didn't think it was wise to deal with his family in the state he was in. Mustafa, though despondent after the day's events, arranged for them to make the hour trip to the city of Casablanca instead. Once they checked into their penthouse suite at the Four Seasons, Mustafa headed to the mini gym in the suite. She sat in the silence of her room and listened to roars rip from his gut as he took his anger out on a punching bag. Later, when he emerged showered and calmer, she ordered dinner. He took only a few bites and went to his room. That was the last time she'd seen him. She spent the remainder of the night working and watching some television. Anything to keep from crowding him.

The emotional drain and anxiousness from the events of the last twenty-four hours still had her stomach in knots. His grandmother's party was in two days, and they should've been in Tweede Kans Cove already. His family was so used to having access to him that his phone had rung nonstop. His siblings and grandmother took turns calling, but he didn't answer any of them. Then he asked her to turn off the device. Zaina understood their concern and was stuck between respecting his wishes and putting his family out of their worry as to his whereabouts. At first, she gave him time to call them. When she saw he had no intention of doing so, she texted Yasmine that he was okay. It wasn't her story to tell so she would allow him to deal with his family when he was up to it.

They were supposed to leave later, but now, Mustafa's silence had her unsure of what their plans were. Zaina rounded the corner and let out a cleansing breath when she saw him on the balcony. His back was to her, as he took in the impressive oceanfront view. His arms were folded across his chest. She moved toward him. The wind lifted the white, unbuttoned dress shirt he wore over dark jeans.

Jeans.

Mustafa never wore jeans. His feet were even bare. His appearance was a sharp contrast to the "put together" Mustafa. Was he falling apart? Mustafa let out a deep exhale, alerting her that he was aware of her presence. Zaina wrapped her arms around his waist and rested her head on his broad back. He moved her hands upward to his chest and sighed. Zaina closed her eyes, taking in the solace the moment provided them both.

"Dear God, we are here before You heavy ladened. Your promise of peace is where we lay our trust. We surrender our pain and hurt at your altar of mercy and grace. Create in us a new heart and renew the right spirit within us. Thank you, Father. In Jesus' name. Amen," Zaina said.

"Amen."

Mustafa turned in her arms. Snaking his arm around her waist, he walked them closer to the railing. Leaning against it, his other hand found its way into her hair. Holding her in place, he gazed at her. After a few beats passed without him saying anything, she cleared her throat.

"*habib albi*, you are the moon that lights my dark world. You saw the real me and still decided to wrap your soul around mine. The intensity of that scares me because I share things with you that I hide from myself. You've helped me reach in and exposed parts I forgot existed. I can't imagine tomorrow without you. We didn't mess up the last time, we just weren't ready. I'm not a hopeless romantic, I…"

Zaina released the breath she was holding and giggled. He was, but she wouldn't tell him that.

"Butterflies and feelings are not who I am. But I do promise to protect your heart, keep you safe, pray over you, support and supply all your desires my money can buy." He pinned her with his gaze. "*uhibbuki*."

Her floodgates opened and tears rolled down her cheeks. Mustafa smiled and thumbed them away. When he called her *habib albi*, love of his heart, she had to remind herself to breathe. She hadn't heard those words since London. When he called her sweetheart in French, he could be endearing or condescending. But when he spoke Arabic, the word had depth. Their eyes remained locked in the soul dance destiny had afforded them. Her lips turned up in a smile.

She sniffled. "I don't need the butterflies. I only need you."

"Then I am yours. I belong to you and only you," he confessed.

She stood on the tips of her toes and drew his head to hers. Her lips met his and they engaged in a passionate kiss. "What does that last word mean?"

"*uhibbuki?*"

"Yes."

Mustafa grinned. "I love you."

Zaina flung her arms around his neck. "I love you too, baby. With everything within me." She rested her head on his chest and allowed herself to bask in the euphoria of the moment before she dampened it with her next question. "How are you? Did you get any sleep?"

Like she knew it would, his body stilled. "Please don't shut me out."

"Never." He kissed her forehead. "I no longer wish to talk about it. I'm fine." His tone cemented the finality of his statement.

She giggled. *Yeah, and there goes vulnerable Mustafa. The incommunicado alpha is back. It was good while it lasted.*

"What's so funny?"

"Nothing, it's mid-morning. I assume we aren't leaving today, so what do you feel like eating?" she asked.

"We'll leave tomorrow. I want to take you around the town. Get dressed." Mustafa turned and made his way to his bedroom.

Zaina stared at him and shook her head. She remembered one reel she watched on Instagram a while ago. Gabrielle Union, the American actress, looked at her basketball player husband in two contrasting pictures. In one, he was dressed up and in the other he looked homeless. She reiterated that he was her man regardless. Zaina felt the same sentiment in this moment. Mustafa was her man, and she was gonna stick beside him. Grumpy, bossy, self-aware, or otherwise. He was hers.

❧

Friday afternoon, the driver travelled down the road leading to the gates of the DuBois Manor. The windows of the car were tinted, affording Zaina a little more time to preserve the bubble she and Mustafa had existed in for almost five months. The time had come for her to meet the

DuBois-Arazis…again. Mustafa was on the phone with Assad. He was back to his CEO mien, directing and orchestrating things that had been pushed back with his absence. Although she had the week off, Zaina still worked to keep herself distracted from the inevitability of this trip.

Zaina exhaled and brought the sweet memories of the previous night to the front of her mind. Anything to reduce her anxiety. After a light breakfast, they strolled through Muhammed V Square, a historical square established in 1916. Then they went to the Moroccan mall where they had lunch and visited a lot of shops. She quickly learned that once she admired something, Mustafa bought it. She wanted to stop gushing over the artwork, crafts, and local jewelry, but she couldn't. The place was gorgeous. They ended their day out with a quick visit to an archeological museum.

Before they left the city, Mustafa took her to a design show-room. His complaint was that her vision was too small. Instead of only designing for clients, she should make custom pieces, so those who couldn't afford her services could still have access to her signature designs. Zaina stood stunned, thankful for a partner who was willing to encourage her dreams. Not everyone had that.

When they arrived back at the hotel, Zaina was glad to see that guest services had her surprise ready. On the balcony, she had them set up two easels, paint, and paint brushes. She ordered a platter of cheese, crackers, assorted meats, and wine. They spent the night laughing, talking, and goofing around. She hadn't seen her man that carefree in a while. She knew his heart was still heavy, but he wasn't burying the hurt under the facade of busy. Her healing was a process, and she knew his would be one too.

Zaina wasn't aware they had reached the gates until the car came to a stop, waiting for it to open. At that moment, her phone buzzed in her hand. Zaina turned to Mustafa who was still on the phone.

"Good afternoon, Mum," Zaina said.

She and her mother were at a place where their conversation was no longer stilted. Zaina even shared more, but with boundaries. Her mother asked about Mustafa almost daily. It was weird. There used to be a time her parents, had to play "Where in the World Is Zaina?" but not anymore.

"My darling, I assume you've arrived."

"Yes, we landed a few hours ago."

"Okay. Enjoy yourself, but make sure *you shine ya eye*. Don't let anyone disrespect you. You're *Naija*," her mother said.

Zaina regretted telling her mother about her run in with Salma a while back. She hadn't meant to. Her father had gotten her mother a new jewelry set that she was gushing over. Zaina sighed and the Salma thing just slipped. Now, her mother thought all the DuBois-Arazi women were going to sabotage her relationship. Zaina wasn't sure they wouldn't but having her mother in her ear about it wasn't her plan.

"Technically, I'm Tanzanian, but I get what you're saying. I'll be fine." As Zaina said the words, she felt Mustafa's eyes on her. She didn't need his overprotectiveness as well. If she would ever be respected, she didn't need his interference.

"Hmmm. Have you talked to your father today?"

"Yeah, earlier. He was boarding his flight to see you."

Her mother giggled. "Yes, I can't wait. I visited Bordello and—"

"Mother! Good grief. I don't want to know that. Besides I have to go."

At the mention of one of London's lingerie stores, Zaina knew she needed to end the conversation. Her own sex life had been nonexistent for years. She didn't think about it because it gave her a chance to focus on God, herself, and her career. With Mustafa, she was still celibate, but it was a serious battle between good and evil. There were times, she wanted to pull her hair out and cave. The previous night they'd come dangerously close. Which was the reason why, for this trip, she'd be staying at the DuBois Manoir while Mustafa stayed in his villa.

After promising to call her mother later, Zaina disconnected the call. She turned to find Mustafa's eyebrows etched with concern.

"Do you not feel safe here?" he asked.

"What? No! Of course, I feel safe. Why?"

"I didn't mean to eavesdrop, but I heard your mother has concerns."

"My mother is being a mother. I'm fine." Zaina gathered her purse.

His piercing gaze prickled her skin. She knew better than to meet his eyes and engage. She had to get herself together. The car came to a stop in front of the magnificent mansion, and Mustafa came around to open the door for her. Holding her hand, he helped her out and pinned her against the closed door. Using his index finger, he lifted her head.

"If anyone bothers you, I want to know about it."

Yeah, that wasn't happening, but arguing with him wasn't something she wanted to do either. Thankfully, she didn't have to respond because they heard a soft voice behind them.

"Mustafa, don't crush the woman before I get a chance to say hello."

Mustafa closed his eyes, causing Zaina to smirk. She would be eighty years old by morning, but Grandma Olly still had it. She had aged gracefully. Her gray hair was in loose waves that stopped at her nape. Her greyish blue eyes, a testament to her French heritage, still had a spark to them. The embroidered, maroon kaftan she wore shaped her voluptuous figure and complimented her radiant, olive skin. Zaina stepped to the side and strutted up the steps to greet the matriarch of the DuBois-Arazi clan.

"Good afternoon, Mrs. DuBois."

Grandma Olly drew her into her arms for a hug. When they pulled apart, she tenderly framed Zaina's face with her hand.

"My dear, I was Grandma Olly to you years ago, and by the look on my grandson's face, I'm still Grandma Olly."

Zaina nodded. Her throat raw with emotion. She really wasn't expecting this warm of a welcome, but she was relieved. "Okay."

The older woman touched her hair, then rubbed her arm. "It's good to see you, baby."

"It's good to see you too, Grandma Olly. I'm sorry about Sir Marcelle."

Grandma Olly paused and squeezed her hand. "Thank you. How are your parents?"

"They are well."

"Good, I'm glad you came. Come on, let's get you settled in while Musa gets the bags."

Zaina observed the way she looked at her grandson. One couldn't mistake the pride in her eyes. Zaina couldn't wait to see the look on the older woman's face tomorrow. She thought everyone was here for a quiet dinner celebration. She didn't know her grandchildren had planned a big party.

~

*L*ater in the evening, Zaina descended the winding staircase as two children zipped by. Their loud screams of "daddy" told her that other members of the family had arrived. After she'd arrived a few hours earlier, she and Grandma Olly had retreated to the great room while Mustafa ensured her sleeping arrangements were in order. He didn't have to as his grandmother had told him everything was taken care of. However, it wouldn't be Mustafa if he didn't check things out for himself. Soon after, he left for the office

after insisting she rested. Zaina and Grandma Olly got reac-
quainted with each other over a light lunch. The longer they
stayed together, the more comfortable Zaina got.

When a couple of her friends came over to discuss some
charities, Zaina excused herself and headed upstairs. Zaina was
glad for the reprieve to mentally prepare to meet everyone. The
kids running and the savory aroma that wafted up her nostrils
told her that the time had come. She looked at the phone in her
hand. No other communication from Mustafa except the last
one saying he was on his way. She lifted the phone to call him
when she heard.

"So, this is how you look all grown up?"

Zaina lifted her eyes to meet Omar's and she smiled. He was
leaned against the door frame adjacent the bottom of the stairs
with his arms folded over his chest. A grin spread across his face
as he pushed himself off the frame and walked toward her. He
was the playful version of her man. And time had indeed done
him well.

"I could say the same for you," she responded.

He enveloped her in his arms. She hugged him back. He was
a bit taller than his brother but leaner. He pulled back and
examined her.

"Does my brother know you have a dress that looks like
that?"

Zaina looked down at herself. She had showered and
changed into a purple and green print layered crop top with a
matching midi skirt. Her flat tummy was exposed, but not a lot.
The slit on her skirt also wasn't distasteful.

"Your brother doesn't dictate what I wear, so..."

He laughed and draped his arm around her shoulder. "If you
say so. Come on, the family is gathered in the great room.
Musa ain't here though." They started to walk down the
hallway.

She stalled. "He's on his way."

Omar turned to her. "Is that why you were dragging down the stairs? You scared?"

"Of?"

Omar laughed. "Nothing. Come on. You with me…"

"No, she's not."

They both turned around to see Mustafa heading their way. There was some amusement in his eyes. She smiled and moved toward him while Omar chuckled and raised his hands in surrender.

"Wow! I never thought I'd see the day again…you're even worse than the last time," Omar taunted his brother.

Mustafa gave him a hard look before he looked down at her. His eyes softened and he bent to brush his lips against hers. "Did you rest?"

"Yes. Was Assad able to get the courier to deliver the papers?"

"Yes." His eyes roamed her frame. "You look beautiful, *habib albi*. Do you have another dress?"

Omar cackled loudly. "Ha! I told you."

Zaina frowned. "You're kidding, right?"

Mustafa shrugged. Placing his hand on the small of her back, he ushered her forward. The three of them reached the great room and Zaina was nearly knocked out of place by two kids that ran up to Mustafa. Omar placed his hands on her shoulders, gently moving her out of the way. Mustafa knelt to their level and hugged them tight until they began to giggle. Zaina admired the way he bonded with them.

"I have someone I want you to meet," Mustafa said after a few moments. He reached for her hand and pulled her closer to them. "This is Zaina. Zaina this is Anisa and Kwame."

Zaina smiled as two pairs of eyes darted from Mustafa to her. They glanced at their uncle again before their eyes settled back on her.

"Hello, Aunty Zaina," they greeted in unison.

"Hello. It's nice to meet you both. Your uncle has told me so much about you two." Even though Mustafa had only started talking to her about his family recently, these two had been what mainly filled their conversation. It led to their discussion on kids for themselves, a topic they never concluded on.

"Are you Uncle 'Stafa's friend?" Anisa asked.

"Like his special friend?" Kwame asked.

Omar found the interrogation funny. Mustafa stared at her, waiting for an answer. Zaina searched for the proper response.

"Girl, if you don't know the answer to that question, then we need to talk."

Zaina turned around to see Yasmine with a gorgeous, dark chocolate man draped over her. It was *the* Kojo Sarbah, in the flesh. She tried not to openly fawn over him. Grandma Olly came in from behind them and took her seat in what Zaina had gathered was her favorite chair. The kids quickly abandoned their fact-finding mission and ran to the older woman.

"Hey, Yasmine. It's so good to see you," Zaina said.

"Baby, move. Let me say hi to the woman whose had my brother MIA." Yasmine giggled. The man she knew as Yasmine's husband nuzzled the crook of her neck before letting her go. Yasmine came over and they hugged. "Zaina, this rude one over here is my husband, Kojo. Baby...Zaina. You can deduce who she is by the possessive look on my brother's face."

"The next time 'let me help Yas with somethin' really quick' turns into all that noise, I'm leaving your children to fend for themselves," Omar fussed.

"O, man. Shut up. I haven't seen my wife in days," Kojo said, then turned to Zaina. "It's nice to meet you, Zaina."

"And who's fault is that? I left dinner to look after these two while you guys..."

"Enough," Mustafa groaned. Kojo snickered and dapped Mustafa.

Yasmine giggled and kissed both her brothers on their cheeks. "Zaina, you sure you wanna deal with this?"

Zaina chuckled. "I've seen worse."

A member of the kitchen staff entered and whispered something to Omar who followed them out. Yasmine drew her to the corner as Mustafa asked, "Where's Salma?"

"She should be here shortly. I had her stop by Beautiful Eyes. Gloria needed the backup list of new residents urgently," Grandma Olly said.

"Zay, come on, let's see what Omar is up to and catch up," Yasmine said.

"Yasmine," Mustafa warned.

Yasmine waved him off. "Give it a rest."

Zaina walked up to Mustafa and kissed his cheeks, then whispered in his ear. "Stop it. I'm fine."

"O, I hope food is ready. I'm starving."

"Grandma, grandma…"

They all turned to the entrance, awaiting the body the voice belonged to.

"In here, Salma. Stop yelling," Grandma Olly said.

A few seconds later, Salma appeared. She scurried to Mustafa who held her in a tight embrace. When they released each other, Salma's warm, bright eyes roamed the room until they landed on Zaina, and the smile she sported dropped. Zaina knew it was probably only a few seconds before Salma regained her composure, but it seemed like a lifetime. A lifetime between when her lips turned down in a small frown and her face displayed the displeasure from Zaina's presence. Salma's eyes turned back to Mustafa in an unspoken exchange. Zaina could feel the dread in the other eyes in the room. The tension consumed the life out of the playful atmosphere of minutes earlier. Zaina decided to be the person to diffuse it.

"Hi, Salma," Zaina said.

Extending grace to the sister who obviously felt protective

of her older brother, she willed herself to recall the first time she met Salma years ago. She wasn't hostile toward her. In fact, she was happy for them. Their eyes locked in a silent battle.

"*aikhti alsaghira*," Mustafa growled

Salma's eyes darted to her brother before she yielded to whatever he said.

"Hello, Zaina," Salma muttered.

Immediately dismissing her, Salma walked over to Kojo and hugged him before doing the same with her sister. Completely ignoring Mustafa, she moved past them and walked over to their grandmother. The kids who had on their headsets with eyes buried in their tablets, suddenly became aware of their aunt's presence, and squealed.

Zaina could feel the heat radiating off Mustafa. That made her feel bad. She knew how close he was to his siblings. The thought of her being the cause of a rift between them knotted her stomach. She didn't owe Salma an explanation, but she did hope they would be able to talk soon.

Mustafa grabbed her hand, dragging her out of the room. A few steps down the hallway, he had her up against the wall. He bent his head to hers.

"I'm sorry," he whispered.

"For what?"

He closed his eyes and let out a harsh breath.

"Baby, you have to let me fight my battles. I'm fine," she pleaded. "Just do me a favor, don't interfere."

"What you ask of me is difficult," he argued.

Zaina placed her hand on his chest. "I know, but you love me so you will try, right?"

"You drive a hard bargain, woman."

Zaina giggled. "I know. Now let's go. We're being rude."

CHAPTER 21

Zaina absently looked on as the cool water ran over her hands. Her mind ran the tape of the last ninety odd minutes. Dinner itself was outstanding. Omar had out done himself. Zaina knew she wasn't the best cook. Ibiso's food was up there, but Omar, that man knew his stuff. Even for a casual family dinner, he didn't mince in presentation. Dinner started with mint tea then morphed into a three-course meal of lamb tagine with olives, herbed couscous, and a tomato salad. For dessert, they enjoyed a seasonal fruit platter and lemon raspberry yogurt cake.

When they all sat down, there was some awkwardness, but that quickly changed. The conversation flowed as they discussed local politics which she knew nothing about, to the continent and world affairs. Pop culture and religion also found their way into the mix. Laughter was boisterous and everyone seemed to be having a good time. Salma didn't talk to her directly. She also was short with Mustafa, so Zaina knew she wasn't alone on her hit list.

Zaina turned off the faucet, dried her hands and disposed of the paper towel. Examining her face in the mirror of the guest toilet, she cringed at the puffiness below her eyes. She needed to sleep. The last couple of days had been an emotional roller coaster. Watching Mustafa fall apart made the offence she'd held toward her parents seem trivial. Her feelings weren't invalid, but at least they had a chance to make it right. She could ask the questions that bothered her. Mustafa would never get the answers he sought. Instead, he'd have to work through how to live without an explanation. The words he had said to her in Rabat flooded through her mind.

"People look at me and think I shouldn't have a problem," he'd said. "But if money was my problem, then I wouldn't really have a problem. Because that, I can control."

Zaina shook her head to rid herself of the memory. It was time to get back out there. Opening the door, she walked down the second hallway she'd done her best to remember. The place was like a fortress, and she'd gotten lost one time before. Voices floating through the air stopped her in her tracks.

"This was supposed to be a family thing. I don't know why he brought that woman," Salma said.

"Sally, leave it alone. Your brother is happy. That's what should matter the most," Yasmine responded.

Zaina wanted to keep going about her business, but the urge to hear what Mustafa's sisters really thought of her kept her rooted in place.

"He was happy the last time too, remember," the younger sister retorted.

"I do. And I had my concerns at first, but people change." Yasmine sighed. "You gave Kojo a chance. You even advocated for him. What's so different about Zay?"

"Kojo was different. What you guys had didn't have a chance to grow before the opportunity was taken away. Besides, you didn't give up your life for him. You got married and had my niece—"

"I love you sis, but this is what happens when you make

assumptions without all the facts. You only knew what I let you know about Kojo. I didn't tell anyone that I saw him some years after he first left Tweedes. It was in London, and he treated me like dirt. Or that he had his manager tell me I was a distraction to him. What I'm trying to say is, back then probably wasn't the time for Musa and Zay. You and I only know only what Mustafa said. As a matter of fact, you know less because you were eavesdropping." Yasmine laughed

"Are you saying you don't believe Musa?"

"No, I'm saying that was his perspective. I've learned from being back with Kojo, that every villain is a hero in their own story."

"Yeah, whatever. All I know is when that Zaina hurt him, he was sad, meaner, and more unyielding," Salma argued.

"One, our grandfather had just died, and two, our brother has always been rigid and mean. He's soft on you; that unfortunately has you being a brat. Can't you see you're breaking his heart by shutting out his woman."

"His woman? Ewww... I'll play nice till Sunday. Then that woman will be gone," Salma finished.

Before Zaina knew it, her legs propelled her forward. She entered the kitchen and was met by two pairs of widened eyes.

"Look, if you can't address me by my name, don't address me at all. I won't be another 'that woman.'" Zaina paused, then placed a hand on her waist. "Now, I understand the Supergirl thing you've got going on for your brother. Really, I do and it's sweet, but and I repeat...but I owe no one an explanation but him.

"You can sit on your high horse and act like a right little princess. But guess what? For most of us, life has kicked our behind. We have things that molded us to make decisions. Good, bad, and ugly. I made a terrible one, but God smiled on me. He brought me back to the one man I ever, ever truly loved. I love Mustafa with ever fiber in me. If he's forgiven me, and we've agreed to be together, that's all that should matter. And you should respect that."

Salma raised her brow, glanced at Yasmine, returned her eyes to Zaina, and scoffed. "I don't have to respect anything that will cause my family pain."

"Ladies…"

Zaina raised her hand to Yasmine. "And that's not my intention. Never was. What I will not do is keep defending my right to be happy. You can't even look past your disdain for me to see that your brother is happy too." Zaina pointed to herself. "I did that. We do that for each other. I'll fight a million battles to protect him and what we have. Even from you."

Zaina stopped short of telling her that she shouldn't make Mustafa choose because he would choose her. This she was now sure of. But since she was still holding on to the issue of her moving to London, she didn't want to jinx herself. Besides, she was in no way trying to break up their family. Their closeness was something she wished she had.

Salma rolled her eyes. "Hmmm, I didn't need the sermon."

"Apparently, you did since you won't give her a break," Yasmine snickered.

Zaina smirked. Her relationship with Mustafa would run so much smoother if she was okay with his sisters, but she wouldn't let them push her around. "Look, we don't have to be friends but—"

Salma waved her hands in the air, shaking her head. "No, no, nope. Not another epistle. You had me at love and protect. If your actions match your words, we're cool. My brother loves too hard and deep for him to not have someone who matches his energy." Salma spread out the dishtowel on the handle of the oven door and exited the kitchen without another word.

"I'm so sorry about that," Yasmine offered.

Zaina waved her off. "It's not your fault. I get her stance; I'm just done with the disrespect."

"As you should be. Now, do you want another piece of Omar's cake? This thing should be banned." Yasmine eyed the cake that was on the island.

Zaina eyed the confection. She mentally calculated how many more laps on the treadmill she would need to shed the extra pounds after this trip. But after the showdown with Salma, she needed a reward.

"Sure, then you can tell me how it feels to be married to a man who has a whole Facebook page dedicated to him and his band mates abs." Zaina laughed when Yasmine groaned. "His face, I get. You did good, but their abs? How did those pictures come about?" Zaina laughed.

"Ugh...please don't remind me. I have no idea and for my sanity, I don't look at that stuff." Yasmine turned to get out two saucers from the cupboard.

Zaina chuckled again and made some tea for them. For the rest of the evening, they laughed and caught up on each other's lives. Zaina smiled when Yasmine's hand kept rubbing her pregnant stomach. She was glowing, prompting Zaina to think of a topic she'd since placed in the recess of her mind.

Motherhood.

~

"Yesterday, I saw a side of you I never thought I'd see," Kojo said.

"That was mild. I think because Grandma Olly was there. When he brought her home the first time, he wouldn't let her around anyone," Omar added.

Mustafa looked at his phone and read the message from Zaina. Earlier, the whole family had gone with Grandma Olly to visit her favorite charity. After a short tour and a sizable donation, everyone dispersed. Mrs. Bernadette met them there and took their grandmother with her to keep her distracted. Zaina went with Yasmine to her favorite coffee shop, after which they'd head to St. Johns to ensure everything was in place for Sunday. Salma was out coordinating with the caterers, event planner, and the other vendors to ensure everything was in place for the party later. They wanted Omar to enjoy the party, so he wasn't handling the food. That left Mustafa, Omar, and Kojo on kid duty. Currently, they were at a café in the town square having a late brunch.

"I know you hear us talking about you," Kojo said.

Mustafa lifted his eyes to his brother-in law. "I do and I'm trying my best to ignore you both."

Omar laughed. Kojo shook his head when Mustafa took a sip of his coffee. He turned to check on his niece and nephew. The kids had finished their food and were now playing in the playhouse.

"What do you want me to say?" Mustafa set the coffee mug to the side. "That's my woman. I belong to her, and she belongs to me."

"Told you it was destiny," Omar said.

Kojo nodded. "I believe in destiny. I also think we can choose to participate with it or not."

"Agreed." Mustafa thought back to the last couple of months. He had chosen to accept Zaina's white flag while offering one of his own. He and Zaina chose each other and in any version of reality, he'd choose her again. They'd gone through everything that was meant to tear them apart and were stronger for it.

"Personally, I think it's beautiful when you find your one true love," Omar said.

"Oh, here comes Mr. Sensitive," Kojo joked.

Mustafa smirked. Omar had a playful exterior, fooling people into believing he took nothing serious. But underneath it all, Mustafa knew it was the shell he'd created to protect himself. Growing up with a father that constantly ridiculed him for not being interested in things that were traditionally male and the fact he was almost always sickly from asthma was very difficult. Mustafa would forever be grateful to his grandparents for nurturing Omar's dreams. He wouldn't be what he was without that.

"Call it whatever, man. I think it's cool," Omar responded.

"Oh, no doubt. Having Yasmine back… I can't even describe the feeling."

"Second chances are great, but not without difficulty. You have to work on not allowing the past to trigger you," Mustafa said.

"Look at you, stringing more than five words together to make a complete point." Kojo grinned, lifting his glass of orange juice to take a sip.

"You are not funny," Mustafa said.

"And he's back." Omar chuckled. "Love you, bro, but I'mma have to stick with the in-law on this one. That was funny."

Omar and Kojo fist pumped, drawing a slight chuckle from Mustafa. His family always teased him about measuring his words. He didn't think it was necessary to talk to hear yourself speak. Only things of importance, which was why he was contemplating on how important it was to tell his siblings of his visit to Rabat. The journey the pastor recommended released him from negative emotions he'd been carrying. However, it was part of *his* treatment plan. He didn't want to expose his siblings to that experience if it wasn't necessary.

"But seriously O, you mean there hasn't been one that got away?" Kojo asked.

"Nope. Not that I can remember anyway. There've been a whole lot."

"Spare us." Mustafa was in no mood to hear about Omar's many sexual escapades over the years. Especially because they spilled over into his life. Like the night he and Zaina broke up and Omar called from a detention center. It was a woman whom his brother wronged that set him up.

"I will." Omar gave Mustafa a two-finger salute.

Mustafa checked his watch. Zaina had helped him pick out a gift for his grandmother and it was set to arrive soon from Marrakech.

"Daddy, did you see that?" Anisa's voice rang out in the air. She was running toward them with Kwame in pursuit.

"Slow down, baby," Kojo scolded.

"I'm not a baby. Mummy is having a baby." Anisa pouted.

Kwame pointed at his sister and laughed. Kojo frowned at his son, who came around the side and took a sip of his father's juice before propping his forearm on Kojo's shoulder.

Mustafa chuckled at his niece. She was almost ten. It amazed him that the tiny baby who was born premature was now this vibrant human. He was pleased to see that she and her step-brother, had developed a natural sibling relationship.

Kojo turned his head. "Stop laughing at your sister." Turning back to Anisa who stood in front of him, he continued. "Correct, you're not a baby. You're my princess and—"

"And mummy is the queen of your heart," Anisa finished.

Kojo raised his hand for a high five. "There you go. Now what's up?"

"Kwame helped me to do a backflip. Did you see?"

"I missed it, Princess. But please don't do that again. Your mum would kill me if anything happened to both of you."

Omar looked over at Kwame and high fived him.

"O, stop encouraging him," Kojo said.

Omar waved him off. "Nephew is teaching his sister life skills. Let them be."

"Mustafa?"

His family turned to see who had called his name behind them. Mustafa didn't have to. He knew that screechy sound from anywhere.

Monica.

Even though he told her where they stood, she still sporadically sent him text messages. The last time, which was about three weeks ago, he called her and reiterated his position. What he hadn't done was tell her he was with someone.

"Hey, you." Monica placed a hand on his shoulder.

In stunned silence, his family stared at him probably awaiting his response. Mustafa rolled his shoulder, hoping the motion would get her to let go of it. No such luck.

"Hello Monica," he said.

"Err, I didn't know you were back in town. I mean I figured since my grandmother and I got the invitation to the party…"

Mustafa tuned out her words as she rambled on about the dress she was going to wear, before shifting to how thankful she was that he was around because she wouldn't know anyone there. It was as though she wasn't aware that they were in the company of others or more importantly, that he'd advised her of their status.

Omar cleared his throat and Mustafa sent him a silent thank you. He didn't want to be rude to her, but Omar knew that was coming very soon.

"Oh, hi everyone. Musa won't you introduce me. Hello, little ones." Monica waved at the kids like they were puppies.

They stared at her, murmuring a greeting in return. Kojo held a fist to his mouth to stifle his laughter. Mustafa should've known that Omar had no such sense.

"Monica, you know they're not pets?" Omar cocked his head at her.

"*shaqiq!*"

Monica tittered.

Mustafa turned to her. She still hadn't let go of his shoulder. He knew the only way to get her to take the hint was to stand. So, he did.

"This is my brother-in-law, Kojo. These are his kids, Kwame and Anisa. And you know Omar. Everyone, this is Monica."

"Hello. It's nice to meet you all. Musa doesn't talk about his family much."

Omar turned to Mustafa. "Much?"

Kojo nudged him. "Nice to meet you."

Monica squinted her eyes and squealed. "Oh my gosh...Keyz?"

Mustafa closed his eyes when Monica referred to Kojo by his stage name. *Not another fan.* He didn't mind it for his brother-in-law, but he knew Kojo didn't like any attention when he was with his kids. He protected his family fiercely, something Mustafa admired.

Kojo gave her a faint smile and nodded his head in acknowledgement.

"I'm a huge fan. Is Niyi here? Please can I take a picture with you?" Monica asked as she ransacked her bag for what Mustafa presumed was her phone. She retrieved it and looked behind her. Mustafa traced her line of sight and saw her grandmother seated at a table. He nodded toward Kojo. Kojo stood and Omar took the picture.

Monica examined the picture with a huge grin on her face. "You have—"

"Yas just sent me a text. KJ, remember you got that thing." Omar dropped some bills on the table and held out his hands for the kids. "Let's go guys."

"Oh, I have to go too. My grandmother is waiting. I'll see you later tonight." She waved again and walked away.

"Good looking out, bro," Kojo said.

"Indeed," Mustafa said.

Omar chuckled. "I didn't do it for you. I did it for KJ. He has enough to deal with while on tour," Omar responded.

Mustafa grunted but didn't offer a verbal response. It was done. That's what was important.

"'Preciate it."

They walked out of the restaurant with the kids skipping on

both sides of Omar. When they got to the SUV, Kwame turned and looked up at Mustafa.

"I want to be like Uncle 'Stafa," the little boy said.

Omar unlocked the door and the kids got in. "Why?"

"He has two queens of his heart."

Mustafa clenched his teeth while Kojo and Omar, who thought everything was funny, cackled. Omar threw the keys to Kojo and walked to the passenger side.

"I do not have two, Kwame. I have only one," Mustafa corrected.

The little boy shrugged. Mustafa made sure both kids were buckled in and closed the back door. He looked at the men, who were supposed to be the adults.

"What? I didn't say anything. In fact, I'm about to check on our women. Catch you later," Kojo responded getting in the driver's seat.

"I'm riding with you KJ. I need a nap. I don't want to miss a moment of tonight's drama when Zay whoops Monica's behind." Omar chuckled. "She had her hand on your shoulder for a few good minutes, called you Musa...the woman won't be able to help herself tonight. And I want to be on the front row."

"*almashaghib.*"

"I didn't make the trouble. But I'm not about to miss it." Omar got into the vehicle. Both him and Kojo kept laughing as the car rolled out of the parking lot.

Mustafa made his way to his car. He needed to get to his villa, then check in on his woman. Omar's words lingered, but he brushed them off. The party would go off smoothly. Nothing short would be tolerated.

CHAPTER 22

For the eighth or ninth time that evening, Mrs. DuBois held Zaina's hand and introduced her to yet another friend. The gesture wasn't strange to her; her mother was fond of it. Her mother, however, knew she had a three-friend minimum. This was Grandma Olly, and it was her birthday party. Besides, it was the least she could do to help the woman calm down. Zaina had expressed her concerns to Mustafa about the shock factor for an older woman when she found out that the plan was to have the guests yell out surprise. He and his siblings seemed to have it all figured out, so she let it be. But she was right, the woman nearly passed out.

When she'd returned earlier, Zaina was stunned at how the mansion and its grounds had been transformed into pure elegance. The gentle breeze of the October night added to the ambiance of the occasion. String lights, flowers, candles, lace table runners, a DJ, bar, and food tables, were all tied together nicely with the gold and silver color theme. With Salma as its head, Grand Amour had many awards for guest service excellence. Now Zaina knew why. The woman was gifted. That, she had to admit.

"Ah, Father Mathew, I'm glad you could make it," Grandma Olly greeted the cleric.

"Mrs. Dubois, I wouldn't have missed it. Happy birthday again."

Grandma Olly pulled her forward and placed her hand on Zaina's back. "I want you to meet Zaina. She's Mustafa's special friend."

Zaina pressed her lips together and smiled as she had done with the other guests. This tag of "special friend" was hilarious to her, but she dared not laugh.

"Good evening, Father Mathew," Zaina said.

He shook her hand. "Hello, again." Turning to the older woman, he said, "I met her earlier with Yasmine."

Grandma Olly shook her head. "They had me fooled. I never expected this."

Zaina heard her voice shake, prompting her to squeeze the arm that was over her shoulder a little tighter. Earlier, her emotion was so raw. Grandma Olly had lost her husband and only daughter. She had her grandchildren who cared for her deeply, but the loss still had to sting. Especially today.

Zaina kissed the older woman in her hair. "You deserve it, Grandma Olly."

The Reverend Father nodded in agreement. When they began talking about breaking ground on some church project, Zaina excused herself. Across the lawn, her eyes caught Mustafa. Two men flanked him on each side. His eyes held her in place until she mouthed, "I'm fine" before blowing him a kiss. She'd been with him in his villa until it was time to get dressed. They had been together since then until his grandmother dragged her away. Zaina turned and walked the short distance to the open bar. She ordered a virgin martini.

"Don't tell me all those introductions have led you to drink?"

Zaina laughed, glancing at Yasmine who had her daughter

with her. The mother and daughter had on the same material, but different styles.

"Nah, not yet. Anisa, have I told you how pretty you look today?" Zaina asked.

Anisa smiled then lowered her eyes. "Yes, thank you."

Zaina turned to her mother. "Should you still be on your feet?"

"Please not you too. Kojo and I already had this argument. My shoes are flat enough." Yasmine turned to the bartender. "What do you have that can mellow me out?"

"Nothing, ma'am," the bartender replied, handing Zaina her drink.

The pregnant woman's murderous look caused Zaina to put her other hand up in surrender.

"I had nothing to do with that." She cautiously lifted her glass to her lips.

Yasmine faced the bartender. "What do you mean nothing? Please give me half a glass of Stella Rosa."

"Yasmine?"

"What? My doctor said it's okay occasionally and this wine has only five percent alcohol. I haven't had a drink in three months."

Zaina was about to speak when the bartender cut in.

"My apologies, Mrs. Sarbah. Miss DuBois-Arazi gave strict orders not to serve you anything but water and—"

"Salma is the baby. How is she giving orders?"

Zaina had never seen Yasmine this upset. She could understand it. Even though their intention was driven by love, she'd watched all weekend as everyone fussed over her. "Remember you're pregnant" was the beginning of all their sentences as though she wasn't responsible enough. Mustafa told Zaina how Yasmine almost died with Anisa's birth. Still, she knew it must be driving her crazy

"Yas, you're scaring the poor man. I'll go in the house and get you something."

She exhaled. "No, it's fine. I wish they'd stop. They're getting on my nerves."

"They love you." Zaina pulled up a stool so Yasmine could sit.

"Mummy, can I go to Daddy?" Anisa asked.

Yasmine agreed and the little girl took off. Zaina's eyes followed her until she got to Kojo who was with Mustafa, Omar, and another man. Her heart swelled with pride at the successful, handsome African kings who looked like they belonged on the cover of a magazine. Her bubble deflated when a beautiful lady walked up to them. Zaina dismissed her unease as she thought the woman could be the unknown man's date.

Seconds later, her bubble completely popped when the woman stood next to Mustafa and placed her hand on his arm. Her intuition told her immediately that it wasn't a friendly gesture. Especially with the way she leaned into her man when she giggled. Zaina was far from insecure, but Mustafa should've known to remove her hand from his body. He had one more minute to do it or she would go do it for him.

Her eyes narrowed and she took a bigger gulp of her drink before placing the half-finished drink on the bar. She smoothened down her dress and looked over at Yasmine who was talking to someone beside her. Zaina was about to move when she observed Salma walk up to the men. After what Zaina assumed were the initial pleasantries, Salma reached over and removed the woman's hand from Mustafa's arm. The mysterious woman frowned. Salma then leaned in and whispered something to her. Right after, she turned and began moving in their direction.

Zaina's eyes expanded as she let out a low chuckle. If Salma was nothing else, she was consistent. *She doesn't think anyone is good for her brother*. Zaina's thoughts wandered to the possibility of Salma having someone she wanted her brother to be with.

"What was that about?" Yasmine asked when Salma reached them.

Zaina eyes danced between the sisters. She didn't know Yasmine had seen Salma's action too.

Salma shrugged and asked the bartender for half a glass of Stella Rosa Ruby Rose Grapefruit. Without answering the question, Salma waited until the bartender returned with the drink. She handed it to her sister.

"Here, I heard you were being a cry baby. If KJ comes at me, I'm telling him you put me in a headlock, so I had to do what you asked."

Yasmine rolled her eyes, took a sip of the drink, and sighed.

"Zaina, I see you got out of grandma's clutches. I was about to rescue you, but then better you than me...so," Salma shrugged.

Zaina didn't know how to respond to that. She looked over to where the men once stood. They were no longer there.

"So, what was that about?" Yasmine asked.

"Nothing..." Salma glanced at Zaina before facing her sister. "Just telling Ms. Giggles to keep her hands off other people's property."

Zaina's eyes bugged. Salma had taken up for her. Her brows creased. "Err, thanks?" That was all she could say. She had nothing else.

Salma winked at her. "No problem, Zay."

Zaina wondered whether Salma was under the influence, but decided it wasn't even worth finding out. This Salma was better than the other.

"Isn't that 'Sim?" Yasmine pointed at a tall, bald man standing next to the unknown man that was with Mustafa minutes ago. "I didn't know he came with Q."

Zaina wanted to ask who they were, but Salma's posture

caught her attention. The man Yasmine was referring to turned. Zaina watched his eyes roam the area before they landed on Salma. He felt her stare. Zaina noticed Salma's breathing hitch as the man began walking their way. She rubbed the diamond earring in her earlobe before her hand landed at the back of her neck. In a split second, her panicked expression turned into annoyance.

Wow...the big and bad Salma can be affected by someone.

Zaina wished she hadn't discarded her drink. This was good.

"It's time to present Grandma with her gift. Let's go," Salma ordered and walked away.

Yasmine and Zaina locked eyes. She was sure her face mirrored Yasmine's befuddlement. The man halted Salma's hurried steps by blocking her path. He placed both hands into his pockets and leaned into her. He whispered something in her ear that must have set her off. She nudged him and walked off. The man grinned, watching the sway of Salma's hips until she disappeared into the house.

"Who is that?" Zaina asked. She needed the tea.

"That is Qasim, and the other guy is his older brother, Qadir. I have no idea what that was, but I'll find out." Yasmine said.

Zaina nodded and was still amused by what she'd seen when a voice flowed through the speakers.

"Ladies and gentlemen, gather 'round," the host announced.

Yasmine and Zaina strolled over to where the family was standing. Grandma Olly sat on a decorated throne-like chair and the family surrounded her. Kojo was absent. Zaina figured out why when the beat dropped, and the spotlight focused on him. He was in the corner with a microphone in his hand. In those earlier days when Mustafa refused to talk to her about his family, she'd obsessively stalked Kojo's Instagram page and the 891 Crew's website. Yasmine wasn't on social media, and she needed any link to his siblings. She couldn't believe the lengths she went to. Their website said he was a producer/songwriter.

She'd been among the four million plus views on the YouTube video of him singing to Yasmine one Christmas. Now, seeing him perform live was amazing.

Mustafa snaked his arms around her, drawing her close. Her back was flush against his broad chest as Kojo continued to serenade Grandma Olly. Looking around, Zaina could tell the ballad had the guests emotional. From the lyrics, Zaina knew he wrote the song specifically for her. He sang about her life journey, God turning her sorrow into dancing, and the Heavenly Father's love for her. It was beautiful. Thunderous applause erupted when he was done. Kojo strolled over and bowed his head before Grandma Olly. She wiped her tear-stained face and blew him a kiss. He walked over to where they stood and kissed his wife before standing behind her.

Next a huge package wrapped in Grandma Olly's favorite color, turquoise, was rolled out. Mustafa and his siblings moved to the front.

"Grand-mère, words can't express our love for you. This town is better because you are in it," Mustafa said.

"What do you give the woman who has everything?" Omar's question drew a laugh from everyone.

"Something priceless," Yasmine said.

Salma moved forward and motioned for the men who stood behind the package to get ready to open it. "Grandma, we know that grandpapa and mummy are watching down from heaven. Remember how you always used to say—"

"I wonder what my baby would look like with her babies," Grandma Olly whispered. She let out a grief laden chuckle.

Zaina wiped the corner of her eye, halting the tear that threatened to drop. One could feel the weight of the tension in the air. Salma nodded and the men unwrapped the portrait. Mustafa walked over and helped his grandmother up. He ushered her forward until she came to a halt. She froze in place when the whole portrait became visible.

Mustafa told Zaina one night that they were having trouble deciding what to get their grandmother. Zaina suggested something sentimental instead of material. What she was looking at was simply amazing. She wasn't sure how it was even possible, but it was a painting of the whole family. Grandparents, their daughter, and her grown children. Their grandfather and mother had been digitally enhanced to resemble how they'd look like presently. It was stunning and so lifelike. The gasps from the crowd drowned out Grandma Olly's sobs as her fingers traced the face of her late daughter and husband. She turned and hid her face in Mustafa's chest as she continued to sob. Zaina and Kojo stood back with the kids while Yasmine, Omar and Salma walked over to join in on the embrace. After giving them a few moments, Zaina turned to Kojo.

"This is supposed to be a happy occasion. What can we do to get it back on track?"

Kojo nodded. "Good looking out."

He walked over to the DJ and soon, "Happy" by Pharrell began to play. As expected, the siblings broke apart and their grandmother kissed each one of them on the cheek. Shortly after, the portrait was wheeled back inside, and the crowd dispersed. Kojo was with Anisa on the dance floor while Kwame sat with Yasmine.

"May I have this dance?" Mustafa came up to her.

"I didn't know you can actually ask questions," Zaina said.

"I don't follow." His forehead creased.

"That lady laughing all over you, why didn't you *ask* her to take her hands off you?"

Mustafa chuckled and kissed her temple. "Because I didn't even know they were there."

"Huh?" She looked up at him.

"Your touch ignites a fire in me. Hers, I felt nothing." He winked at her.

Zaina twisted her lips. "Hmm, good save, buddy."

He smiled. "Let's go, *habib albi*, you owe me a dance."

Zaina giggled. "You're lucky I love you."

"I know."

She took his hand and he led her to the dance floor.

~

It was Monday evening and instead of relaxing to her favorite show, Zaina was in a local crafts shop trying to distract herself from reality. Since leaving Tweede Kans Cove, the last three weeks had flown by like a blur. After Mass at the family's church, St. Johns, where Father Mathew preached about the need for legacy, the family gathered for brunch. Later, they said their goodbyes and headed for the private airstrip in Marrakech. Zaina had exchanged numbers with Omar, Yasmine, and was shocked when Salma offered her number. Qasim and his brother stayed for brunch and Zaina noticed Salma's mood was subdued when Qasim was near.

Zaina didn't think it was possible, but since they'd been back, she and Mustafa had become inseparable. The saying was true, you make time for what's important. Zaina was sure Mustafa's schedule hadn't lightened up, especially with the safari audit being the next day. However, they spent almost every evening together. Date nights consisted of flying to Gaborone to catch a theatre performance, a visit to an art gallery or the museum. The evenings always ended with a private dinner in some of the finest restaurants that she'd ever seen. On Sundays, they streamed service, enjoyed brunch on the deck, watched some television, or prepared for the work week while listening to Mustafa's favorite jazz playlist.

The trip to Tweedes had been enriching for her in so many ways. Not only did she get to see what family could be, but it helped her appreciate hers more. The sermon on legacy also triggered something in her. She'd heard the Ephesians 2:10

verse so many times, but this time, *"being the workmanship of God, doing good works that He has called you in advance to do"* stuck with her. It jolted her into replacing the excuse that she needed more clarity about her vision with the courage to act. God had already given her what she needed. She had to be courageous enough to move and let Him fill in the blanks along the way. This was why she was currently refreshing her email every five seconds.

Mustafa was in Cape Town while she had just wrapped up from the office. Instead of heading to her room, she decided to take a trip to the local crafts shop. The day after they got back from Tweedes, she'd stayed up all night finishing up the proposal for Irek Designs. After her boss shut down her request and Ibiso had encouraged her, Zaina still felt intimidated by the prospect, so hadn't followed through. She looked at her phone and sighed again. The first time she reached out to them, thanking them for the opportunity and promising to send them a proposal soon, she had gotten a personal response back. Now that she had sent the proposal, all she got was an automated reply saying they would contact her shortly. It'd been three weeks.

Maybe they no longer needed her. If that was the case, she was going to have to tell Mustafa soon that she would be leaving for London in two weeks. Zaina stared at the decorative clay pot in front of her. The intricacy of the design mirrored her life. Her eyes tried to trace one of the lines when her phone buzzed. It wasn't an email notification, but a call. She answered, knowing her friend probably could help calm her nerves.

"Any news?" Ibiso cut straight to the chase.

Zaina sighed. "No, not yet."

"They said two to three weeks *sha, abi?*"

"Yeah, today makes three weeks and a day. I need to hear yay, nay or something. So—"

"When do you leave?"

"Contractually, I'm done after the audit report comes out. So, a week from today. The audit is tomorrow. I'm sure we'll pass, but the results come out two days after."

"Are you sure you don't want to tell your man? Hmm, I'm worried."

Zaina was too. "Well, I'm in too deep already. Might as well see it through."

"I can call and see what's up. The person is my husband's friend. I—"

"No, just as I didn't want Mustafa's involvement, I don't want yours or your hubby's. You opened the door, that's more than enough. I'm thankful."

"Okay, where are you?"

"I went to the neighboring town to one local craft shop. Trying to distract myself. I'm kinda glad Musa is away because of my nerves." Zaina picked up the clay pot and headed to the register.

"It's gonna be fine. We're about to sit down for dinner, but I wanted to check on you," Ibiso said. On cue, one of her kids yelled that they were waiting. "Let me go before someone gets slapped upside the head."

Zaina laughed. "I'll call you the minute I hear something."

She disconnected the call and paid for the clay pot. As she stepped outside, the driver of the resort's official car she rode in hurried out to help her. Zaina got in the back of the car and rested her head on the headrest. Shutting her eyes, she let out a heavy breath.

"Father, I need Your intervention, please," she murmured.

Her phone buzzed and her eyelids flew open. *That was fast.* She searched for the phone in her bag. A disappointing sigh left her nostrils when she saw it was a text from Mustafa.

habib albi, I'm delayed in Cape Town.

The manager will take the lead with the auditor tomorrow.

Talk to you later tonight.

MDA

Zaina placed her hand on her forehead. She willed herself to swallow the frustration that threatened to rip from her throat. Nothing was going according to plan.

CHAPTER 23

"Ms. Bakari, you've done an outstanding job. I must admit when you joined us years ago, I was skeptical, but I am thoroughly impressed."

Zaina stared at her boss through the screen, calling for the help of the Holy Spirit to stop her eyes from rolling. This man had given her a hard time when she first moved to Abuja. At first, he threw a slew of menial jobs at her. Then he put her on projects where she had no voice, passed her up for promotions and finally sent her to Botswana. All to frustrate her.

"Thank you, sir."

"As I am sure you've heard, we've received the preliminary audit results. They are favorable."

"I heard, sir."

The resort manager had left her office a few minutes before her boss called. It had been two days since the audit took place and the initial results were a pass.

"I have a meeting with Mr. DuBois-Arazi later today for the final steps. In the meantime, I need a favor from you," he said.

Mustafa. She missed him. Her heart ached with longing for his presence. Three days. This was the longest he'd been gone since returning from Tweede Kans Cove. In fact, this was the first time he'd been away since then. He was still in Cape Town. He was meeting with some developer and the negotiations were taking forever.

"I'm all ears, sir."

Zaina knew that there was no such thing as a favor. He was giving her the illusion of choice, but they both knew she had none. She took a breath. Her renewed animosity for him was totally misplaced. It wasn't his fault that he finally gave her what she wanted, and she no longer wanted it. It wasn't his fault she had found love and the thought of leaving Mustafa behind again made her sick. Neither was it his fault that Irek Designs still hadn't responded to her email.

"The Botswana government is hosting a gala for all the African expats doing business in Botswana. I want you to attend on behalf of Safi Kijani."

"I thought Amadi was supposed to do it?" She knew about the party, but last year, the company sent someone from Nigeria. Even when she asked about it earlier in the year, she was told it wasn't for her level and Amadi would fly down. Now, they needed her to attend. She had things to do, especially if she was to report to the London office in two weeks.

"He still might make it. But I want you to be there in case he doesn't. Right now, he's dealing with a personal issue."

"But sir, I'm due in London soon. I'm done with this job. What will I be doing here until then? I have to come back home to prepare."

"Per the contract, you're to move out of the resort once the audit report is released. That's today. I know this is an inconvenience, but your apartment is paid for until the end of the month. Use this time to wind down."

Zaina wanted to argue, but remembered that when the contract was being negotiated, her personal relationship with the owner wasn't a factor. She didn't want to wind down. It was time for her to face her life head on. Her plan was to discuss her job situation with Mustafa over a celebratory dinner later, then head to Abuja to start preparing to move to London. Not to be here for two weeks doing nothing.

"Ms. Bakari?"

"Yes, sir. I got it. Thank you so much."

"You're welcome. Once again, good job. I'll delay your start in London by two weeks since you are staying for the gala."

"Yes, sir."

They discussed a few more projects before they disconnected the call. She closed her laptop and swiveled around in her chair. She played around with the idea of coming up with some health emergency to delay London. But she quickly tossed it. Her stomach growled and she looked at her phone. She stood to head to the restaurant when there was a knock on her door. She smiled when she saw a tray being wheeled in with flowers. Mustafa. She honestly couldn't wait to see him. She strolled over to the tray and picked up the flowers. Sniffing them, she read the card while the waiter set the tray on her table.

Thank you *habib albi*,

You saved the resort.

I'm proud of you.

See you tonight.

MDA

Zaina picked up the phone to call him when an email notification interrupted her. It was from Irek Designs. Her finger shook as she opened it. Her eyes browsed the email and she let out a scream.

"Oh my God. Thank you!!!"

"Madam. Is everything okay."

She fanned herself with her hand. "Oh, yes. I'm sorry. I just got fantastic news."

"Oh. Okay madam, enjoy. I'll be back for the dishes later."

Zaina danced around her office, food forgotten. She couldn't wait to share her news with Mustafa. They'd offered her the subcontract to redesign the lobbies of a chain of banks. She had her first client under Kutoka Duniani. She resisted the urge to call Mustafa. The dinner she was going to prepare would be so much better with them face to face and her sharing her news.

Everything had come together. Well almost, but now if Mustafa asked why she didn't tell him, she could pacify him by telling him what she had been doing to fix it. It was perfect. Zaina fell to her knees in reverence to the One who made it all possible.

Later that evening, Zaina sat on the edge of the couch, tapping her foot on the floor. She'd just blown out the candles and put up the food. Gritting her teeth, she glanced at the place setting before her eyes landed on her phone. Wrapped up in the euphoria of her news and anticipation of seeing Mustafa, Zaina had rushed to her room to start dinner preparations and await his arrival. About an hour later, an unsettling feeling crept up her spine when she realized he hadn't called. Neither had he responded to her call or text. She called two more times but didn't get any response. Thinking he was probably in flight, she continued making dinner and set the table.

He never showed up.

Three hours after he was supposed to arrive, he never showed. Not able to contain her anxiety, Zaina called Yasmine. She didn't know what she knew and hated to alarm her if it wasn't necessary, but she was at her wits end. To her surprise, during the conversation, Yasmine casually slipped in a question about how she was managing his absence since he was in Tweede Kans Cove. Totally oblivious to her shock, Yasmine went on to compare it to the situation she found herself in with her husband. After talking about what Zaina couldn't even remember, Zaina hung up the phone.

Lost in thought, with no explanation, Zaina strolled to her room. What changed? What happened? Why was he shutting her out? Desperate for answers, she dialed his phone again. This time, it didn't ring, but when straight to voicemail. His phone was now off.

~

Monday morning, at the staff meeting, Mustafa absently looked at the presentation before him as the heads of departments gave their updates. His mind was disoriented, but his body functioned. Which was what it was doing as he sat barely comprehending what was being said. The detachment wasn't new to him. He'd relied on it as a coping mechanism for years. But he didn't think it was something he would use again so soon.

His business in Cape Town wasn't complete when he received the news that the resort had passed the audit. Cutting the talks with Rice Holdings short, he asked that the jet be prepared to fly him back to Botswana. He had the insatiable need to see Zaina. To celebrate with her. His chest tightened with the knowledge that she would be headed back to Nigeria. He had willed himself not to think of it. With it now being a present reality, he couldn't get it out of his mind. Neither was the separation from her something he was willing to tolerate.

He wanted to marry her. He wanted her in his home every day. In his bed, every night. Admittedly, he knew he wouldn't be there every night, but knowing she was there when he got back pleased him. His peace depended on it. Nothing short of it would do. These six months had been torturous on his libido, and it had to end. Yasmine had lucked up, so maybe he could too. He'd never stand in the way of Zaina's job, but he could make a few deals.

Zaina didn't want to work for him. But he could broker a deal with Safi Kijani to hire them on as permanent consultants. An external body to oversee the ecosystem structure, compliance, and improvement of all Grand Amour locations. On his way to the airstrip, he decided to call Zaina's boss, to make the offer. The conversation still played in his head like a bad song.

"Mr. DuBois-Arazi, I'm glad we handled everything to your satisfaction. Congratulations again, Sir" Mr. Ladi had said.

"Very well then. I trust you'll handle the other matter with expediency," Mustafa said.

"Yes, sir. We're glad to be of service. I'll have legal prepare the draft contract and send it over. As soon as both parties agree to the terms and sign. A consultant will report to Tweede Kans Cove to familiarize himself with the initiatives you presently have in place."

"Himself? Since Ms. Bakari is already familiar with our systems and processes, letting her continue will lessen the learning curve," Mustafa said.

Mustafa was aware that he'd incur Zaina's wrath for interfering. While they were in Tweede Kans Cove, they had discussed marriage and their future. If she was going to be upset about him taking the steps to stabilize that future, he'd gladly take on her anger.

The man chuckled. "Sam is a great worker. Unfortunately, she won't be available."

"Why?" Mustafa's eyebrows drew together.

"Oh, no, it's nothing bad. She interviewed for and got a promotion to our London office several months ago. Now that your project is over, she's to report there. She's supposed to leave at the end of the month. I promise you, this person trained with her and is equally as good."

Everything else the man said was like birds chirping out of harmony. London? When was she going to tell him? Once again, he'd totally miscalculated when it came to her. Exactly like the last time. He'd thought they were on the same page, but she had other plans. How did he keep missing the signs? She talked about her work, but not the specifics. He should've known.

When they broke up years ago, reading people, to detect sincerity was something he'd become skilled at. How did he allow the same woman to deceive him twice?

Overrun by his anger and disappointment, he waited for the pilot to apply for a route change and headed back home instead.

"Will there be anything else, sir?"

Mustafa observed the pairs of eyes that were on him. His mind made its way to the present as he tried to recall the last thing any of them said. Unsuccessful, he stood and buttoned his jacket.

"No questions. That will be all. Good work everyone. Mr. Phiri, please stay on."

"Yes, sir," he said.

As everyone filed out of the conference room, Mustafa was grateful none of his siblings could attend. They all had previous engagements, and sent their representatives instead. Salma was finally out of his business. She was the only one who could sniff out his moods, and he didn't want her making up stories in her head. He didn't need the complication.

Mustafa placed his hands in his pockets and faced the projector. "I got the final audit report over the weekend. Good job."

"Thank you, sir. Ms. Bakari is the real champion, sir. I'm happy, you found that company," he said.

"Indeed. Wh—"

"We were sad to see her go," Mr. Phiri said. From his expression, he wasn't aware his news was coming as a surprise.

Mustafa's chest tightened. "Go?"

"Yes, sir. She moved out of the villa on Saturday."

Mustafa hadn't talked to her since Thursday morning. After the discussion with her boss, he'd ignored all her calls. He knew that if he spoke to her then, he would explode with the fury that rumbled his heart. A tiny bomb detonated in his heart each time he let her calls go to voicemail, so he had ended up turning off the device altogether.

She knew what he had been through. She knew he had issues with trust. He'd asked her so many times not to keep things from him and the most important thing, she did. Deception from her could alter his world.

"Okay, Thank you."

"Oh sir, I have to give the Ministry of Investment, Trade and Industry the final count of our entourage for the evening with African Expats. Will you be joining us?"

Mustafa knew of the annual event. He'd attended it only once in all the time the resort had been in Botswana. He wasn't up for schmoozing with anyone, but it would be rude to ignore the invitation again.

"Yes, I'll be there."

Mr. Phiri nodded, and they disconnected the call a few moments later. Mustafa walked up to the window. The view of the mountains was always spectacular and soothing. The snow-capped mountaintop was something only God could've designed. The serenity was something he wanted. It'd been five days and he knew he had to talk to Zaina. Closing his eyes, he prayed for wisdom.

~

Mustafa resisted the urge to run his fingers through her hair that was fanned out on the black satin pillow. The only reason he knew it was satin was because she told him what she did to maintain the wild mane he loved. Late afternoon, he left Tweedes for Gaborone. On the nine-hour flight, he'd thought about all the things he wanted to tell her. Now, her beauty silenced his words, but they had to be spoken.

It was about two a.m. and he'd been in the dark watching

Zaina sleep for about five minutes. From her boss, he learned she was back in her apartment, so he came straight from the airport. They'd stayed here a few times after their nights in the city, so he had a key to let himself in. As he stared at her, he desperately needed to understand why she was willing to destroy what they had. Mustafa caressed her cheek.

"How do lips like yours manage to weave lies so easily," he whispered.

He watched her stir at his voice. Her eyes sprang open, and she scurried to sit up. His eyes roamed to her supple bosom under the loose night shirt she wore. How could something so sweet be so manipulative? Zaina followed his line of sight and raised the sheets to her neck. He smirked. She moved against the headboard. She reached across her nightstand and turned on the lamp.

"Musa? What are you doing here?" The expression on her face went from confusion, then concern before resting on indignation. "Where have you been? Why are you here?"

"You know where I've been."

"Because I had to call someone else to find out. Do you know what I've been through these past five days?"

"Now you know the torture of receiving important information about your significant other from someone else."

"I don't care what you heard. So, you decide to punish me without talking to me first?"

He lifted his hands to trace her lips. "How do lips like these tell such lies?"

Zaina slapped his hand away. "Now I'm a liar?"

Mustafa saw the minute it dawned on her that he knew about London. Her eyes fell, then she lifted them to him.

"You found out about London? Let me explain."

The fire from his feet shot him up to his full height. "Why do you always have to explain?" he roared.

She flinched and he couldn't be bothered to assuage her

unfounded fears in the moment. Maybe she should be afraid. Afraid enough to think twice about keeping things from him.

"I cannot build a life with someone I can't rely on. Someone I can't trust."

"What? You can trust me. Listen…" Zaina got out of the bed, reaching for her robe at the foot of it. "Listen, I didn't tell you at first because I didn't want to. Then you disappeared not giving me room to. As time passed, I just didn't know how. Look, I have been working…" She walked over to the table in the corner of her room to retrieve some papers.

Mustafa had no interest in what she wanted him to see. He'd fought to better himself for her. Well, for him, but it was because he needed her in his life. He'd racked his brain trying to figure out what was it about him that made her want to keep things from him? Not share what was on her mind. Or allow him to take care of her, fix her problems? Was he that inadequate of a partner that her first response was to lie to him? Wasn't he enough?

"Look. See." She stretched out a paper to him.

Mustafa's eyes darted to the paper. He didn't take it from her, but a quick scan of the document showed the name of her business and another company's name. His jaw clenched.

"I don't know what this is. Neither do I care to. Why did you lie to me?"

"I didn't lie. I waited to tell you," she yelled.

"I asked you so many times. You made me believe something else by not telling me the truth." He strolled toward her until her back was against the wall. He lowered his head to her ear. "An omission is a lie. I know you were taught that in those fancy schools your parents sent you to."

Zaina's jaw dropped as she stepped to the side. He turned to her. The plea in her eyes gave way to fury. Her parents and her upbringing were a sensitive topic for her, but so was trust with him. His victory at inflicting as much pain in her as she had done to him turned sour when she thumbed away a tear. Squaring her shoulders, Zaina walked out of the bedroom.

Mustafa followed. "Where are you going?"

Zaina ignored his question and continued her march to the door. She opened it and turned to him. "Nowhere. But you are. Get out."

Mustafa moved toward her. He opened his mouth to speak when she bellowed again.

"No! Out now!"

After a few seconds of contemplation, he realized it was wrong to come here sleep deprived. He hadn't had a good night's rest in days and from the weariness etched on her face, neither had she. Nothing was going to be hashed out now. He strolled to the door.

"Five days," he said.

"Huh?" Irritation laced her tone.

"That's how much time you get to punish me." He lifted his hand and curled her loose tress around his finger. "I can't imagine my world without you in it, so there's no way your permanent absence will be a reality."

Zaina scoffed. "You have a whole lot of nerve. Well, I'm about to welcome you to the real world. Out."

"Don't test me, *habib albi*." Mustafa walked out of her apartment and the door slammed behind him. He came to a halt when he heard Zaina's frustrated scream. It was like the one he had in his head.

CHAPTER 24

"What do you mean, you feel him? SoSo, I love you, but I'm going to hang up on you. Seriously."

Zaina glanced at her friend who was on a video call before returning her attention to the two dresses hanging on the closet's door. She took the dresses off the hangers and walked back over to the dresser where her phone was propped up.

"Which one? Emerald or Black?"

"Turn them around. Let me see the back."

Zaina did as she was asked.

"Hmm. Are you going for apply pressure or let's get this thing over with?" Ibiso tapped her chin.

"Huh?"

"Never mind. The goal is always to apply pressure. The black will have their necks hurting. Then again, Mustafa will be there. I don't know how a dress with that much skin showing will work out for you." Ibiso laughed.

Zaina rolled her eyes and flung the black dress on the bed. "How many times will I tell you he's a non-factor?"

"I guess as many times as it will take you to believe that lie."

Zaina sighed. "I'm being serious."

"And this is Mustafa we're talking about. That one time I talked to him, I thought I was in the principal's office."

"Yea, Mustafa Benoit Dubois-Arazi, that's his full name. I'm aware of who we're talking about." Zaina shook her head. "He can take several seats. I mean, can you—"

Ibiso raised her hand. "Yeah, yeah, you've given me the story. In detail…but you must accept some of the blame. I'm not going to say I told you so, but you made the man feel inadequate. The outside world does that to them enough. Black men, but African men specifically. To the world, they're already considered subpar because people haven't taken the time to see that we're not monolith. We don't come from one big jungle or that our accent isn't a measure of our intelligence. I'm all for you being independent, and I know your reasons, but this was a new dawn for both of you. You can't be independent in a relationship. Please, stop letting your trauma make decisions for you."

Zaina stared at her friend, then let out a cleansing breath. She picked up the phone and plopped down on her bed. She was so angry with Mustafa but missed him terribly. She hadn't spoken to him in a week. True to his word, he hadn't bothered her for the first five days, but yesterday he was on a roll, and she sent his call to voicemail each time. Why couldn't he understand that her decision had nothing to do with him?

"I have so much to tell him," she whined.

She wanted to show him her designs, tell him about the plan she had for London and that she was going to be an aunt again. She walked into a coffee shop the other day and a jazz song was playing, and her throat clogged with emotion.

"Then tell him," Ibiso said.

"I don't want to."

Ibiso laughed. "Well, good luck with that. I'll be at the airport tomorrow to pick you up if somehow, your Arab lets you go."

Zaina laughed. She blew her friend a kiss, disconnected the

call and walked to the shower. She decided not to drive, so the car service she hired would be here in an hour. Her eyes caught her packed bags in the corner. She rubbed her chest to ease the tightness. Did she stand a chance without him?

~

"The ease I've become accustomed to seeing from you is missing."

Mustafa steepled his fingers under his chin and leaned back in the chair. The pastor's assessment was correct, but he wasn't sure he wanted to talk about the reason. He'd cancelled his last session with the pastor, but in his current state of mind, he knew missing anymore sessions would be a mistake. For himself and all those connected to him.

"Interesting," Mustafa said.

Pastor Mensah studied him. "You were happy. What happened?"

Mustafa's eyes darted to the time at the bottom of the computer screen. He needed a sense of the time. The hotel he was in was about forty-five minutes from the venue of the night's events, and he couldn't afford to be late.

"I don't think I've mastered this thing of acknowledge and release."

"I don't expect you to master it. If you do, then I need to come study under you," the pastor chuckled.

Mustafa found no humor in what he was going through. He knew that by the end of the evening, he and Zaina would come to an agreement. He would make sure of it. What he didn't want was for it to happen again.

Seeing he wasn't partaking in the joke, the pastor stopped laughing and asked, "Do you want to talk about what happened?"

A few beats passed between them before Mustafa gave the

pastor the abbreviated version of what took place between him and Zaina.

"From one of our past sessions, it is my understanding that you consider Zaina to be your life partner, correct?"

Mustafa nodded.

"Since that's the case, you can't go through a relationship avoiding fights. You will fight, but your disagreements should be from a place of progress instead of perfection. Your issues with trust and feelings of inadequacy took years to develop and won't go away after three months. At the root of your anger is self-preservation. I understand she wasn't entirely truthful, but it wasn't done from a place of malice."

"Why did she do it at all?"

"I can't answer that. She's human and we make mistakes. Mustafa, you can't expect everyone to tiptoe around your trauma. This is a process, a journey. If you think about this as a destination to reach, you'll keep setting yourself back. Instead of thinking of it as lying to hurt, why couldn't she have lied to ease your worries? That's what a partner does, right?"

Mustafa grunted.

"I'm not championing the deception. What I'm getting at is shifting your perspective. Remember?"

"Yes. I understand."

Pastor Mensah nodded.

Zaina and their life together were Mustafa's end game. The risk of love was a small price to pay compared to the thought of losing her.

"The line you crossed to hurt her isn't one she'll always forgive. Her parents are a sensitive topic and the ability to properly govern yourself around it, even in anger, will do well for your relationship."

Mustafa winced. That wasn't his proudest moment and he needed to make amends. The pastor then did something he didn't normally do. He asked for permission to pray for him. A request Mustafa granted. He needed the extra help to get his woman back. Their session ended soon after.

Several hours later, Mustafa stood at the far corner of the ballroom with a drink in his hand and his eyes trained on Zaina. He hadn't made his presence known. At first when he arrived, he saw her laughing and joking with a man. His first instinct was to march over and claim what was his. But then he knew that humility was what was required to get her to listen to him. Especially since she'd avoided all contact with him.

When she stood, his eyes burned with desire and anger at what she had on. He had no problem with the way the black sequin dress drew attention to all her curves. Or how high the slit was. Or how only one sleeve held the dress up, displaying her silky skin. What he did have a problem with was that she wore the dress without him by her side. Her hair was up in a loose bun, the auburn tips gently bounced against her delicate neck. He couldn't contain the beast within when she stood, and her companion placed his hand on the small of her back. Mustafa finished off his drink and began to move. As though she could sense him, Zaina shifted and turned around. Their eyes connected and he saw her jump. He smirked.

Good.

As he got closer, Mustafa watched as Zaina excused herself and started walking toward him.

"Musa—"

"I wanted to say hi to your friends."

"No, you don't, and they are not my friends."

Mustafa studied her. "I see you decided to test me." He held out his hand. "Let's go."

Zaina hesitated. "Where are we going? It's not over yet. I'm here for my company."

"I know that, but I'm not spending another minute at odds with you. We can talk in the middle of this room, or you can follow me. Which is it going to be?"

To his pleasure, Zaina didn't offer up an argument. Instead, she placed her hand in his, and he led them out of the room. They moved in silence until they got to the balcony that was opposite the ballroom. He moved Zaina to the corner to provide them some privacy. He took a moment to take her in. It was hard giving her the space he knew she deserved after their argument. He understood his shortcomings, so he had to be patient, a virtue he'd never possessed. He tried to gather the words he wanted to say to her. He couldn't mess this up.

"What are we doing here, Musa?" Zaina snapped.

Ignoring her tone, he asked. "Do you love me?"

A frown creased her forehead. "Of course, I do. My anger doesn't negate that."

"I'm sorry. I—"

"Yeah, I got that in your voicemail." She sighed. "But here's the thing, I don't want your apology. I want your complete trust. I deserve that. Anything short of that, I can't be a part of."

"I know—"

"We both had traumatic childhoods. Our traumatic responses are the key reason we didn't work the first time. I didn't tell you, yes, but there was a reason."

"You said that but—"

She jabbed his shoulder with her finger. "I'm not out to hurt you."

"I know—"

"Do you? I love you, and I know you love me too. If this thing is going to work, we must live without worrying when one of us will eventually hurt the other. You left me!"

"Woman, I can't get a word in. Stop cutting me off and listen." Mustafa exhaled. "I am sorry. You're correct. But I don't need there to be a reason you keep things from me. I can't operate that way."

"Okay, I won't. But you should—"

"Enough with the scolding, *habib albi*." He walked her back until she was at the rail. He brushed his lips against hers.

Zaina chuckled. "Something is wrong with you. I—"

The rest of her words were caught in her throat when he dropped to one knee. Her eyes widened and she cupped her mouth.

"The only person who gets to scold me is my wife. For her, I'll endure it. Some of the time."

She tittered. Her eyes pooling with tears at the small box in his hand.

"Zaina, will you marry me?"

He opened the box and her mouth hung open. There was never any doubt that he wanted her to be his wife. Their time in Tweede Kans Cove solidified that. That was where he bought the quad, princess-cut, diamond 14k white gold ring. When he saw the ring with a group of four princess cut diamonds in place of one stone, he knew it was befitting of his future wife.

She nodded her head vigorously.

"Speak, *habib albi*."

"Yes. Yes. Yes."

Mustafa removed the ring from its encasement and slipped it on her finger. It fit perfectly. He stood and wrapped his arms around her, crushing her to him. He brushed light kisses on her neck before he captured her face and delivered a passionate kiss cementing their commitment. He thumbed away her tears as she admired the ring

"Bu…but…what abo…"

"Everything else, we'll discuss later. No matter what, you're mine."

"Yes," she answered breathlessly. "Yes."

Mustafa enveloped her in his arms. The familiar peace she always brought him resurfaced. His hands went to her back, and he felt her bare flesh. He remembered what made him walk over to her in the first place.

"Why did you wear this dress wit—"

She waved him off. "Oh, come on. Let's go dance. Besides, I knew you'd be here."

"So, this was a deliberate attempt to poke the bear."

"All is fair in love and war. I want to dance in my fiancé's arms. Come on."

Mustafa chuckled. Hand in hand, they reentered the ballroom and danced the night away.

THE END

EPILOGUE

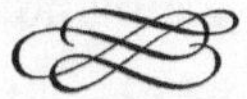

"*B*aby, you do know that you're not helping my case with Salma." Zaina pulled out two plates from the cupboard.

"One will do."

Zaina tilted her head and chuckled at her shirtless husband of one week. He wanted them to eat from the same plate. His pajama bottoms hung low on his waist as he sauntered toward the fridge for something for them to drink. She still found it hard to balance his ultra-alpha with his need for her attention. She set one plate to the side and removed the leftovers from the microwave. They'd arrived in Zanzibar a few days ago and had been basking in the serenity of their bubble.

The day after Mustafa proposed, they told their families. With the announcement, a makeshift wedding planning committee of two was formed. Her mother and Salma. Zaina had other things that needed her attention so had no time to fret about a wedding that was, at that time, a year out. But they wanted to, so she saw no harm in indulging them.

"Salma will be fine." He set two bottles of water on the island.

"Easy for you to say." Zaina opened the drawer and removed two forks.

Mustafa patted his leg. "You can let her plan an elaborate reception."

Zaina smiled at his unspoken command for her to sit on his lap. She walked over to the island, swaying to the melodic jazz playing in the background. Zaina adjusted herself on Mustafa's lap as his arm circled her waist. She shuddered as he nuzzled her neck and peppered it with kisses.

"She wanted to plan a wedding, Musa."

He shrugged. "And I wanted you as my wife sooner."

Zaina giggled. "When did you become so spoiled?"

"I'm not spoiled. I'm obsessed with my wife. There's a difference."

Zaina rolled her eyes. They said grace and began to eat. They'd spent the last two days exploring the island and engaging in various activities. With this being their last day in the safety of their cocoon, they decided to stay indoors. The clock on the wall chimed signaling three a.m. After a day of movies, swimming, and playing cards, they showered and ended the day in bed. Mustafa refused to let her up, not that she was complaining, but that caused them to miss dinner. They'd woken up about thirty minutes ago hungry and decided to raid the kitchen. A lazy grin eased up her face as she chewed on her food. They ate in comfortable silence, allowing her thoughts to travel back to the past six weeks.

On target, she'd resumed her position in London while working on her designs for Irek. The first week of her stay, she was miserable. Her ache for Mustafa was so palpable that it physically hurt to be away from him. Thankfully, Mustafa felt the same way which led to him flying to London every weekend after that. Although their misery was mutual, much to Mustafa's annoyance, Zaina refused to give her boss her notice until Irek approved her final designs. The day after they were approved,

Mustafa flew to London for them to celebrate. A celebration that ended with them married in a London courthouse.

Luckily for her, the meetings with Irek were still remote. She would have to go to their headquarters in Lagos after her prototypes were done. But that wouldn't be for another three months. Now, her office would be set up in Tweede Kans Cove, and her first order of business was getting a warehouse, sourcing materials, and hiring labor.

Zaina examined her wedding band. "I guess the difference is the reason you called in that favor."

"Correct. Are you happy?"

Zaina cupped his face and gazed into his eyes. "That your old college buddy was able to expediate the marriage notice you secretly applied for? Or that you whisked me away afterwards for a romantic picnic at Turner's View. Or with the euphoric high you have me on with the things you did that night and keep doing to my body. Things I didn't even think were possible. Yes, I am happy." She captured his lips in a passionate kiss.

She was ecstatic. She'd had underestimated how much stress would accompany juggling her job, business, and still having to look at designs and colors that her mother and Salma sent her almost every other day. Once again, Mustafa had anticipated her needs and eliminated her stress. That didn't mean she was looking forward to explaining to her mother and Salma that they were already married.

Zaina moaned when she felt Mustafa take control of their tongue battle. He stood, shifted the empty plate to the side and lifted her onto the island.

His palms caressed her bare thighs. "Careful, woman. We have a flight to catch in the morning."

"Hmm. Don't remind me."

"It will be fine. Blame me, I can take it." His hands threaded through her hair. "What I can't take is your discomfort."

"Thank you, baby. I love you." Zaina ran her hands up and

down his back. "So, the plan is still the same? See my dad before we fly to Tweedes?"

Mustafa nodded and lifted her. Zaina's legs naturally circled his waist as he carried her to their bedroom.

"Musa, I have to clean up."

"I'll do it later. Now I have more pressing matters that demand my attention." He grazed her neck with his teeth while making his way to their bedroom.

Zaina giggled as he placed her on the bed. She scooted back to give him room. Mustafa crawled toward her. Pinning her with his stare, mischief laced his eyes as he moved closer like a lion after its prey. She was amused at his silliness and slid back. Mustafa caught her ankle to stop her movement. Hovering over her, he stared into her eyes. Zaina saw the exact moment his aura shifted. The jest in his eyes was replaced with an unreadable intensity.

"Musa..."

"'ant hayati waruhi waqalbi. 'ashkuruk ealaa alsamah li bihubik libaqiat hayati."

Zaina's throat clogged. Even though she had no idea what he'd said, the intensity of his words pierced her soul.

"Translate..." she whispered.

"I'll show you instead."

The next words out of her mouth were cut off as she surrendered to her husband's kiss.

GLOSSARY

<u>French/Arabic/Swahili Translations</u>

Although Tweede Kans Cove is a fictional town, it is located in Morocco. Therefore, the culture of Morocco is threaded in the story. Moroccans speak Arabic and French mainly. However, with foreign influences, English is also spoken to some extent. Zaina grew up in London, so there are a few British slangs in here and she's from Tanzania where Swahili is spoken.

Below are translations (done to the best of my ability) to the languages I used in the story. I have this in the order in which they appear.

aikhti alsaghira: little sister (Arabic)

al'akh al'akbar: Big Brother (Arabic)

Avez-vous: Have you? (French)

Je ne peux pas attendre: I cannot wait (French)

Knackered: Tired (British slang)

Wahala: Trouble (Nigerian Pidgin)

How now: How are you? (Nigerian Pidgin)

No vex: Don't be annoyed (Nigerian Pidgin)

Na wa o: An expression of awe (Nigerian Pidgin)

Look scruffy: Look like a hot mess (British slang)
Chérie: Sweetheart (French)
shaqiq: Brother (Arabic)
hasan: Good (Arabic)
bahir: Fantastic (Arabic)
Abeg: Please (Nigerian Pidgin)
Binti yangu: My daughter (Swahili)
Las, las: If Push comes to shove (Nigerian Pidgin English)
tatasaraf binafsik: Behave yourself (Arabic)
habib albi: Lover of his heart (Arabic)
uhibbuki: I love you (Arabic)
Shine ya eye: Be wise (Nigerian Pidgin English)
Act like a right little princess: Act like your mess don't stink (British slang)
almashaghib: Troublemaker (Arabic)
'ant hayati waruhi waqalbi. 'ashkuruk ealaa alsamah li bihubik libaqiat hayati: You're my life, my soul and my heart. Thank you for allowing me to love you for the rest of my life (Arabic)

FINAL NOTE

Thank you for reading Mustafa & Zaina's story. Please consider leaving a review on the platform you purchased the book. I greatly appreciate honest feedback. They really go a long way. The number of reviews a book receives greatly improves how well it does.

If you liked this story, I trust you might like some of my other titles. But before we get to those, never miss a sale, new release announcements, or freebies. You can ensure that by joining my mailing list. I'd love to stay connected.

Next up in the DuBois-Arazi family is Salma DuBois-Arazi. Join here to be the first to see the cover and get release information.

New Year's Kiss (Prequel)

Rent-A-Bae